NEVER CRY
WEREWOLF

L. A. BANKS

St. Martin's Paperbacks

This is a work of fiction. All of the characters, organizations and events portrayed in this novel are either products of the author's imagination or are used fictitiously.

NEVER CRY WEREWOLF

Copyright © 2010 by Leslie Esdaile Banks.
Excerpt from *Left for Undead* copyright © 2010 by Leslie Esdaile Banks.

Cover photograph © Barry David Marcus

For information address St. Martin's Press, 175 Fifth Avenue, New York, NY 10010.

ISBN: 978-0-312-94300-4

Printed in the United States of America

St. Martin's Paperbacks edition / April 2010

St. Martin's Paperbacks are published by St. Martin's Press, 175 Fifth Avenue, New York, NY 10010.

10 9 8 7 6 5 4 3 2 1

intricacies are carefully woven throughout, but Banks piles on the danger, making this one exciting thrill ride!" —*Romantic Times BOOKreviews* (4½ stars)

"Banks takes on werewolves and makes them her own…A blast to read." —Kelley Armstrong

"Shadowy, sexy, intense." —Cheyenne McCray

"An action-packed thrill ride!"
—#1 *New York Times* bestselling author Sherrilyn Kenyon

The Vampire Huntress Legend™ series

THE THIRTEENTH

"Wow! As usual, Banks blows your mind. This book is exciting from the first page, as all hell has broken loose…World religions, vampiric lore, and myths come into play, and overlying it all is a wonderful spirituality, as people of different cultures join forces to fight a pervasive evil. This powerful story makes you watch current events and wonder."
—*Romantic Times BOOKreviews* (Top Pick)

THE SHADOWS

"Steamy and chock-full of action."
—Vampirelibrarian.com

THE CURSED

"A wild amalgam of Christianity, vampire lore, world myth, functional morality, street philosophy, and hot sex…fans couldn't ask for more." —*Publishers Weekly*

THE WICKED

"A complex world of Good vs. Evil . . . The story is so compelling, the whole series must be read."

—*Birmingham Times*

THE FORSAKEN

"Readers already enthralled with this sizzling series can look forward to major plot payoffs."

—*Publishers Weekly*

"In the seventh book in her incredibly successful series…Banks presents interesting myths—both biblical and mythological…with prose that's difficult to match—and most certainly just as difficult to put down." —*Romantic Times BOOKreviews* (4½ stars)

THE DAMNED

"All hell breaks loose—literally—in the complex sixth installment.…stunning." —*Publishers Weekly*

"In [*The Damned*], relationships are defined, while a dark energy threatens to destroy the entire squad. Banks's method of bringing Damali and Carlos back together is done with utmost sincerity and integrity. They have a love that can weather any storm, even when dire circumstances seem utterly overwhelming. Fans of this series will love *The Damned* and, no doubt, will eagerly await the next book."

—*Romantic Times BOOKreviews*

THE FORBIDDEN

"Passion, mythology, war, and love that lasts till the grave—and beyond....Fans should relish this new chapter in a promising series."   —*Publishers Weekly*

"Superior vampire fiction."   —*Booklist*

"Gripping."   —*Kirkus Reviews*

THE BITTEN

"Seductive...mixing religion with erotic horror dosed with a funky African-American beat, Banks blithely piles on layer after layer of densely detailed plot...will delight established fans. Banks creates smokin' sex scenes that easily out-vamp Laurell K. Hamilton's."

—*Publishers Weekly*

"The stakes have never been higher, and the excitement and tension are palpable in this installment of Banks's complex, sexy series."   —*Booklist*

THE HUNTED

"A terrifying roller-coaster ride of a book."

—*Charlaine Harris*

DEDICATION

A book in and of itself is only words, thoughts, and feelings spilled onto paper . . . that truly doesn't come to life until readers breathe their energy into it. I want to thank you all for hanging with me through two paranormal series that I've had the most fun of my career creating, namely, the Vampire Huntress Legends series and the Crimson Moon novels. BIG PHILLY HUG to my Street Team, without whom I couldn't run around the country feeling like I was at home everywhere I go . . . to the book clubs that have embraced me, and to each and every single reader who stayed up nights to read my sagas, especially those who felt inspired to drop a beautifully enthusiastic e-mail. Believe me: I don't care what any writer tells you, those notes of encouragement inspire us on our darkest days. Thank you all for the love!

SPECIAL ACKNOWLEDGMENT goes out to Manie Barron and Monique Patterson, my fabulous agent and editor extraordinaire as always. Thank you both for believing in me even when I hit a few rough patches.

Holly and Rachel, St. Martin's crew—thank you for "making it do what it do," smile. I also want to thank Randall Recknagel, owner of Castle of Dracula wine, for showing me the breathtaking beauty of New Hampshire and for being a good friend! Thanks for showing me "Stephen King country," man. Awesome.

But I would be remiss if I didn't give a special shout-out to West Point buddies, Chip Armstrong (a fantastic writer in his own right—look for him in the near future), and Phil Beaver, Ph.D. Colonel, U.S. Army (Ret.) (another new author with forthcoming work), for their EXPERT military guidance in helping me master "military speak" (trust me, for this civvy it was like a crash course learning a foreign language), along with helping me to understand the complexities of rank, branches of government, and all the nuances of a life in uniform. You guys are both "Great Americans." THANK YOU for your service to this country and for helping a crazy writer-lady, *moi* (to steal Chip's designation for me, LOL!).

PROLOGUE

New Orleans . . . deep within the bayou

"Bring her to me," Elder Vlad said through his fangs, his voice slicing the stillness of the night with a hissing whisper.

Vampire sentries vaporized into a dark mist, moving swiftly and silently between the trees. The ancient leader of the Vampire Cartel narrowed his gaze as he inhaled deeply, then vanished, only to reappear at the far side of the chase. Quickly moving orbs of darkness had an invisible quarry on the run. Branches snapped, underbrush crackled, but Elder Vlad remained steadfast and patient, watching them drive his prey directly to him. She would tire soon; she was no immortal . . . just very, very old and strong.

The moment the animal scent came within a yard of him, he cast out a thunderous black charge from his gnarled, hook-like fingers. A blue-black spider's web of dark energy spread across the ground, and a feral growl, then female shriek, sent bats and owls into an aerial frenzy. His sentries immediately stopped their pursuit and touched down in the damp mud, their black leather trench coats billowing on an unnatural wind behind them and their boots displacing fertile soil. They all watched dispassionately as the invisible entity that had been snared slowly lost power and had to reveal itself.

"Such a beauty and such a waste," Elder Vlad said with a slight taunt in his voice as he walked forward and watched the gorgeous entity thrash against his black-charged netting. Her unstable image flickered, finally showing glimpses of a pristine white coat that was mottled with velvety black spots. The pattern on her fur was so carefully created that he reached out his fingers to touch it, and then laughed as she yanked away and tried to savage his hand. "I am not your enemy, Empress," he cooed.

Panting and clearly winded, the snow leopard became still. Her face was distended by saber tooth–length fangs, but it slowly began to normalize as she stared at the ancient Vampire.

"Lady Jung Suk, why didn't you come to us first?" Elder Vlad asked, and then tapped a hooked nail against his thin lips. "I don't understand why you would put your fate in the hands of the Unseelie Fae—not even a main political player, at that?"

Her image continued to phase in and out in a pulsing throb, allowing her captors to witness the partial metamorphosis that had left her body in leopard form and ready for attack, but made her face an eerie combination of woman and beast.

"Kiagehul promised me that he was in alliance with the Vampires through the baron," she said, breathing hard.

Elder Vlad shook his head. "That was indeed unfortunate."

"Only Vampires can grant immortality," she said, slumping and no longer fighting against the black charge. "I knew that."

"And an entity of your age didn't know to even fact-check such a claim?" Elder Vlad smiled. "Come, come, milady, let us not toy with each other."

"He got me out of the country," she said, clutching the black charge in desperation but quickly letting it go with a painful wail. "Then he took me to see the baron—there were discussions that led me to believe that Kiagehul could pull this off, and Geoff promised that if he did, he would pick out a young body and—"

"Enough," Elder Vlad said, holding up his hand. With a wave of his palm he dropped the black-charged barrier, causing Lady Jung Suk to fall to the ground. He held out his hand to her and she looked at it for a moment, clearly afraid, as his sentries surrounded her. But the old Vampire stood his ground. "Have you decided what type of body you'd prefer?"

Lady Jung Suk slowly placed a clawed paw in his hand. "I cannot shift back . . . I am a disembodied. I am trapped," she said quietly.

"I know. And if I bring you a young, nubile body to inhabit, then you will be indebted to me . . . say . . . forever?"

She closed her eyes and nodded. Elder Vlad snapped his fingers and two of his sentries instantly disappeared, moving the underbrush with their invisible velocity.

"I am sure as an ancient sorceress you are able to

perform the spell. Should we provide you with the proper resources?"

"Yes," she murmured and then stared into the elderly Vampire's eyes with an unblinking gaze.

"My apologies for any part our representative may have played in misleading you. Baron Geoff Montague was not authorized to enter into a negotiation of that nature—one that had vast political implications." Elder Vlad released a weary sigh. "However, we do have great use for someone with your dark arts talent, as well as your obvious fighting capacity as a Were Leopard. Perhaps as a royal assassin . . ."

Lady Jung Suk bowed. "My apologies for not more thoroughly investigating the scenario presented to me . . . my eagerness led to the blunder. But I am at your complete disposal . . . for the generosity of your amnesty."

Elder Vlad offered her a sinister smile and then graciously kissed the back of her hand. The sound of a struggle and a muffled scream made the entire retinue in the swamp turn to stare at the source of the disturbance.

A young girl held in a vise-like grip twisted against one of the Vampire guard's hold while the other gestured toward her with a toothy smirk as though imitating Vanna White.

"You approve?" Elder Vlad said, leaving Lady Jung Suk's side to closely study the terrified Asian co-ed. "She seems to be no more than twenty years young," he said, deeply inhaling near the young woman's throat. "We thought that you might want to stay with that which is familiar, but you can change ethnicity, if you'd like . . . we can bring you a blonde, or—"

"She's exquisite," Lady Jung Suk breathed out, walking closer. "Drain her, but not to the point of death. I need to pattern over her soul with the spell just as she expires so that I can be a strong conjuring source for you. This is the advantage of the covens—they have souls that can be sold or bartered to the Ultimate Darkness . . . I am of minimal use as a sorceress without one."

Another muffled scream was caught into the sentry's hand. Elder Vlad simply laughed as he looked at the traumatized girl.

"Oh, do uncover her mouth . . . the screaming is the best part."

CHAPTER 1

NORAD . . . Denver, Colorado

It was surreal, really. Captain Sasha Trudeau stood at attention in the war room with her gaze focused on a point on the wall. She was two thousand feet below the surface of the earth again and surrounded in a granite-encapsulated city. There were no shadows within this fluorescent hell to escape into. Twenty-five-ton steel doors had closed behind her and her team. This was just another one of the military's citadels, but today it felt like a prison.

Now she understood what Doc had meant: A political schmooze trip on Air Force One to meet the president and the first lady had nothing to do with what was about to go down. The military was, in essence, its own government and its own country. It didn't matter if a civilian president was the commander in chief, there would always be things known by the Pentagon and the military intelligence community that flew under the radar. This meeting was obviously one of them.

What the president knew and understood was so far

removed from the tactical realities of what the Joint
Chiefs had cooked up that Sasha felt numb. The new
president had been excited to talk to her, curious, and
awed by the knowledge that the supernatural existed.
They'd met at his insistence. His wife had warmly embraced her, and Sasha had vowed to never wash the
shirt that had the first lady's elegant touch on it. Never
in Sasha's life had she been so proud to serve as in that
moment when she was told "job well done" by two
people who seemed to have it all . . . intelligence, honor,
love for each other, their children, and their country.
They were world leaders in her opinion, had respect for
other nations, and yet kept it all together as a couple
and a family despite the stress that went along with that
leadership. Simply being in their presence had instilled
hope. Maybe she and Hunter could have that, she'd
thought for all of two days . . . until now.

She hated these sessions. Sasha's mind had latched
on to the positive, clinging to it in military silence as
her entire mission was lambasted as a complete failure.
Talking heads on the video teleconference made her
swallow a snarl. She hated VTCs. Old bastards. What
did they know about *this* kind of war? The Cold War
didn't have jack on a confrontation with the supernatural, if the Unseelie or Vampires decided to retaliate.

Sasha looked at the stern expressions that appeared
on the huge screen at the end of the war room. The
broadcast was coming from multiple sources—the Pentagon and USSOCOM at MacDill Air Force Base in
Florida—and everything that was being said made the
hair on the nape of her neck bristle as she cut Doc a sidelong glance. He never returned it. That was probably

best. One didn't blink or stutter in the face of U.S. Special Ops Command.

Before the inflexible scrutiny today, she'd been complimented by the president on her brave handling of the situation in New Orleans, despite the human casualties that couldn't be avoided. The president, a man of reason, had spoken to her frankly, openly, asking her opinion about how they could address potential future threats, as well as her best guess at how they could do PR damage control—knowing the public would freak out.

Down here in the bowels of NORAD was another world. The Pentagon was broadcasting from *the tank,* their situation room. The whole array of brass was on the teleconference—the freaking secretary of defense, the chairman of the Joint Chiefs, the vice chairman, the army, as well as the air force chiefs of staff, plus the chief of naval operations and the commandant of the marine corps. *Sheesh.* All of her general's chain of command was present—starting with the U.S. Army Special Ops Com commander from Fort Bragg. This was so not good. She wouldn't be surprised if General Westford didn't just retire after this fiasco. Her general was getting his ass chewed out by the secretary of defense . . . and as always, the shit would roll downhill.

But the next words spoken drew Sasha's full attention to the screen. Disbelief made her slack-jawed.

"This is why we've always had a backup team in waiting," the bulldog-jowled General Rumsford said, glaring into the screen. "Ever since the tragic death of General Donald Wilkerson, we knew there was potential for this project to get out of control, and it finally did."

Sasha felt her lip beginning to curl but took a slow, steady inhale to keep her cool. *Is this the same cleanup squad that mowed down Rod Butler's entire squad in Afghanistan? Same SOBs that tried to drop Woods and Fisher!*

"Now, wait just a minute," General Westford said, the crimson spreading up his neck to begin to color his ruddy face. He dragged his fingers through his damp blond crew cut and narrowed his hard blue gaze as he leaned forward, slapping a meaty palm down on the polished mahogany. "Yes, there were civilian casualties during this particular operation—but as you well know, and have all experienced in any battle theater, that is bound to happen when dealing with urban warfare. Collateral damage is regrettable but often unavoidable. That is the price of urban warfare. So don't act like this is some new outcome! With all due respect, each of us in our long careers has experienced this. I stand by my Paranormal Containment Unit. These men and women did an outstanding job in keeping this entire thing from escalating to a level that might have otherwise been catastrophic."

"Paranormal *Containment* Unit," the bulldog reiterated with disdain. "It wasn't *contained,* Westford."

"And neither was Iraq or Afghanistan!" General Westford shot back. "I've only got Trudeau, Holland, plus a biotech crew of three hired civil service specialists backing her up, with two soldiers, Lieutenants Fisher and Woods, to keep a lid on a threat that is bigger than all the bull going on in the Middle East and Pakistan combined! Give me more resources, and we'll have the threat contained."

"That's precisely what we intend to do—Colonel Madison and his squad will be the new boots on the ground. This time out we want an all-human squad on this, one that cannot be compromised by potential interspecies affiliations or that we have to worry might flip out under duress—or given the phase of the moon . . . no offense to Captain Trudeau. We would like to offer you an opportunity to continue your fine work in an army staff position, General . . . while Colonel Madison takes over command of PCU."

"You're burying me in the army bureaucracy," General Westford said, pushing back from the table. "You might as well draw up my retirement papers, then. This is an outrage."

"General," the secretary of defense said in a conciliatory tone. "Let's allow cooler heads to prevail before you make such a monumental decision. *We value you.* Know that. You are not being buried. We need a man of your skill and knowledge on the policy end of this very new threat—because, believe me, the president wants smart people making smart decisions about how to handle all of this. We need a military liaison to the secretary of state, given the potential international issues this paranormal problem raises."

General Westford didn't respond but released a guffaw as his noncommittal answer for the moment.

Sasha just stared at the screen, now so angry that she was seeing spots before her eyes. They were replacing her general and pulling her team off the mission? All of the uniforms and the colorful braid on the high-definition-broadcast stuffed chests began to bleed together, but she didn't blink.

"Sirs, I have to interject," Doc Holland said, bracing his aged ebony hands against the table. "There are delicate—no, *fragile* relationships down there in the paranormal community. Have you read Captain Trudeau's full report? If you send an unfamiliar human team down there with a *shoot first, ask questions later* mentality, you are asking for military casualties. Even worse, you have no idea what long-standing retaliatory aggression this course of action might create."

"It has already been decided," the secretary of defense said calmly, gaining a grim nod from the other Joint Chiefs. "This was a rogue project under the late General Donald Wilkerson, as you are aware, Doctor Holland . . . and while we know that it is difficult to bring closure to your research, the time has come where we must shut down the PCU in its current form in favor of a more strategic, and more secure, way of interfacing with this threat. The moment we all learned about it, a phase-out strategy was set in place . . . but as long as the PCU showed signs of viability, we were willing to go along with the experiment and learn what this new environment—or rather, this new universe—actually held. But with rising political pressure and the growing public alarm, there is only one solution. The PCU has to go dark, and if there are still any targets of value out there in the New Orleans area—on North American soil, for that matter—they have to be eliminated."

Now Sasha *knew* they were crazy.

"Permission to speak freely, sirs," Sasha said as respectfully as possible.

"Permission granted," the bulldog on the screen barked back.

Sasha hesitated for a moment. She wasn't directing her comments to Rumsford, but rather toward the more reasonable new secretary of defense, who'd clearly come under General Rumsford's sway. For a second she wondered how the hell some of the old political hacks got to remain at the decision-making table when there was a fresh, new administration—but there wasn't time to dwell on that. It was what it was, and the Pentagon didn't do change well or quickly. Drawing on all the political correctness in her bones, she simply stated the jarring facts.

"Sir," Sasha said in a monotone voice, "to engage the supernatural community with threat of extermination will start a war on U.S. soil that we, as a nation, are unprepared to fight. It would be akin to dropping a nuclear bomb in the middle of Times Square or, in this case, in New Orleans's French Quarter. The fallout will be catastrophic, the recovery in half-lives . . . Your primary foes, Vampires and the Unseelie Fae, are immortal, sir." Sasha dragged her gaze back to the benign point on the wall and lifted her chin.

Pandemonium broke out at the table and on the screen. Finally, after a few moments, order was restored.

"This is why it is imperative that Colonel Madison and his team do an impartial assessment," the secretary said. "A second pair of eyes, a second report. If Captain Trudeau's claim has merit, then we will undertake a new course of action. Colonel Madison has already arrived at NORAD and will need you to fully debrief him, Captain. General Westford, we expect your full cooperation in this transition, your request for retirement notwithstanding."

"And until then, Captain Trudeau is to remain under house arrest," the bulldog said with satisfaction coating his words. He clasped his thick hands together, obviously enjoying the newly bestowed power that came with his secret new cabinet post as secretary of containment. "Her movement is to be restricted to the base, and she is not to make contact with any of her New Orleans—"

"What?" General Westford shouted. "Are you saying that she and her team are being brought up on some sort of charges?"

"No . . . and 'house arrest' may be too strong a term, General Rumsford," the secretary said calmly. He glanced at the general to his left, making the man concede with a gruff cough. "Captain Trudeau is not under house arrest, per se, but New Orleans is off limits to her and her team until Colonel Madison completes his mission. We would like the captain's area of operation to remain highly visible and within the state of Colorado until further notice. Colonel Madison's squad is highly trained, Delta Force, not unlike members of the captain's team, and he has a blend of support from our military intelligence community as well. His job is to not only assess the problem caused by the last series of incidents, but also to go down there, unhindered by anyone else's efforts, to develop a public containment strategy. We have got to get this under control. Have you watched the news, General?"

General Westford pushed back farther from the table. "I've seen the news, sir."

"The area is crawling with every crackpot ghost hunter, paranormal investigator, psychic who thinks he can talk to the dead, and journalist who wants to get the money-shot of Big Foot. Civilians are coming out of the woodwork with outrageous claims; everyone who can is trying to get paid for their fifteen minutes of fame. Cell phone video has proliferated on the Internet, and social networking sites are causing additional hysteria, while we're analyzing what is bogus and what is authentic, which is eating up vital resources in a way we hadn't anticipated. For damage-control purposes, we need a highly visible black-ops team to go down there, kick in a few doors, rattle a few cages, and hopefully drive what's underground way underground, so that we can do a full media report to debunk the evidence of any so-called paranormal activity. They have a clear mission—if they encounter anything, contain it or eliminate it. They are not going down there to negotiate with it."

The secretary released a long and weary breath before continuing. "Captain Trudeau, we thank you for your service, but on this mission, you and your team are hereby relieved of your PCU duty until further notice."

The Seelie Court . . . New Orleans

Sir Rodney weaved, stumbled, and caught himself against a bedroom tapestry as he made his way toward the dining table in his master suite. Rupert, his trusty valet, dropped the breakfast tray he'd been carrying and rushed over to Sir Rodney's side.

"Milord, are you ill?"

Sir Rodney waved him off. "Nah . . . probably too much of the ale last night. I'll be fine."

Ignoring the monarch's words, Rupert helped him into a chair and then rushed to the door to call the guards.

"Please call Sir Garth and the king's top advisors immediately! I fear milord has been poisoned!"

"You're making too much of a little stumble, old friend," Sir Rodney called out, but he was barely able to hold himself up where he sat. "It was a wonderful night of debauchery, is all."

Rupert gently closed the door as the guards rushed off. "Milord, I have been your best man for many a year and have yet to see a night of debauchery turn your blue eyes to pure black."

Denver, Colorado

"You okay?" Bradley asked, going over to Clarissa quickly and holding her by both arms.

She nodded weakly and then slumped against him. "I'm just a little nauseous," she said, dabbing at her brow. "Could've been the takeout we had last night."

Bradley felt her brow and stared into her eyes. "Or it could be the residual effects of the possession you experienced a few weeks back when trying to save this team in the shadow lands."

She hugged him and tried to laugh off his concerns.

"Or you could be ultraparanoid, which is why I love you so."

He stooped down beside her. "I love you, too," he said softly, "and that's why I'm paranoid. I saw what that Unseelie black spell almost did to you."

"Stop worrying," she said and then winced. "It could be something as basic as a girl getting cramps."

"Your skin is clammy and—"

"I just need to go to the ladies' room," she said, standing with effort.

Unconvinced, Bradley stood with her and began walking with her.

She stopped, turned to him, and smiled weakly. "I know we're a couple, but there are still some things I'm not ready for you to see—and going into the bathroom with me is—"

"Okay, okay," he said with a nervous smile. "Then I'll wait out here for you."

"Brads, we're in NORAD, okaaay? Nothing can get down here on the base. It's demon-protected—"

"Yada, yada, yada," he said flatly, not moving from the bathroom entrance.

"If the guys see you standing guard on the ladies' room, they'll get all freaked out. So why don't you just go back to the lab, all right? I don't want to have to explain to Winters, Woods, and Fisher that it was that time of the month, I got a little queasy, and you—"

"Okay, okay . . . for the sake of your privacy, I'll go back. But—"

"I'll be fine," she said, pasting on a smile and then slipping beyond the door.

She waited until she heard Bradley's footsteps ringing out in the corridor and then rushed into a stall and hurled. Greenish, gooey phlegm bubbled up her throat and spewed into the toilet. The awful taste and hard, brackish smell made her close her eyes with a shiver. But she did feel better. She flushed the refuse away and then hugged herself.

A cold, hard sweat had broken out all over her body, and after checking that her period hadn't come on, the next worry assailed her. It was time to buy an at-home pregnancy test, even though she and Bradley had been pretty careful . . . then again, *almost all the time* wasn't 100 percent.

"Damn . . . ," she murmured and then exited the stall to wash her hands and face. She so did not need this right now, but if she was pregnant, then so be it. If there was anyone in the world she'd be happy to have a child with, it was Bradley. But she didn't want him to think she'd tried to trap him. She hadn't. This was unplanned.

She knew how he'd take it. Bradley was so old-fashioned, he'd want to marry her and would insist that she stop doing anything related to the paranormal that could possibly injure their unborn child. As she approached the sink, she shook her head and chuckled to herself. Here she was projecting a whole scenario and she didn't even have the facts yet. Okay, that was a sign to not do that. "Get the facts first McGill, before you start emotional drama on the team." Hell . . . maybe she was having a hard bout of PMS.

Clarissa turned on the faucet, washed her hands, and then bent to splash cold water on her face.

But when she lifted her head to dry her face with a towel, she froze. Her blue eyes were pitch black.

Not one word. Sasha would not say one word until after the general said his final piece. Hunter had been so frickin' right that her elevated blood pressure was causing her ears to ring. She just stared at General Westford once the monitors went black. Fury made her fist her hands at her sides. The desire to flee, to just find a hallway shadow and be out, was so strong that she bit her lip.

Under house arrest? The mere suggestion was absurd, even if the secretary did recant and give her the state of Colorado to roam—WTF? They could kiss her natural wolf ass! *And* they had fired her general—had reassigned her ally and mentor? She was going to tell her team the bullshit news, go back to her apartment, find Hunter, and then find the nearest bar.

Once she got out of earshot and could get Doc in a room alone, she'd blow. But not now, and not in front of the general. His eyes said it all, even if his tone of voice was gruff. The apology in them made her feel only slightly better. However, the fact that the man's career had been shredded by one botched mission weighed on her soul.

"This is bullshit, Captain . . . but my hands are tied. Those poor dumb bastards are gonna go down there and get themselves killed if they stumble on the wrong nest."

"Sir, yes, sir," she said, not hiding the sarcasm in her tone. It wasn't directed at General Westford, and he seemed to know that. He caught her inflection with a nod, acknowledging that he felt the same way. It was the most either one of them could say without crossing the insubordination line no matter what they felt.

"Just stay in the area and stay in touch—don't go dark on us. I suspect we'll be calling you soon for a rescue-and-recovery mission. I'm not throwing you in the brig or locking you in your damned apartment. You aren't an enemy combatant and haven't done anything wrong; I don't care what they say. And you damned sure aren't going to flip out into some monster—if that was going to happen, you would have long before now. This is political jockeying and gamesmanship, because this is about to be the new president's favorite secret initiative. You and I both saw the look on his face when you debriefed him . . . This, Captain, is about *power*. It's all about who is going to run the real PCU, and who is gonna get the unlimited black-ops budget to go with it, trust me. But one thing for sure, I'm not going to put a good solid soldier who has risked everything for this country out to pasture . . . just give me a little time to work this out—and keep your nose clean until I do. Right now, I've got nothing to lose. I'll be retired soon enough."

She stared at General Westford and saluted him. "Thank you, sir."

"No . . . thank you," he said and then glanced at Doc Holland. "They don't understand. Hell, at first I didn't understand, until you all showed me what was at stake . . . told me things that will never allow me to get another good night's sleep for the rest of my life. All of us with an ounce of common sense know that Captain Trudeau is right, but that young arrogant prick, Madison, doesn't know it. That's the problem." General Westford shook his head. "I met him this morning when he came on base. Thinks he knows it all. Those poor young bastards that they're sending into New Orleans will pay the price for the political one-upmanship that's going on at the Pentagon—but then again, what else is new? That's just Washington as we know it."

"It's suicide," Doc Holland said, shaking his head. "Fools, all of them. This isn't any kind of conventional war—this is madness."

The general let out a weary breath. "No, Doctor—this is fear . . . and fear makes fools of us all."

CHAPTER 2

"You cannot be serious," Winters said, glancing around at the others in the lab.

"Figures," Bradley muttered and then fixed his gaze on Winters for a moment. "You're the youngest here, so you still haven't learned that the little guy always gets screwed."

Clarissa slipped back into the lab, picking up on the conversation. Bradley cast her a worried glance, but she gave him a discreet look that allayed his fears and told him they'd talk later.

"What'd I miss, guys?" Clarissa glanced around at the haggard expressions in the room. "I take it the meeting with the Joint Chiefs didn't go well."

"You got it," Sasha said with a scowl. "I'm on house arrest for a botched mission and some new, arrogant . . . ahem, a new colonel, guy named Madison, is taking over and we've been told to stand down."

"So, like, nothing we did mattered?" Fisher said in disbelief, opening his lanky arms and then dragging his fingers through his sweat-spiked red hair. "First they fire on us, and then clear us as nonwolves, but now we're downgraded to this BS spectator position? What gives, Captain?"

"Might as well get used to it, bro," Woods said, pushing off a lab stool. "Face it, we're cannon fodder. They don't give a rat's ass about us. We were an experiment born out of a petri dish who happened to get the right concoction that made us familiars and not full-blown Werewolves." He turned to Doc Holland and saluted him with bitter sarcasm. "Much obliged, sir!"

"This sucks, big time," Clarissa said, her hurt gaze holding Sasha's.

"I know," Sasha muttered, beginning to pace and not caring that the walls had ears. "It blows, it sucks, yeah, yeah, and what? There isn't jack we can do about it right now but take it on the chin. Wish I had better news, but I don't . . . and we've gotta debrief—"

Sasha stopped mid-sentence as a colonel entered the room with Doc Holland and General Westford. She and her entire squad stood at attention, as was protocol for the general—but she was really having a tough time even thinking about saluting the guy she assumed to be Colonel Madison.

There was instant dislike between them; it was in his haughty glare and the vibes that radiated from his aura. Sasha stared into a pair of hard, dark brown eyes and a stone-chiseled face the hue of dark walnut. He was almost a full head taller than her; that put him at about six foot three, and he was clearly proud of it. She could tell by the way he looked down his nose and surveyed the lab as though something in it were rotten, like old garbage—or her and her team. Instinct told her that Madison would be the kind to use his height advantage to try to loom over others, invading personal space to get the psychological advantage. His stance was more than perfect military posture; there was an arrogance to it that went beyond fit-body male swagger. She'd seen his kind before; the kind of officer who assumed that because she was female, she was somehow inferior or inept. Part of her wanted to chuckle—the part that was on the side of her DNA that could rip his fucking throat out if he blinked at her wrong.

"At ease," the general said, and then tensely began the formal introductions. "Captain Sasha Trudeau, Colonel Keith Madison."

Out of respect, Sasha forced a salute. "Colonel." She waited for a nod or some form of recognition that never came. Okaaay. "Sir, I take it you have already been briefed on Doctor Xavier Holland's stellar reputation. Permit me to introduce my team. Our civilian hires who come with phenomenal university résumés are Doctor John Bradley, who is our dark arts spec; Doctor Clarissa McGill, our resident bio expert; Mark Winters, who is our computer and technology spec; and Lieutenants Woods and Fisher are—"

"I know, I know, Captain—the guys, like yourself, with compromised DNA," Madison shot back, cutting Sasha off.

"Wanna see how compromised?" Sasha said with an angry half smile. "In the interest of a thorough debriefing, sir," she amended to stay just within the very fine lines of insubordination that she was treading dangerously near.

Colonel Madison nodded, a challenge clear in his eyes. "Any day or night, Captain."

"Under a full moon might be better, sir," Sasha said as the hair began to bristle at the nape of her neck. Human or wolf, an alpha challenge was an alpha challenge.

"No, I think you might be more impressed by one Max Hunter, sir," Woods said, his gaze now locked on Madison. "He's a friendly with a mean overbite."

"Are you threatening me, soldier?" Colonel Madison asked, stepping in close to Woods. "Tell me you aren't that stupid with a commanding officer present."

"Not at all, sir," Woods said, not backing down in the least, but keeping his answers politically correct. "Our orders were to give you a full briefing on the enemy combatant's full capabilities. That was my suggestion—a demonstration of that by a friendly, sir."

"Gentlemen," General Westford said, clearly conflicted, but staying within the authority of his office to keep order. "This transition from one team to another is a hard choice that has been made, but it has been made nonetheless. Period." He stared at Colonel Madison for a moment to get his point across. "This is the finest team that I have seen to date. No matter what you may have heard from the brass in Washington or out at Mac-Dill, this Paranormal Containment Unit has brought us valuable intel while engaged with new species and threats to our way of life that almost defy explanation. Captain Trudeau and her squad have my utmost respect—they should also have yours. They know this enemy and have seen what it can do on the ground."

"I have read the reports *thoroughly,* sir," Colonel Madison shot back, staying just within the bounds of propriety.

"And they have *lived* the goddamned reports, Colonel," General Westford said between his teeth. "Do I make myself clear?"

"Sir, yes, sir," Colonel Madison said, looking past the general to a point on the wall, obviously peeved.

"Then carry on," the general said to Sasha. "Maybe if Colonel Madison opens his mind, he just might learn something."

"Send Sasha Trudeau a Fae missive," Garth urgently commanded the captain of the Fae Guards.

The lithe archer drew a silver, iridescent arrow from his quiver and waited as Sir Rodney's top magic advisor prepared his wand to infuse the arrow with the critical information. He watched with ancient eyes as an arc of white static charge flitted from the tip of his wand into the tip of the arrowhead.

"If this falls into the wrong hands, it will self-destruct," he said with unwavering confidence. "Demons cannot infiltrate the white light, nor can they abduct the silver. It is programmed to follow her until it finds her, but to not reveal itself until she is alone."

"Aye," the archer said, drawing the arrow into his bow. "But if she's in that blasted human underground hell hole they call NORAD, my arrow will not reach her until she's aboveground."

Garth sighed, and nodded. "Do it, man. Before the Seelie declare war on the Unseelie for this most recent act of aggression against our king, we must inform our battle allies. We must know that the wolf Federations stand at the ready to bear arms alongside the Fae, as they ever were. An attempt to send residual possession spells against Sir Rodney is an act of war. It is a full declaration!"

"But she was called in by her human commanders. They have her sequestered . . . it could be days before we know that she's received our missive." He pulled a long Phoenix feather off the end of it and handed it to Sir Garth. "Once this burns, we know she's read it and it's burned into the ether. Until then . . ."

"We wait," Garth said. The aged Gnome lifted his chin and stuffed the feather inside the sleeve of his long monk-like brown habit. "What other choice have we got?"

News trucks clogged the French Quarter as news helicopters beat the night air. Bright television crew lights added an unnatural glare to the sunset. Martial law had been declared, making it illegal for civilians to be on the streets past nine PM, but the media would take that right up to the last possible moment in an attempt to get a story.

Russell Conway swirled his beer in the bottle and then turned his longneck up to his mouth while looking out of the bar's window. The Fair Lady was a paranormal joint, as word on the street had it . . . then again, the private blood clubs might have been a better choice, if only he could get in. But you had to know somebody who knew somebody—Vampires definitely weren't going to let him in without an intro.

With all the bright lights and human curiosity, anything that was remotely paranormal most likely had been driven way underground, especially Vampires. For some odd reason, he was drawn to them tonight.

Something in his gut told him that if anyone would have direct access to what had gone down here in New Orleans, it would be that species that foolish humans refused to believe existed. He knew otherwise.

The bartender signaled Russell when he set down his empty bottle. "Want another?"

"Yeah," Russell said, his time-hardened gaze roving the establishment. "Tell me," he added when the bartender brought him a new bottle, "who do I have to see to get into the Blood Oasis?"

The hefty bartender smirked. "Yo, buddy, you're obviously new around here. Half of New Orleans and the rest of the United States want to get in that joint, or joints like it. You been watching the news? So what brings you to town all the way from probably Texas—judging by the way you dress? You a ghost hunter or paranormal investigator, or something?" He looked over Russell's worn fringed leather jacket, cowboy hat, dirty jeans, and cowboy boots. "Bounty hunter or trapper, right?"

A pair of hard hazel eyes stared at the burly man behind the bar. Russell smiled a strained half smile. His getup had worked, and yet it had also told on him. He'd have to amend that. He was a long way from South Dakota, but no one needed to be the wiser. However, he'd been correctly pegged as a bounty hunter.

"I'm not a ghost hunter or bounty hunter," Russell said and then took a swig of his fresh beer. The cold ale felt good going down, and he winced with satisfaction and then rubbed the five o'clock shadow on his jaw with a callused palm. "I'm just a guy from a small-town rag wanting to get an angle. Might put it on my blog."

The bartender laughed. "Okay. So you came all the

way here to get the story that'll get you a job with the *New York Times,* huh?" He shook his head and began wiping out glasses with a rag of questionable cleanliness. "Looking at the long hair and the outfit, I'da swore you was a bounty hunter looking to get yourself in a world of hurt over there at the Oasis."

"Why, is there something over at the Oasis that will hurt me?"

"Only the mob, maybe, if you go placing screwy bets and trying to sneak into their upscale club, son. They don't want any part of this circus going on in New Orleans. All of it's bad for business—especially shutting down the city as soon as it gets dark." The older Creole man leaned forward. "All the business during the day don't make up for the loss of late-night carousing, if you follow. People don't drink the same during the day as they do at night . . . not as hard and therefore tips be slow, you understand?"

"So, I take it you don't know anybody who knows anybody . . . not even for the right price?" Russell studied himself in the mirror behind the bar for a moment. The bartender was right. He needed a good shave, some preppy clothes, something that said *college professor interested in making friends with the supernatural world via a sighting,* or maybe *hungry reporter.*

The bartender laughed again. "Listen, son, let's not be hasty . . . everything is negotiable in the Big Easy. This *is* New Orleans."

"Can you believe that asshole?" Sasha muttered under her breath as soon as Colonel Madison had left the lab with General Westford.

Everybody on her team just shook their heads. Bradley and Winters pointed toward the ceiling tiles to remind her that they were probably being monitored.

"Well, since we're officially off duty for the foreseeable future . . . I say we go find the Road Hawg, then find a fifth of Jack Daniel's and get snot-slinging hammered," Woods said, looking at Sasha. "What say you, Captain?"

"My call is tequila—that's even uglier," Fisher said. "Shots are called for, in my humble estimation."

"Salt, lime, then brrrrr—tequila," Winters agreed. "Isn't that the order, Cap?"

"Nah . . . Kamikazes just seem like they'd be more appropriate, given the frickin' circumstances," Clarissa said, raking her plump fingers through her short blond bob. "I don't even want to remember this conversation until maybe three days from now."

Bradley just gave Clarissa a look.

She smiled at him. "What?" She seemed slightly disoriented. "That oughta kill any leftover bad takeout in my system—that or bring it all up."

"I'm going home," Doc said. "You all might want to do the same. I'm going to order a nice steak dinner, open a beer, and take my high blood-pressure meds— I'm too old for this shit. Then I'm going to watch a movie and just go to bed. Tomorrow morning, I'll begin working on my overrun garden. Might just follow General Westford's lead and retire. I fulfilled my initial service obligation a long time ago—put in my thirty years, retired at the mandatory age, and came back to work the next day as a civil service hire. And I've served in that role long enough to get another pension. I'm going home to think about all my options; you all might want to do the same."

Sasha just stared at Doc for a moment. "You'd really retire?" The thought was incomprehensible to her—not that he'd leave the military, but that he'd leave the team . . . would leave her.

"I refuse to have a stroke about what I can't control," Doc said in a weary tone. "One day you'll hopefully get to my age and see the wisdom of my approach. Self-destruction is—"

"Gratifying," Woods said, kicking over a chair.

"Totally," Fisher said, punching the wall. "Hell, me and Woods are beyond our initial service obligation as commissioned officers, just like you are, Cap." Fisher held Sasha's stricken gaze. "Just say the word. We can resign at will, just gotta give ninety days' notice."

"No contract to break like enlisted men," Woods said, staring at her. "No contract re-up, no end of time served to worry about, no reenlistment NCO sweating us about bonuses for signing our lives away for another five or six years . . . your call, Captain. If this bullshit is too thick, we're with you."

Clarissa nodded. "We're civvy hires," she said, glancing at Winters and Bradley, who also nodded. "We could probably all resign and then go government consultant on them to make ten times what we make now just for providing vital expertise, without you guys being in harm's way, ya know?"

"My point exactly," Doc said, rubbing the nape of his neck. "With this change of leadership and all the political games about to go down, it might make more sense to be free agents. Who knows? Time will bear all that out. But I need to go somewhere quiet to think."

"I need to go debrief Hunter," Sasha said. "He's waiting for word at my place. Save us a seat and start lining up the shots. And, Doc, you might not want to get too comfortable at home. After I explain this bull to Hunter, both of us might need a Jack Daniel's IV drip."

CHAPTER 3

"What!" Hunter stalked away from her and punched the wall, taking out a huge chunk of plaster with his fist. "This is bullshit, Sasha—complete bullshit!"

"Yeah, tell me about it," she said, and then motioned with her arm around the room. She knew her apartment was being monitored. It was a fact she hated but lived with. "Care to discuss this somewhere else, where I'm pretty sure it won't end up in an MI report?"

She flung open the coat closet door and then waved her arm in front of the dark shadow within it. "After you."

Hunter shook his head. "Ladies first."

The Fae missive hit the wall just as Sasha slipped into the shadows with Hunter, and then pulled out—hovering, waiting, sensing, trying to relocate its delivery target, who was once again unreachable.

Two seconds after they'd entered the shadow lands, Sasha's voice exited her body in a sonic boom. "I cannot believe it—but I do believe it! That's the pure tragedy of it all. You told me one day this would happen," she shouted, walking a hot path back and forth in the misty cavern. "You have no idea how hard it was to keep from shape-shifting right there on the spot! *Oh!* And that arrogant son of a bitch colonel they replaced me with—he's going to get an entire squad slaughtered, not to mention however many innocent civvies in the streets of New Orleans! You should have seen the way he disrespected me and my men. I thought Woods was going to get put in the brig for insubordination . . . right after I showed the colonel what a real live wolf combatant looked like. I swear I wanted to rip the guy's throat out, the way he spoke to us and blew off Doc! Even General Westford had to check him. I thought Westford was gonna have a coronary—the man retired on the spot!"

Sasha whirled on Hunter and folded her arms over her chest, breathing hard. "Go ahead. Say it. You told me so. Said that I couldn't live a double life—being a part of a Shadow Wolf pack and being a part of the human military. Just go ahead and get it out once and for all."

"First of all, I'm not the enemy." Hunter looked at her, his eyes blazing. "I have no interest in saying those things to you, Sasha," he added in a low, threatening tone through distended canines. "My only interest is with those who have injured you. Give me their names—starting with the colonel."

For a moment she didn't move. Then, quickly realizing that her mate had gone into hunt-and-protect mode, she held out her arms in front of her. "Whoa, whoa, whoa—I was just metaphorically talking about ripping out the guy's throat."

"And you know I don't deal in metaphors, Sasha,"

Hunter said in a low rumble. "Give me the bastard's name, and I guarantee you he won't ever disrespect the alpha mate of the North American Shadow Wolf Clan."

Perverse gratification flitted through her spirit for a moment, before logic overruled it. "Thank you," she said, more calmly, now not nearly as enraged as she'd been. "But I can't let you do that."

Hunter cocked his head to the side as though he'd heard her wrong. "Let?"

Sasha rubbed the nape of her neck and then released a hard sigh. "You know what I mean." She looked up at him. "I'm not the enemy."

"To be sure," Hunter said, beginning to pace. "Nor am I about to stand by and allow your territory to be challenged! That is a matter of principle. What gives them the right to take your position?"

"You understand hierarchy and rank, Hunter," she said flatly. "That part is the same in both the wolf world and in the human military world." Her true statement caused him to walk away from her, but she pressed on, feeling more defeated as she spoke. "They have much higher rank than I do and replaced me with someone *they* could trust, since I'm a hybrid . . . a being with one foot in the human world and one in the wolf world—all because Doc created me in a lab." She blew out a weary sigh. "I'm probably not even defined as a human being. I wonder if I even have the same civil rights as the average citizen . . . and as long as I'm in uniform, most of that shit doesn't apply anyway."

Hunter turned to look at her and pointed out toward the mist. "I don't care about their stupid, short-sighted laws—*you exist,* therefore you are a being with inalienable rights. They summoned you down into the bowels of their military base, which to me is no different from one of our clan dens, and then set upon you like a ravenous pack! Then they replaced you under the command of a full-blooded human who knows nothing of our ways or those of the paranormal community! They have done what they have always done—broken a treaty, a covenant that would keep the peace between the nations . . . and yes, Sasha, this is like having a human diplomat who was well liked and well respected get replaced by a fool. You do realize that if the humans make a preemptive strike on the paranormal community, this is undoubtedly going to be war."

"I know," she said quietly. She then closed her eyes as she let out a slow breath.

"This time, they will not be able to just exterminate what they find. Genocide will not be allowed."

"I know," she repeated, now staring at him.

"As alpha clan leaders, we have to make the packs aware of the situation, as well as alert our allies."

Sasha just nodded, too weary at the prospect of what this could all mean to even speak.

"I'll alert my grandfather. Silver Hawk can carry the message throughout the region. I can also contact my brother, Shogun. However, we should both speak directly to Sir Rodney. If he's still in the sidhe where human technology doesn't work, then—"

"I can't leave the area, remember," Sasha said flatly, and then turned to begin to walk deeper into the mist.

"Then where are you going?" Hunter jogged to catch up to her.

"To the bar to throw back a fifth of Jack Daniel's with my very dejected squad."

Hunter grabbed Sasha's arm. "I've never seen you like this," he said quietly.

"Like what?" she said, blowing out a hard breath and blinking back tears.

"So angry that you've lost your drive to fight. You're letting them win."

"Maybe you haven't noticed, but they *have* won, Hunter." She released a sad chuckle and then looked away from him. "I've been put out of my human pack. One botched mission and they turned on me."

"It wasn't a botched mission," he said, not letting go of her arm and forcing her with his voice to look at him. "It wasn't," he added more gently.

"But that doesn't matter now, does it?"

"Yes, it does." Hunter's gaze searched her face. "It matters to the countless paranormal nationals who got saved. The humans aren't the only ones that exist. Sasha . . . you are a head of state."

"In a secret world," she said more quietly than intended. "An unrecognized, secret world—but to them, I'm just a grunt."

"Never, ever say that in front of me again," he said in a low, firm murmur. "You are not a word I refuse to dignify by repeating. You are not a lab mistake. You are a North American Clan alpha she-Shadow." Hunter lifted his chin and cupped her cheek with his palm. "You are majestic, Sasha Trudeau. You are a warrior and it is time for the wolf within to decide which pack she wants to belong to—theirs or ours . . . but that is always going to be your decision. I will wait, no matter what."

Deep conflict tore at her insides, and her mouth simply couldn't form the words to tell him that she would abandon all she knew to go AWOL as a wolf. Just as her wolf was second nature, her military uniform was her second skin. Her entire adult life had been spent in the service of her country. It was all that she knew . . . then there was her team—her family. How could she leave them to fend for themselves in a system that would brutally interrogate them, ruin their careers, and possibly court-martial them for her defection? No one would ever believe they hadn't known in advance or didn't know where she'd fled. She'd have to do this by the books, not by primal instinct, and properly resign.

Still, right now she just wanted to transform into her wolf and run wild and free in the unadulterated North Country.

Hunter seemed to understand all of that without words; it was in his patient eyes as she closed the small gap between them and took his mouth. When his warm arms enfolded her, that's when the silent tears fell in earnest, making their kiss wetter and saltier. And seeming to know that she needed a hug more than anything else right now, he pulled his mouth away from hers and simply enfolded her in his arms.

The tenderness in his touch set off an avalanche of emotions within her—fury, frustration, doubt, panic . . . and the knowledge for the first time that she was really trapped in the existence she'd been manipulated into choosing. She clung to the strong mountain of muscle and bone and flesh that surrounded her and hid her face against his shoulder, refusing to sob, just breathing hard. It wasn't fair—none of it was fair . . . but knowing that life was never fair still didn't make the bitter truth go down any sweeter.

"No matter what you choose, I will not leave you." His promise came out in a firm tone against her hair as his embrace tightened around her.

Sasha nodded and sucked in a shuddering breath, trying to compose herself. He had to go, had to warn the various supernatural communities to lay low while a cowboy colonel came to town.

"I don't want anybody to get hurt," she said on a thick swallow. "No civilians . . . nobody from our side . . . and not even that asshole and his squad." She pulled away from Hunter a bit to stare up at him. "He's just following orders—hasn't a clue. They pumped him up, filled his head with a lot of BS, and the old bastards who play these games aren't on the front lines."

Her body relaxed when Hunter nodded. "The only thing I ever agreed with the Vampires about was when they ripped off Wilkerson's face. Maybe if the war went directly to the source more often, there'd be less war?"

She nodded and blew out a breath, and then rested her forehead in the center of Hunter's chest.

"Are you going to be all right for a few hours . . . or do you want me to come with you to the Road Hawg?"

"I'll be fine," she said, still talking to his stone-cut chest. "Thanks for letting me get it all out."

"It's not out," he said, gently brushing the crown of her head with his lips. "Not by a long shot." Hunter lifted her chin with a finger. "This isn't like a cold that you get out of your system, Sasha . . . this is like cutting off a part of your body. What you're feeling now is only phase one—the realization that the limb has to come off. Just know I'll be there through the process, however long it takes."

She closed her eyes, knowing that what Hunter had said was true. Her general had retired, Doc was talking about doing the same, and her whole squad was toying with the idea of resigning. Everything was coming apart at the seams. It had hurt like hell just acknowledging that change was probably imminent. Then what the hell was it going to feel like if she actually did it, actually left the military? Would there always be phantom pains reminding her of what she used to have? All of it crushed in on her, and right now she could only sort out segments of the problem one at a time.

"I wish I could go with you to explain to our allies what's about to happen," she said, now holding his gaze. "I want them to go underground for a little while . . . but I don't want anybody getting jumpy and deciding to go after the colonel and his squad. That won't make things better."

"You go have a beer or something stronger. I'll be back shortly to join up with you guys for shots—by then I'm sure my nerves will need it." He gave her a tense half smile.

"I'm serious, Hunter," she said with a straight face.

He nodded and lost the smile. "I know—and we want the same thing. No bloodshed."

Sir Rodney stood in the bayou with his retinue of sidhe guards, all eyes angrily surveying the Vampire contin-

gent and those from the Unseelie Fae court. Other
paranormal parliaments were represented by nervous,
well-guarded diplomats. But none of the locals were
present. This meeting in the clearing was for the leadership class only. All other members of the paranormal
communities had gone into hiding following the disas-
trous human invasion of television cameras and human
supernatural seekers.

Elder Vlad gave Sir Rodney a wicked smile that
looked like a cross between a threatening grimace and
a sneer. "The wolves are not here. How fitting."

"You know they abandoned the area when Captain
Trudeau returned to Denver and had her meeting with
the human leadership," Sir Rodney snapped. "I will
carry word." He then looked at the Unseelie represen-
tatives who were present. "I also have a message for
your queen. You tell her that any aggressive act against
me is a declaration of war. I want you to ask Cerridwen
if she's ready to try my hand."

"But can you proxy for the wolves' vote?" Elder
Vlad said coolly as the large court structure rose from
the swamp at his command. He dismissed Sir Rodney's
talk of war with his ex-wife with a wave of his hand.
"Whatever your battles are with Cerridwen, they will
have to wait. The more pressing issue at hand is that
I don't believe it is possible to vote on behalf of your
allies without express proof of their consent in written
form."

"There was to be no vote cast tonight," Sir Rodney
volleyed back as nervous delegates shot one another
worried glances.

"No vote?" Elder Vlad said, raising an eyebrow.

"How naive. Did you think we would have called an emergency meeting of the United Council of Entities' leadership to merely debate the merits of the human invasion taking place in New Orleans?" Elder Vlad clucked his tongue with a sinister smile. "After a week or two, the human media will die down. Humans are like cattle—they have short attention spans. Once the cameras find the next interest, our constituents can again come out of hiding . . . This has just been an inconvenience, not a paranormal-world-shattering event."

Sir Rodney cast a worried glance around at his advisors and leaned down so that Garth could murmur in his ear.

"The Vampires do not appear to be aware of the attempted possession, milord . . . perhaps it would be best not to make them aware that our sidhe was breached and a weakness still exists until we have word back from our allies."

Sir Rodney nodded and stepped away from Garth to address his ancient Vampire enemy. "Then what vote is required that cannot wait until the wolf Federations are present?" Sir Rodney called out into the night. Those around him muttered in agreement.

"Read *the law*," Elder Vlad said, causing the huge black book reserved for court events to appear and hurling it with sudden fury to slam Sir Rodney in the chest. The moment Sir Rodney caught it, the senior Vampire's fangs crested. "Without due diligence and without provocation, our assets were attacked. We sustained significant property and collateral damage. You later learned in court that you and your wolves were wrong!" He pointed at Sir Rodney, making the now airborne Fae archers draw and hold the Vampire leader in their bow sightlines. "The law states that my cartel is due recompense for these unwarranted acts of aggression, and as you know we are not likely to allow those vile acts to go unchallenged. We are due a body for a body, and financial remuneration for all reported property damage—fair exchange is no robbery."

"You heard the circumstances under which your assets were laid to siege! The late Baron Montague, exterminated in court by your very hand for his part in this travesty, was involved in duplicity that created mistaken identity!" Sir Rodney shouted. "You come here under the cloak of darkness demanding a death—"

"This is our afternoon," Elder Vlad said coolly, making his Vampire henchmen snicker. "One man's darkness is another man's daylight . . . but no, we did not come to haggle over bodies. And as you well know, if you'd suspected the baron of wrongdoing, then the proper way to address his crimes would have been to call an emergency session of the UCE, which *you did not do.* Thus your recklessness—or rather, the primal response by the wolves at your beck and call—violated our laws, causing undue property damage and the unnecessary loss of Vampire existences that went well beyond the baron. Had he been found guilty, we would have brought him to swift justice, just as you saw us execute in court. He is no longer with us . . . and now it is time to review our other losses—the illegitimate ones you and your *wolf* allies caused."

"Then what do you want, if not dead Seelie Fae or

wolves at your feet?" Sir Rodney shouted, hurling the ancient tome back toward Elder Vlad, who caught it without effort.

"Come, come now, Your Majesty . . . you *know* we are much more sophisticated than that." Elder Vlad smiled, but his black eyes remained void of emotion. "We want a fair exchange."

"And that would be exactly what?" Sir Rodney asked, his tone wary as he glanced at his allies.

"Your forces have laid siege to a prominent member of our cartel's lair, thus causing undue human awareness . . . You do remember the destruction of the baron's manor house, yes? You then attacked one of our prominent private clubs, the Blood Oasis. Many of our trained human helpers and Vampire security forces were killed at those sites. You allowed your wolves to openly threaten us in court—shall we review the record?" Elder Vlad flung the tome into the air to allow it to hover between him and Sir Rodney. "Read it and weep," he said in a threatening murmur as the book opened to the smoldering pages that held the proceedings of the last UCE meetings.

"You still have not stated your purpose here tonight!" Sir Rodney said, ignoring the book.

"The waver in your tone, no matter how much you protest, tells me you know *exactly* what we want as recompense," Elder Vlad said with a smile. Moonlight reflected off his black, black irises, and he released a satisfied sigh. "Instead of the several bodies you owe us for the multiple unjustified attacks you have waged against us, we want a reinstatement of our leadership at the UCE—"

"Impossible without a full vote!" Sir Rodney shouted as pandemonium broke out in the swamp.

Elder Vlad placed a hooked finger to his thin lips for a moment as he shook his head. "You did not allow me to finish, Your Majesty . . . In addition to my being reinstated as leader of the UCE, we want those who have committed the worst offenses, those who actually led the atrocity against my people, to be sanctioned by an immediate loss of their voting power at the UCE. Therefore," he added, smugly looking around, "the wolf Federations, by violation of their leadership, are no longer voting members of this council. It is *the law*. Thus, under the circumstances, I do believe we have all voting parties present."

"No," Sir Rodney said. "We do not!" His gaze tore from Elder Vlad's deadly eyes to stare at the clearly frightened leadership around him. "The Vampires willingly stormed out of the UCE before this last incident." His gaze shot back toward Elder Vlad as he pointed at him. "It was *your choice* to leave the council once you were voted off as the head of that ruling body. Therefore, if you study the record, we do not *owe* you reinstatement!"

"We were publicly humiliated by those same animals that attacked our assets—the wolves," Elder Vlad said, curling his lip. "But if you'd prefer that we seek our redress the old-fashioned way—a body for a body— remember, we get to choose the bodies. I think you should confer with your allies to see which tack they would like you to pursue—ousting the wolves for their crimes against genteel Vampire society and a reinstatement of leadership . . . or blood in the streets. Either way, we are fine with the outcome. We just thought we'd keep the discourse civil by asking you first and putting it to a vote."

"No one wants another war," a burly leader from The Order of the Dragons called out. "And without the wolves, our voting blocs will not be as strong . . . our membership will recoil from another war or the sacrifice of bodies to replace the Vampires' losses."

Other paranormal leaders murmured their assent with the moans of Phantoms, and chaos erupted again while Elder Vlad chuckled.

"According to the law, those accused and scheduled to be stripped of their standing must be present!" Sir Rodney shouted, turning to face his weakening allies.

"Or voted off, if deemed too dangerous to attend the proceedings . . . and then a messenger is sent."

Sir Rodney glared at the crafty Vampire and then whirled on his allies. "Would any of you be the messenger to the wolves to bear such news?"

Silence echoed loudly. Sir Rodney spun back to meet Elder Vlad's gaze. "In the absence of anyone willing to take the news to the wolves—"

"*We'll* take the news," Elder Vlad said flatly. "Now vote."

Again, silence strangled the attendees for a moment.

"You are the ones gaining from the challenge . . . therefore you cannot be the messengers," Sir Rodney said as calmly as possible. "The opposing side has a fortnight to prepare a rebuttal to the request." He sent a blue streak toward the hovering tome before Elder Vlad could answer. "Let it be written that we accept Elder Vlad's request for a possible restoration of his former office and the possible removal of the wolf Federations from the voting leadership bench of the United Council of Entities pending the customary fortnight recess and rebuttal."

The book blazed and then snapped shut while Elder Vlad and his guards hissed their bitter disapproval.

"Time will buy you nothing!" Elder Vlad shouted, his fangs glistening in the moonlight. "A fortnight is but a blink of an eye in time to Vampires!"

"Then it is all settled," Sir Rodney said, his mouth forming a wry smile, but his eyes burning with pure hatred. "We will reconvene in a fortnight . . . and as we say in the Fae world, 'May perpetual daylight shine upon you and your family.'"

CHAPTER 4

Too much time had passed since she'd crossed the threshold of Ronnie's Road Hog Tavern, affectionately known to her and all the locals as simply *the Hawg*. Sasha hopped down out of her jeep and took a deep breath, shaking the tension out of her limbs as her boots hit the parking lot gravel. Summer in Denver was particularly sweet. This little oasis well off the main highway was surrounded by a fragrant pine bluff. She smiled to herself as she walked, remembering how she'd first met Hunter here—and how she'd almost shot the man.

The absurdity of it all nearly made her laugh out loud. Bitter irony that the wolf was her friend, while the fighting force she'd always been associated with had turned on her, kept the sound from exiting her throat. Right now, though, she just had to forget it. There was a bigger problem than the acute sense of betrayal wafting through her soul; there was a loose cannon headed down to New Orleans about to get himself killed or—worse—get his men butchered and possibly innocent people mauled. And . . . with the firepower she knew Madison had access to, wolves could die, too—not to mention friendly Fae.

But there was no choice at the moment other than to wait for word from Hunter. She hated feeling boxed in. Sasha flat-palmed the front door of the tavern and welcomed the cool air-conditioned temperatures and convivial spirit that instantly enveloped her just like the loud country music. The scent of sawdust and the crush of it underfoot made her release a quiet sigh.

Admittedly, it felt good to get out of her uniform and into jeans and a T-shirt, even if she'd had to change in the dark in her closet to avoid whatever surveillance she was sure had been reinstalled while she was gone. Didn't they know by now that she could tell when someone had been in her apartment? Wolves always knew. There was the vibe, the energy tracer, and last but not least the human scent, for crying out loud. Not only was she gonna have to change careers, but she was definitely going to have to move to Shadow Wolf country just to take a shower in peace.

Too much knowledge was sometimes a dangerous thing. She could feel herself getting more and more wound up again about the invasion of her personal space as she walked deeper into the tavern. All of her territory had been violated, truth be told. However, the moment she spotted her guys, her shoulders relaxed.

They'd commandeered several tables and had pulled them together. Cheese fries, hot wings, and nachos littered the tops of them, creating a messy, high-calorie defeat feast. Shots were lined up, as promised, and two empty pitchers were on the tables with a smiling wait-ress hustling in their direction holding a sudsy refill in each hand.

"You're shit-faced already, soldier," Sasha said, coming up to Woods's flank, laughing. "That's a good thing."

"Sir, yes, sir," Woods said, pounding her fist and then slinging a Jack Daniel's shot at her across a table-top.

"Got burgers on the way, but figured we'd start with tradition. Plenty of alcohol," Fisher said, knocking back his shot as the one Woods sent to Sasha whizzed down the table.

Sasha caught the shot and knocked it back, then set the shot glass down with an exaggerated wince. "Line 'em up, ladies and gentlemen."

"Hunter took it that well, huh?" Clarissa said, filling a beer mug as the waitress set down a pitcher.

"I knew the big guy would be pissed off," Winters said, shaking salt on his wet fist. "Tell him plenty of tequila will bite the snake that bit him."

"Our alpha is baring fangs, no doubt," Bradley said calmly and tossed Winters a fresh lime wedge.

"Ooohhh, yeah," Sasha said, accepting another slingshot from Fisher. "Where do I even begin?"

"So someone is playing a very deadly game of cat and mouse," Cerridwen said, looking into the icy mist. She drew away from the glacier table in her war room and placed a delicate finger against her lips. "And they are so eager for Rodney and I to war . . . hmmm . . ."

"Milady," her advisor said quietly, lowering his

head. "Sir Rodney will take an act of attempted possession as a clear act of war. Perhaps we should prepare for a potential Seelie onslaught."

She nodded and narrowed her gaze. "Yes, that is wise. But in the meanwhile, let us also hedge our bets."

Hunter heard his grandfather's howl echoing in the shadow lands long before he'd exited into the lush Uncompahgre wilderness. The etched amber amulet that had been passed through his family for generations burned white-hot against his T-shirt, and the silver chain that it hung from was now uncomfortably warm around his neck.

Instinct led him through the underbrush. Every sense was keened as he neared his grandfather's cabin and sniffed the air. The full pack leadership had gathered. Something was terribly wrong.

Mounting the front steps in one bound, he landed on his grandfather's cabin porch without a sound, but the door opened. His grandfather greeted him with expectation in his eyes and then clasped his forearm in the time-honored tradition.

"We've received important news," Silver Hawk said, ushering Hunter into the emergency meeting. "Sir Rodney sent a Fae missive. The Vampires are on the move and are calling for our ousting. We have one fortnight to gather evidence to show we had cause for the actions we took against Baron Montague and his enterprises and must clearly demonstrate that they were complicit in the chain of events."

"We have that evidence!" Hunter shouted, looking at his grandfather and then his pack lieutenants. "When we brought in the Unseelie Fae traitor, all of that was discussed!"

"True . . . but the Vampires are claiming that we did not follow protocol as established by the United Council of Entities." Silver Hawk released a weary breath. "This time I do not know if we will be able to beat their charges, unless we can show a valid reason that we breached due process. We did act prematurely, Hunter. We did attack his manor house when he was merely a suspect. The correct process was not a preemptive strike, but rather to bring charges against him at the UCE."

"That's bullshit," Hunter said, his voice exploding with rage. "We all know what happened. We all know how the baron sat on the sidelines egging Kiagehul on, helping to twist his already bent mind!"

For a moment Silver Hawk only stared at Hunter. "I know, son . . . but you as the alpha leader also know that just because something is legal doesn't make it ethical—or if it is ethical, that doesn't make it legal. We are caught in such a dilemma, the cobweb of such contradiction as can only be spun by the Vampires. Sir Rodney said the other parliaments are beginning to waffle, becoming shaky in their commitment to hold the voting bloc together. This could be a very bad moon for the wolves."

"Does my brother know yet?" Hunter dragged his fingers through his hair, further loosening the leather thong that held his ponytail in place.

"I sent word to Shogun the moment I learned. I carried the missive myself through the shadow lands and gave it to his top lieutenant."

Hunter held his grandfather by both arms and stared into his ancient eyes. "Grandfather . . . to travel that way without the family amulet to protect you against the demon doors, during these uncertain times, could have been suicide. I would have gone."

"There wasn't time," Silver Hawk said calmly, staring at Hunter with ageless wisdom.

"You need to rest," Hunter said in a quiet tone, now thoroughly inspecting the elderly man before him. "What do we need to do to make this right?"

"I will go on a vision quest," his grandfather replied, gently slipping from Hunter's hold. He landed a hand on Hunter's shoulder. "This time we must allow cool heads to prevail. We must go back to the scene of the treachery and collect witnesses, evidence, anything we can to show that we were under attack in principle and had a right to defend ourselves."

"Consider it done," Hunter said. He turned to Bear Shadow and Crow Shadow.

"We stand at the ready," Bear Shadow said.

"We've got your back," Crow Shadow said, but then cocked his head to the side. "Where's my sister? Been thinking about her all day—worried, you know, man?" He smoothed the hair at the nape of his neck. "Doesn't feel right. For something as serious as this going down, Sasha should be here, too."

Hunter nodded as renewed fury threaded its way through his system. "The human military has relieved her of her duty, temporarily. Her general was dressed down for the civilian human casualties and the media circus." He turned to his grandfather and let out a breath of defeat. "Doc, the entire team, have all been cut off from the Paranormal Containment Unit. They cannot leave Denver until further notice. A new colonel is sending a team . . ."

"A wolf hunt?" Silver Hawk asked in a low tone that made every set of eyes in the room begin to glow gold. It wasn't a question; it was more of a statement.

Hunter nodded. "This is what it could turn into the moment that new military force hits New Orleans, if the Vampires have their way. So I want you to stay to the shadows and lay low. I need to talk to Shogun and his men about staying out of harm's way until we know what we're dealing with—but we cannot have any human casualties attributed to us. None."

"Agreed," Silver Hawk said, his gaze narrowed with repressed anger. "But collecting evidence under such circumstances will be hard."

"Just like old times," Hunter said, determination blazing in his eyes. "But I am prepared to show them all the way of the wolf."

"What were you going to tell me?" Bradley said, holding Clarissa's hand. He leaned in closely and sent the private comment into her ear.

"Later," she murmured back, and then took a sip of beer.

He frowned. "If it's important, we should just step outside. All right?"

She looked up at him blankly. "No . . . because I can't remember what I was going to say."

The group gave Clarissa and Bradley a smile.

"You guys are whispering like a couple of teenag-

ers," Fisher said laughing, pouring more beer for
Bradley. "Geez, get a room."

Bradley shoved him playfully as Clarissa shook her
head and downed her beer, holding her mug out for a
refill. "Can't anybody have a private conversation without your minds going directly into the gutter?"

"Not while we're drinking," Woods said, laughing.

Winters knocked his glass against Woods's. "Right!"

A slurry of nachos, cheese fries, and Jack Daniel's
competed at the bottom of Sasha's stomach, but the
warm buzz and camaraderie were beginning to make
her problems temporarily fade. Woods was setting up
another round of shots to sling across the tables when
the hair stood up on her arms and the back of her neck.

"Look alive, soldier," she said, slowing him down.
"Twelve o'clock." Sasha held up her hand and then
nodded toward the bar door.

"You have got to be fucking kidding me," Woods
said, elbowing Fisher.

"That just ain't right," Fisher said, wiping the perspiration from his brow with his forearm. "This is our
bar."

"Aw, man, this sucks—big time," Winters complained and downed his shot anyway.

Clarissa leaned in, weaving from the effects of the
multiple kamikaze shots she'd just consumed with a
beer chaser, and spoke to the group in a hissing whisper. "You guys are off post, right? This is a civilian
establishment."

"It may be a nonduty location, 'Rissa," Bradley
warned, clearing away alcohol from in front of everyone

and bringing food baskets closer, "but anybody in uniform is still subject to military code . . . and just from a political standpoint, it wouldn't do to give the colonel any additional ammunition against us—asshole though he may be."

"Yeah, especially since he and his men are wearing sidearms off-post. That tells me the SOB is just looking for trouble," Woods muttered.

"He's headed our way. Be prepared to get on your feet," Sasha said to Woods and Fisher. "Maybe he won't be a dickhead and will just grab a beer and a burger and go about his business."

"There's a hopeful thought," Fisher said, eyeing Colonel Madison and the four soldiers who came in with him.

Sasha studied the men striding into the bar with Madison. The man standing closest to him on the left was a burly black guy who seemed as though he had Madison by a few years; on his flank was an extremely tall, corn-fed white guy who had MIDWEST stamped across his forehead. Bringing up the rear was a Latino kid with zero percent body fat and hungry eyes, who couldn't have been more than twenty years old. Beside him was a laid-back–looking Asian guy whose age was hard to judge, but his eyes told her he was deadly. All of them, including the colonel, were wearing sidearms.

So this was who was replacing her squad, a bunch of cowboys? Sasha's eyes met Madison's immediately and she got to her feet, even though he was across the room. Behind her she could hear Fisher and Woods slowly getting to their feet, followed by the disgruntled sounds of the rest of the team following suit. But she didn't have to wait to know that Madison was going to be a real prick about making his authority known, even in the Hawg. It was all over his face as he parted the bar crowd and strode toward her, head held high, shoulders back, his squad walking as though they were MPs on the way to make an arrest.

"Good evening, sir," Sasha said, trying to force some cordiality into her tone. She stepped away from the tables and moved toward him, hoping to draw his attention to her solely and to spare her team any unnecessary interaction with the colonel. He wasn't taking the bait.

Madison looked right past her to Woods and Fisher. "Lock it up, soldier."

From her peripheral vision she saw Woods and Fisher straighten up to stand at full attention, rather than the customary at-ease stance that was generally acceptable under social conditions. That was so unnecessary. In a nonduty civilian location it was enough that they'd gotten to their feet and had addressed him with courtesy. This was pushing it. Adding insult to the injury, Madison hadn't even introduced the men with him to her and her guys. It was a total slap in her face that said they weren't a team, weren't welcomed. She hated only being able to identify the colonel's men by their ethnicities.

Sasha counted to ten, her judgment doing hand-to-hand combat with her wolf and the liberal dose of Jack Daniel's that was coating her nervous system.

Madison returned his attention to Sasha, looking her up and down for a moment. "Is this how you led your squad, Captain—allowing them to take liberties in your presence and to lose discipline and focus? Then it is no wonder you got the results that you did. You are property of the U.S. government at all times while you wear our uniform, whether you're physically in it at the moment or not, so is this any way to dignify that privilege?"

A reply caught in her throat. She wasn't sure if it was a rhetorical question designed to simply humiliate her or if the prick actually wanted an answer. But the three seconds it took her to assess all of that sent him into a rage.

"I asked you a question, Captain!"

"Sir, yes, sir," was the fastest response that came to her mind. It was the one that every soldier learned how to say faster than his own name.

Now all eyes were on them. Onlookers craned their necks as Madison's men smirked. That's when she knew she was being set up. If this guy could push her buttons and could get her to react with blatant insubordination, he could get her court-martialed—apparently forcing her out of the unit was not enough.

"Yes, sir?" Madison said, circling Sasha. His tone carried both disbelief and disdain. "This was how you managed your team?"

"No, sir," she said flatly, keeping her gaze past him and on the tavern's door.

"Which is it, Captain? Yes or no? Soldiers don't equivocate!"

"Yes . . . *sir*," she said, now through her teeth. Jack Daniel's was winning; then again, maybe it was her wolf.

"Your tone is out of order, Captain."

"Step away from the lady," a low, threatening voice rumbled.

Sasha closed her eyes in a slow blink and turned, only to see Hunter step out of the shadows of the pass-through near the kitchen. Madison's attention snapped toward the voice, and his lieutenants took aggressive stances.

"Good to see you, man," Winters said, offering Hunter a fist pound that Hunter ignored as he passed him. "That's cool . . . We were all just getting acquainted."

Sasha stepped between Hunter and Madison. "Hunter, don't . . ." She gave Hunter a look but could tell he'd heard enough to put him well past reason.

"I suggest you listen to the captain and stand down, soldier," Madison said, striding up to Hunter. "Is this another one of your out-of-order—"

"I'm not the property of the U.S. government," Hunter said as he tilted his head and rolled his shoulders. "Back off the lady. She's off duty."

"The lady is under my command," Madison fired back. He looked at Sasha. "I see you run your personal life as sloppily as you run your squad. No wonder your mission failed."

"If you have a problem, state it," Hunter said, his voice bottoming out. "But don't be a punk bitch and hide behind your so-called rank."

Winters released a long, quiet whistle.

"What?" Madison took two steps closer to Hunter but stopped just short of being within his swing range, clearly not liking the fact that Hunter was taller.

"I think you heard me," Hunter said, moving in. "Circle her again and it will be your last time to invade her space."

"Are you threatening me?"

"Okay, okay, c'mon," Sasha said, going to Hunter. "Don't do this, all right?"

"What I said was no threat and the lady will tell you I am no liar. *That was a promise*," Hunter said, not moving forward, but speaking to Madison over Sasha's head.

Madison turned to his men. "You did hear that, correct? This civilian threatened me—thinks he's a Billy Badass."

"Affirmative, Colonel. We heard it, sir," the burly lieutenant to his left said and then smiled at the rest of their squad.

"Then, since we have received a threat, it is my duty to protect U.S. property from misuse by unauthorized hostiles," Madison said, lolling his neck. He returned his attention to Hunter, chuckling with overconfidence. "Care to take this outside so the rest of the civvies don't have to see you bleed?"

"Colonel, that is not a good idea," Sasha said. She turned to Hunter. "Just let it go, all right?"

"Property? Call her that again . . . ," Hunter said with his gaze steady on the colonel.

"Dude, I mean, Colonel," Winters said, raking his damp hair, "this is like such a bad idea."

"What did you say?" Colonel Madison wheeled around to stare at Winters hard.

"I'm not a soldier, for one," Winters said, lifting his chin. "So I'm not about to give you the *sir, yes, sir,* crap that Sasha has to—and for the record, if you go out there in the parking lot . . . you're gonna get your ass kicked. So you might just wanna go order a brewski and a burger and relax."

"Oh, man," Bradley muttered as he popped Winters in the back of his head with a flat palm. "Just add gasoline on the fire, why don't you, genius."

"Hey!" Winters said as he grabbed his head. "Quit it, man—it's the truth and everybody knows it."

"Shsssh!" Clarissa hissed, and gave Winters the eye.

"Like the captain . . . or somebody said," Fisher added crisply, keeping his stance at attention and his gaze toward the door. "This is inadvisable, sir."

"Affirmative," Woods said, matching Fisher's stance.

"I think this civilian needs a lesson in manners from Delta Force Bravo Company," the colonel said with pure hatred in his eyes as he looked Hunter up and down.

The man on the colonel's flank patted his sidearm. "And if the she-wolf and her dogs make it an unfair fight by flipping out . . . well, we're locked and loaded for any eventuality, sir."

"Okay, now *I know* it's time for everybody to just stand down before someone gets hurt," Sasha said, looking at Hunter.

"You and your men threatened her with a firearm—one of your own?" Hunter said, moving closer to Madison.

"Just think of my lieutenants as peacekeeping forces so your girlfriend doesn't get nervous under the full moon and decide to break rank, turn wolf, and jump into what should be between men when she sees you getting taken to school," Colonel Madison said. He gave his men a half smile. "I don't think it's going to take much for you to learn what a real leader is made of."

"Believe me, if you pull a weapon on Sasha in my presence, it won't help you. Your arm needs to be connected to your body when you squeeze the trigger."

Hunter hadn't blinked, hadn't stuttered, and was so close to a shape-shift that she wanted to drag him out by his arm.

The colonel looked at Hunter and hesitated for a second and then laughed. "Overconfidence is always the best teacher."

"Yeah . . . Let's go outside and learn together," Hunter said as the muscles in his shoulders bunched.

CHAPTER 5

This was beyond crazy, but there was no stopping the events that were unfolding too quickly. Patrons began flowing out of the tavern behind them, but thankfully Ronnie and his bouncers got between them and the small group that stalked off toward the tree line, telling people he'd call the cops if a crowd gathered.

Yet appalling as the situation was, there was also a small, glowing ember of satisfaction alive within her. The night air fanned it, brought it alive, just as the full moon stoked it, and the sound of her once dejected team trudging behind her made whatever repercussions were sure to follow all seem worthwhile.

The only saving grace was that she was on the record as having tried to intervene. According to military code, Hunter was not her spouse—he was a civilian, a private citizen, and she'd also warned her commanding officer . . . who had pressed for the fight, even after she, Woods, Fisher, and Winters had suggested he stand down. This one wouldn't make it to the general whom Madison reported to, and would undoubtedly be a brawl that remained under the radar . . . the sort of thing this asshole was clearly used to doing—command by intimidation. So be it.

Sasha threw her shoulders back and stood taller when Hunter stopped walking. The shadows were long tonight. The trees, the parking lot trucks, all of it was beyond what Madison could comprehend. However, that also told her how foolish the man was, not realizing he'd been lured into a wolf trap. She watched the man take off his sidearm and hand it to one of his men, a smug look of confidence marring his sharp features in the moonlight. From the corner of her eye she thought she saw a fast-moving silver blur go past the tree line, but then it was gone. She couldn't focus on that now; there was just too much else happening.

"You are so screwed," Winters muttered and shook his head.

"Check him to see if he's armed," the Asian lieutenant said, glancing at the others quickly.

Before one of them could cross the wide circle the two teams had made, Hunter pulled up his jean legs one at a time with perfect balance on one leg, showing them there was nothing in his boots. Without a word, he then lifted his shirt and took it off, stripping it over his head. Methodically, moving like a tai chi instructor, Hunter then took off his amulet and tossed it to Sasha. She caught it with one hand, wishing she hadn't left the mate to it on her dresser at home.

Moonlight washed over Hunter, adding definition to the tight ropes of sinew that made up his torso. Now that he'd passed inspection and been deemed unarmed, Madison began to slowly circle Hunter. The group backed up, giving both combatants wide berth. Sasha's grip on Hunter's amulet tightened as she watched the contest, then Madison lunged.

It was a skilled judo move, an impressive one that combined speed and impact, if only it had landed. But what Madison obviously hadn't gleaned from all her reports was that wolf speed and agility were unmatchable by a human—especially when that wolf was pissed off. The sad part was that Hunter was just toying with his prey. It was all so reckless; Madison just couldn't seem to grasp that he was dealing with a wolf, a being stronger and faster than he'd ever be, and not a regular human. The man's own prejudice had clearly blinded him to the facts and had left him in a state of twisted denial.

Every aggressive move Madison made, Hunter countered with an avoidance move, choosing not to land a blow. The first lesson that Madison would learn tonight was that he was expending precious energy and Hunter was just wearing him out. He'd also have his confidence shaken, as he continued to try to land blows that Hunter easily avoided. Soon frustration would make Madison sloppy and he'd know that Hunter could have put him down at will, but didn't . . . and that would inspire fear. Sasha cringed inwardly watching it all unfold, and knowing how it would probably end.

Then Hunter did the unthinkable. On the next lunge, he spun out of Madison's way and then bitch-slapped the colonel. Sasha's mouth flew open.

"Teach me!" Hunter shouted. "We've been out here for ten minutes and all we've been doing is dancing."

Oh . . . my . . . God.

Madison ran in, fury propelling his body forward in a near-blind rage. This time Hunter allowed their bodies to connect, flipping Madison and body-slamming him to the ground. Hunter moved away with an angry smirk and allowed Madison to get up.

"If you go to New Orleans like this, you'll die, you stupid bastard," Hunter said, slipping into a shadow and coming out behind Madison. "You'll get your men killed. Not that I care, but it's good information for you to have."

Madison spun and stepped back, giving himself safety space. His men immediately drew on Hunter.

"You're one of them!" Madison shouted, and then turned toward Sasha. "He's a goddamned beast like you!"

"Oh, you don't know the half of it," Hunter said, canines ripping through his gums as his eyes changed. "Lower your weapons. Threaten my mate and instinct takes over."

Frightened men backed up, brandishing weapons, turning wildly. Sasha's team remained still as stones, their gazes nervous as they shot glances among the jittery second squad.

"Easy, everybody . . . no need for an accident," Woods said.

"Back away from the two known targets of value," Madison said to Woods and then glanced at Clarissa. "Now! Or we will have to assume that you're all infected."

"Back up, people," Sasha said quickly, watching Madison's men toss him his sidearm.

"Get out of here, Sasha," Hunter said in a low growl.

"This insane bastard won't hesitate to come up with a reason to blow you and your entire squad away."

"You've got that right!" Madison said, pulling back farther to stand with his men.

Sasha backed up and stood close enough to enter an SUV shadow if necessary. She watched Hunter ease back toward the long shadow of a tree.

"Put the guns down. This was supposed to be a fight, man-to-man, Colonel." Hunter's gaze held Madison's, the threat implicit within it.

"But that's just it," Madison said, looking between Hunter and Sasha. "It never was man-to-man. It was man-to-wolf. Fuck you!"

The second Madison's bicep contracted, Hunter spun into a shadow. Gunshot report cut through the night. Clarissa screamed as Woods and Fisher pushed her to the ground, yelling for everyone else to get down. Shells ripped though bark, chasing the direction Hunter had disappeared, and before Sasha could draw her next breath they had spun around to aim at her.

She was gone in an instant, a blur that became one with the shadow beside her. Hunter came out of his in milliseconds to land a knockout blow at the back of two of Madison's lieutenants' skulls, dropping them on the spot before seeking cover in another car shadow. When Sasha came out, she was on the far side of the lot, but she could see what Hunter was doing. He'd gone into a wood-source shadow, come out and landed blows that would be like striking a man with a two-by-four, then eluded them again. But that was indeed showing con-siderable restraint—especially since they'd threatened her. He could have come out of the SUV's shadow and hit both men with the force of metal, rendering them brain-damaged . . . or gone straight wolf and simply ripped their weapons arms out of the sockets.

Regardless, a ricocheting bullet could still hit any of her squad who couldn't escape into a shadow. This was so irresponsible that she wanted to really show them what primal wolf was all about. Picking off the closest lieutenant, she went in for a quick arm twist, stopping just short of breaking it, and stripped him of his weapon, then was gone. Hunter popped out of the shadow by the last man standing and threw an old-fashioned haymaker, dropping the man where he stood. As Madison spun around to follow the sound, Hunter came out of the shadow behind him with a weapon at his temple.

"Drop it," Hunter said in a threatening rumble in Madison's ear.

He waited until Madison released his weapon and then glanced at the lieutenant that Sasha had stripped.

"Tell your man not to be foolish," Hunter said, practically growling.

"Stand down!" Madison yelled.

"Good boy," Hunter said and then shoved Madison away from him. "And what have we learned tonight?" He circled Madison slowly, clearly enjoying the fear in the man's eyes. "Maybe you learned that if you can't run with the big dogs, you might want to stay on the porch?"

When Madison didn't answer, Hunter gave in to a full canine presentation. "I asked you a question, soldier!"

"Sir . . . yes . . . sir," Madison said slowly and quietly with hatred, and then spit on the ground.

"I didn't hear you!" Hunter shouted, flinging the weapon he held away from them both.

"That's enough, Hunter," Sasha said, coming up beside him. She placed a palm on Hunter's chest and then looped his amulet from around her neck. "Enough for one night . . . sirens are getting closer."

Hunter inclined his head, then finally nodded, hearing what the rest of the team wouldn't hear for five more minutes. Her squad slowly stood, dusting themselves off, each glaring at Madison and the one lieutenant whom Hunter and Sasha hadn't dropped.

"This isn't over, Captain," Madison said though his teeth.

"It had better be," Hunter said, rolling his shoulders. "Next class won't be the remedial one like tonight's."

"You guys okay?" Sasha said, glancing at her squad.

"Yeah . . . just sucks to get shot at," Winters said, glaring at Madison. "You tell on us, and trust me, we're gonna tell on you. We were unarmed civilians and this shit got out of control—you egomaniac! You drew a weapon on a fellow officer! I'll bring charges!"

"C'mon, let's get outta here before the local cops get here," Clarissa said. "All of this needs to be off the record."

But before anyone could react to Clarissa's sensible observation, she doubled over and retched up horrible green slime. She shut her eyes tightly and held on to Bradley. "I'm all right. I'm all right," she said, wheezing, and then waved Sasha and the others away. "Drinks, a case of bad nerves, and then getting shot at, all of it went down the wrong way."

Sasha looked at the ground and then at Clarissa as

she turned away with her eyes closed, leaning on Bradley. She watched Madison's men begin to stir, then glanced at Hunter and back at her team. "Get outta here, guys."

"Sir, yes, sir!" Woods said sarcastically, mocking the colonel as they passed him.

Hunter grabbed Sasha's hand. "You're off duty and coming with me."

"What was that?" Sasha shouted the moment they entered the shadows.

"That was me saying enough!" Hunter shouted back. "That guy is a jerk, he was—"

"My commanding officer until I decide differently!" She walked away from Hunter, raking her hair, trying not to grab it in bunches within her fists and begin pulling. This was insane!

"But—"

"It's my choice, Hunter! My career!" she said, walking in a circle with her eyes closed now. "Jesus . . . there's no coming back from this."

"I did not injure the man," Hunter said in a low growl.

"Oh, yeah, ya did," she said, and then stopped and folded her arms over her chest. "You just fly-kicked his ego out of the—"

"Like he didn't deserve that?" Hunter paced and spun on her. "Do not ask me to stand by and watch him breach your personal space, your territory, threaten your life, and that of your team—which is your family . . . even your familiars, Woods and Fisher, whom I have come to respect, and not react. *That* goes against nature, Sasha!" Hunter slapped the center of his chest, eyes glowing a rich, deep amber. "I am what I am, alpha Shadow—do not ask me to pretend to be a beta . . . you wouldn't like that in me, anyway."

Although it was a standoff, the man had a point.

"That's true," she said after a bit, frowning at the concept. "I can't see you as a beta."

"Thank you!" He walked away from her and gave her his back to consider, arms folded.

"I appreciate where you were coming from . . . but it's just that, I was sort of thinking about making the career change, haven't completely committed to the concept, and you're forcing my hand. That's what I don't like."

Hunter turned around slowly and stared at her with an unblinking gaze. "You know what *I* don't like, Sasha, is how you are straddling the border between worlds in this critical time."

"Okay, now *that's* not fair," she said, defensiveness weighting every word.

"It is fair!" he said, opening his arms wide, and gesturing wildly. "What's not fair is having to live in the shadows like your pet! Like your faithful, obedient dog that you call when you want comfort or affection and then gets put in the yard to guard your house—but who has no authority or decision-making involvement in your life! I never signed up for that tour of duty, Sasha! Never! What's also not fair is having to always put the national interests of the Shadow Clans second to those of your human leadership, no matter how ill informed or misguided—people who know nothing about our sovereign nations! For all intents and purposes I have been your goddamned beta, Sasha—but no more!"

"Whoa, whoa, you haven't been—"

"I haven't been what?" He glared at her and stalked away, deep into the mist. "I haven't been honest? I haven't been loyal? I haven't had your back? I haven't understood? I haven't been invisible? I haven't loved you more than my next breath—and haven't been faithful to you as my mate? I haven't been hurt by you in ways I don't want to revisit?" He turned away. "Tell me what I *haven't* been."

She so wished she hadn't been doing shots. This was not how the night was supposed to go. She had never seen him like this, and something very quiet within her told her this wasn't just a fight, this was a very fragile transition that could easily snap a final branch in their relationship. Searching her mind for a response that made sense, one genuinely from her heart, she chose her words with care . . . but that process apparently took too long.

Hunter shook his head and released a sad, bitter chuckle. "You can't even answer me, can you, *Captain*?"

"Don't do this," she murmured.

"Don't do what? Tell the truth?" Hunter looked at her hard. "I told you when we met I was no liar . . . and of all men, I'm the only one you never believed."

The charge was harsh, but she couldn't challenge it. Words were again slow to form in her embattled mind.

"I'm going to New Orleans," he said flatly. "There's work to be done down there—work important to the wolf Federations. Ask your brother about it, I don't have time to debrief you. Maybe when I get back you can let me know what you want to do about us. That's the part you've always needed to figure out—you've always been clear about your military career. My question is, where do I stand? Then again, maybe that's a question that I need to ask myself—because, right now, Sasha, hell if I know."

CHAPTER 6

Hunter was gone. The mist surrounded Sasha and folded in on her with an eerie silence that was all too sudden. There was nothing left to do but give in to her wolf and run. The North Country called her, summoned her, as did the moon. But there was an important stop she had to make to ensure her safety.

Bolting to freedom, she left her clothing in a pool at her feet and then ran long and hard back through the shadows toward her apartment. Her goal was singular—to claim the sacred amulet that she'd laid on her dresser in the darkened room. Then she'd blend into the nothingness once again.

But the moment she entered her closet, she became aware that she wasn't alone. Her space had been violated; men were walking around, throwing things about. Unfortunately for them, her human was pushed way down deep inside her spirit, and her wolf was what they'd encounter for their trouble.

Ears flattened against her skull, head low, Sasha moved forward as though she were a piece of living

night. The closer she got to the source of the disturbance, the more her instincts registered the threat as a
familiar one. The human scent stung her nose—it was
that of the one lieutenant who hadn't been injured . . .
and she smelled Madison.

Sasha remained still and took in another deep inhale. The urge to leap at the intruders and fiercely defend what was hers was so strong that it made her limbs
tremble. Then the unmistakable scent of gunpowder
assaulted her nose and brought with it the sting of common sense that acted like smelling salts. She knew they
would fire on her if they saw her. It wouldn't matter if
she were back in her human form or remained as a
wolf. That was what Madison wanted: a confrontation
that would give him the justification to blow her away.
She swallowed down a low growl, wondering if that
was also a part of his mission, or just a sick sign of his
overt prejudice against anything supernatural.

Battling her kill instinct, Sasha crept to her dresser,
transforming into her human just long enough to drape
her amulet over her neck. She stared at herself in the
mirror for a moment, seeing her eyes glow amber in
the darkened room. A year ago that would have frightened her, too, but did that give someone the right to
take her life just because she was different?

However, there wasn't time for the mental philo-
sophical debate as she heard her living room wall unit
crash to the floor. Did they have any idea what it had
taken to put that together? It represented the last time
that she and Rod and the whole team were together,
having a beer, laughing . . . eating pizza, enjoying life,

before Rod turned and had to be put down. Anger collided with grief. They had no right to take that from
her, to destroy it! Shit!

Her muscles tensed and she had to grip the edge of
the dresser to keep from lunging at the men who were
trashing her place. It was a trap; they were baiting her
and Hunter. As much as it had hurt her, she was glad
Hunter was pissed off and had headed to New Orleans.
There'd have been no stopping him if he'd witnessed
this. And she wasn't sure she would have wanted to this
time.

Yeah . . . things were way too fragile; it was time to
go and stay gone.

Sasha took one last glimpse through the partially
opened bedroom door, turned away from her vandal-
ized apartment, and then became her wolf-self again to
stalk into her closet.

A cold green flame spread along the outer edge of the
carpet, eating up nap with icy fire and sending the sick-
ening stench of sulfur into the room. Gathering into
itself, it coalesced into one tall glittering pillar. He sat
mesmerized, staring at its beauty, drinking in its
power . . . knowing its absolute commitment to wanton
violence.

"You must feed me soon," the disembodied voice
from within the flame murmured, causing the column
to sputter and dance in an eerie throb.

"I will . . . just tell me what you need," he whispered. "The area is crawling with ghost hunters and
paranormal seekers."

"I want one of them. Every feed now must be strategic." The green flame lapped the ceiling and then pulled itself up to crawl across it.

"Tell me what to do," he murmured, staring up at the miasma.

"Come closer for the joining," the voice murmured in a teasing coo.

A long tendril of green flame stretched down and caressed his face. He closed his eyes as pleasure from the sensual touch coated him, burning deep within his groin. It had been so long since his personal demon had come to him like this that his body involuntarily arched toward the fire. Quiet laughter filled the room and entered his bones as he leaned up and then reached toward the roiling flames on the ceiling.

It all happened so quickly—the searing pain, the echo of his scream, and then the bliss of complete consumption.

Hunter stood next to Sir Rodney staring down at the body that was shredded on the bayou floor. Limbs had been shattered, and most of the viscera were missing. The victim's chest was caved in, and Hunter was sure that this was the killing blow before the attacker had begun to feed. Shogun sat back on his heels and shook his head before uncoiling from the squatting position he'd been in to stand again.

"Second human tonight," Sir Rodney muttered. "Judging from what's left, it would look like a wolf did this, but we know better."

"It was cat," Shogun said and then spit on the ground. "My aunt—Lady Jung Suk."

Hunter nodded and inhaled deeply. "It is the same

scent we've picked up before . . . but this time she fed."

"Yes. Before she'd only cast nasty spells to do her handiwork, carving sigils on her victims to make them burn to death. Not this time." Shogun wiped his forehead with the back of his sleeve, clearly disgusted. "She needed a body to feed. She's no longer in the state the Unseelie Fae left her in."

"If she is no longer disembodied, then she will be easier to track," Hunter said, staring at his brother for a moment. "Fortunate for us . . . but unfortunate for the humans. Time is not on their side. We must find her soon. Whoever returned her to a bodied state had to employ dark magic—and that is the beginning of our countercase at the UCE."

"Damn it all!" Sir Rodney shouted and then paced away through the wide opening his Fae archers allowed so he could pass. "Ever since the UCE event I've had sleepless nights knowing there would be repercussions, and now my friends and allies are being set up? This should have never been! You and Sasha came to the aid of my court. We were under attack, and you helped us hunt down and exterminate the source—now you are being brought up on charges? This is insane! What's just as bad, I have been attacked in my own sidhe by a possession spell cast by the Unseelie."

"True, but typical," Hunter said, stalking away from the rotting-body stench. "The Vampires are strategic. So are the Unseelie. We knew Cerridwen was in with them since we brought Kiagehul to trial. She and Vlad left arm in arm, so is there any wonder? They know if they break our backs, we of the wolf Federations, then an unchallenged return to rule will be easy for them."

"You have permanent asylum in the sidhe," Sir Rodney said, lowering his sword in Hunter's direction. He glanced around at his men. "Always will the fortress be at your behest."

"But where will we run under the moon?" Shogun said calmly, moving in a slow, zigzag path among the trees. "Where will we hunt?" His calm gaze locked with Sir Rodney's. "I am sure you have heard the slogan 'Live free or die,' yes?"

"Yes," Sir Rodney said with sad eyes. "Yes."

"And there is a complication that we must not forget now," Hunter said, staring at the men before him. "The humans. This has moved beyond the realm of our hidden communities. Humans have been fed on, one of the bodies at least has been found . . . and before it's all over I am sure more will conveniently find their way to the human authorities to inspire a wolf hunt."

"This is why I've said to seek asylum, man!" Sir Rodney shouted, becoming exasperated. "Our Fae magic can hide you; we can give you glamour to ensure—"

"Appreciated, but not as effective as you would believe in this era," Hunter said, cutting him off. "I have been with Sasha's military. The humans have become more sophisticated, their weapons beyond our comprehension from years past. These are not mere villagers who are fighting demon-infected werewolves with wolfsbane and silver-tipped crossbows from the eleventh century. This is what the Vampires know, too. Our biggest advantage had been that humans didn't know we existed in the modern era. But now that they do, their tracking devices and DNA forensics are effective. With full military cooperation, they can monitor from the air, from satellites so sensitive that they can pick up the correct digits on a license plate from beyond the earth's atmosphere!"

Hunter walked away and punched a tree. "Rodney—when they do a wolf hunt, this time they have RPGs, machine guns, C-4 to blow dens . . . tanks. Do you understand what I am saying to you? If humans feel threatened by an entity that can die, that actually bleeds red blood, they will have no compunction about initiating an extermination directive—especially if they believe that species is feeding on theirs."

"But what about the Vampires, brother?" Shogun's quiet, steady voice drew everyone's attention. "If the Vampires are fanning the flames of a human wolf hunt, and the Unseelie are attacking our ally here, might we return the favor? *The Art of War.*" He bowed slightly and then waited.

"Harder to do," Hunter said, "and against our beliefs." He waited until Shogun nodded. "Are any of us prepared to grab innocent humans and then try to drain their bodies of blood by inflicting a deep jugular vein wound? Or would we set a possession spell upon an innocent human, to incur a witch hunt and burnings at the stake like medieval times, just to have evidence drawn toward Cerridwen for revenge? The evidence would soon fall apart if we did anything less dramatic. As I said, the humans' knowledge of the different supernatural species is in-depth in this modern era. Their forensic gathering techniques are to be respected."

"Especially since Sasha helped them understand,"

one of the Seelie archers muttered. "And she has not yet responded to a missive we sent hours ago."

Both Shogun and Hunter turned toward the sound with a snarl as Sir Rodney wheeled around.

"She was doing her job and has not been where she could receive it!" Sir Rodney shouted toward his men. "Never forget that! She is a head of state, the she-alpha of the North American Shadow Wolf Federation who kept the humans at bay as long as was possible. This was not her offense! Captain Sasha Trudeau will have our respect at all times, and any challenge to that order is treason—are we clear?"

Tense silence strangled the night, and Hunter looked at Sir Rodney with thanks as he paced away from his men.

"We need her here," Shogun said carefully.

Hunter couldn't immediately answer. "I know . . . but her own have turned on her and her travel has been restricted."

"Then she is in danger," Shogun said, coming up to Hunter. "We must—"

"Do *nothing*," Hunter said evenly, leveling his gaze at his brother.

"I don't understand." Shogun landed a hand on his brother's shoulder. "What happened?"

Hunter shrugged away from him. "She is safe in the North Country for now. We have work to do here to save our clans."

"Redirect the missive to locate her there," Sir Rodney ordered his missive archer. "Make sure it contains all that we have recently learned. Call the other one back. It is dated." Sir Rodney and his men looked between the huge male wolves with confusion as Shogun pursued Hunter deeper into the underbrush.

"What work is more important than ensuring her safety, brother?" Shogun called out behind Hunter.

"She is coming to her own conclusion about which comes first—us or the humans!" Hunter shouted, wheeling on his brother. "Do not allow your personal feelings for her to eclipse what is our priority as Federation leaders."

"Unnecessary and way out of line," Shogun said, taking a stance. "As a Federation leader, she is a priority—her safety is no less an issue than yours or mine would be if we were being tracked by the human military. Maybe it is you who has allowed your personal feelings to eclipse what is a priority of our national interests."

"Gentlemen . . . the war is with those who seek to destroy us, not one another," Sir Rodney offered in a solemn tone. "We cannot afford to be divided or conquered."

The night wind parted Sasha's silvery coat with each bound as she ran wild and free across the Uncompahgre. Summer scents of lush flora in bloom filled her nose and broke her heart as she raced through the breathtaking land that Hunter had once shown her. He'd coaxed out her wolf, had shown her its majesty, and had opened her eyes to an entire new plane of existence that she'd once thought was frightening and evil. But it was so beautiful, his version of wolf, that her soul wept.

So she ran to keep from throwing her head back and releasing a mournful howl. Everything she'd known was being stripped away again, being savaged from her grasp. As vast as the open country was, there was no escaping her thoughts, no getting away from Hunter's words—or the look on his face. The hurt that she'd caused him cut her to the bone as though they were linked, as though they were the same body and owned a singular spirit. Yet the independent wolf within, or the fiercely independent woman, would not allow her to easily relinquish her old military life that she'd fought so hard as a woman to prove herself within.

What was it all for, though?

The words echoed inside her brain, chasing her like a predator, making her heart slam against her rib cage as her body defied gravity, leaping, stretching, to outrace herself until she collapsed.

That's when the tears came—the private purge, the private mourning. Wolf paws receded into human female fists that hammered the broken grass. Her hair spilled over her arms and shielded her face from the moonlight as bitter sobs racked her body. She was a soldier, goddamn it! She had worked so hard, saved so many lives, had followed all the rules . . . well, enough of them, given the circumstances. She'd endured the humiliation of being different, being a lab experiment. Had overcome the so-called limitations of being a woman in a male-dominated profession, those of a combatant . . . and had dominance-battled her way to the top of the Shadow Wolf Clan. Yet none of that seemed to matter. Still, in this day and time, she was defined by her mate-status in one world, Hunter's—and by her DNA in the other.

Fatigue and slowly accepted defeat ebbed her sobs. Sasha pushed up and wiped her grass-stained face with dirty hands to stare at the moon. But the sight of the large, luminescent disk made her vision blur again with sudden moisture. The realization that this was the first full moon she'd spent alone since she came into her wolf stabbed her so unexpectedly that she could barely breathe.

Sasha closed her eyes and allowed the tears to flow down her cheeks without censure. There was no getting around it, she loved that man.

"I heard they found another body," one nervous bystander said as a crowd gathered on the balconies of the French Quarter hotels.

Police lights flashed an ominous red and blue stain against dim bar windows and asphalt. Onlookers craned their necks to see the carnage, ignoring warnings from authorities to go back inside. Cell phone video ruled; digital cameras set off a paparazzi bonanza.

"It's a free country!" one man shouted from a balcony with a beer in his hand.

"Yeah!" another called out from across the street.

"Whatchall 'fraid of, huh? Tell the truth and shame the devil," a huge woman shouted, holding her children close under her meaty arms.

Black police helicopters hovered over rooftops warning people to go back inside, to no avail. Crowds had gathered wherever was possible without being directly down on the street in violation of martial law. It was a fine line, a balancing act, but a defiant refusal to disperse nonetheless.

Russell Conway used the telephoto lens on his camera to get a better view, and judging by the size and strange angles of the body tarp in the side alley, there wasn't much left of the victim. He cringed inwardly and took the shot, adding it to his collection of paranormal incident photos. When were humans going to realize that really horrible things owned the night? If the government wasn't going to put down these beasts and exterminate them, he would. He owed the memory of his little sister and mother that much.

CHAPTER 7

A hot shower after her run had helped a little, just as the good clean cry had helped wash some of the pain out of her spirit. The combination had relaxed some of the tense muscles in her back and neck, if nothing else. Right now she was simply numb.

Sasha sat on the porch kneading the nape of her neck and watching the aimless pattern of fireflies. Their haphazard blinks had a hypnotic quality that she latched onto, trying to find some semblance of peace. They seemed to know as much about where they were going as she did at the moment. Tomorrow she'd have to deal with all of that . . . would no doubt have to face Colonel Madison, would have to figure out how to shield her team . . . would have to figure out what to say to Hunter.

For a moment she looked around at the rustic cabin that had become her second home. This was indeed a refuge that Hunter had created, a place that had once hid her from her people when they didn't understand her transition. It was a place where he'd healed her after a nasty she-alpha battle . . . and it was the place that he loved her hard and good and true. Sasha squeezed her eyes shut. There were so many things that had been left unsaid.

But a swoosh and the hard *thunk* of an arrow hitting the wooden post beside her put Sasha on her feet. The Fae missive instantly unfurled from the arrow that carried it. She read the words carefully. She had to get to New Orleans, no matter what. Someone had tried to send another possession spell through the sidhe barricade and this time had nearly succeeded?

Panic filled her as she thought back on everyone who might still be vulnerable to the old discharged spell. Clarissa had puked, and it didn't smell right—not that vomit ever did, but something was definitely wrong. Conflict tore at her. If she went to New Orleans, she'd be violating a direct order, which was grounds for court-martial. But if she stayed, her people could die. The choice was basic: She was going back in.

Sasha held the missive in her fist and spoke to it. "Tell Sir Rodney I understand. I may have a civilian squad member who's been affected—Clarissa McGill. I'm coming in, but I need a body double . . . some type of Fae glamour for a couple of hours so I can do a quick recognizance and get out without my brass being any the wiser. Can you do that? I'll wait for a reply." She flung the arrow back into the air and shut her eyes tightly as it sped away. "What are you doing, Trudeau?" she murmured to herself. "This is crazy!"

A familiar howl broke her concentration and made her eyes snap open. Sasha listened intently as the bushes moved and then noises came from within Hunter's shed across the clearing. She waited until Crow Shadow opened the door wearing a pair of Hunter's jeans without the benefit of a shirt or shoes.

"Just wanted to borrow these for a minute so we could talk," her brother said as he loped across the clearing. "Will drop them in the yard on my way out. Good thing Hunter keeps changes in there and in the cabin for when we come out of the shadows . . . makes it less awkward."

"It's all good," she lied, looking at a taller, darker, lankier version of herself. There was no reason to bring her brother into this madness. She needed to know more before she got the entire clan in a lather.

Her brother hesitated at the bottom step and stared at her, his eyes still glowing with his wolf. "It doesn't sound all good."

Sasha shrugged. "What can I say?"

"Hunter told me what happened." Crow leaned against the stair rail for a moment before taking the porch steps in one easy bound.

Sasha just looked at him.

"About how you're confined to the state," her brother added, coming to sit on a pine chair in front of her. "But from the way you just looked at me, my wolf instinct says it was more than that."

Sasha sent her gaze out toward the darkness to study the fireflies again. "Got busted for the New Orleans situation . . . the paranormal didn't remain 'contained,' " she added, making little quote marks with her fingers in the air. "The news got out to the general public, human civilians got killed, and they took the mission from me. I'm stranded here until they can figure out what to do with me. Not much to tell—other than it kicks my ass because we've got a ticking clock at the UCE. That's the part the military doesn't get—there's a whole bunch of paranormal nations involved and I have to keep the lid on *that* or else things will really blow."

"Sis, can we just be real with each other?" Crow Shadow said, leaning forward on his elbows. "I got that part—that's the warrior-to-warrior conversation. Hunter gave us all a debrief before he headed out. Bear is to watch Silver Hawk's back, and to be sure the old man is cool when he goes on his vision quest. I'm supposed to be your backup, with Woods and Fisher, and to be sure your human squad isn't jumped by those assholes on the base. But that's not what I'm asking you."

Their eyes met in a standoff before she looked away. "There's not much more to tell," Sasha said in a quiet tone.

"How's your head?"

She returned her gaze to Crow Shadow and shrugged, then bit her lip.

"I thought so," he said, and let out a long breath. "Look, Sasha, we're family . . . albeit we found out late in the game."

She nodded and swallowed hard, biting down harder on her lip as her brother spoke.

"I mean, who knew?" Crow Shadow opened his arms wide and let his head drop back. "Shit . . . I was grown and thought I knew who my father was." He sat up straight and stared at her with a pained expression. "Then I found out about Doc, that he was the one. It made all the parts and pieces of my life fall into place . . . why the father I grew up thinking was mine always looked at me funny, always was extra hard on me, as though he was carrying a grudge that I was even born."

"I know," Sasha murmured. "So much came out that year—but I don't blame Doc."

"I don't blame him, either," Crow said, leaning forward and clasping his hands together. "He was never told about me, and he made you to keep you from being the kind of monster the boys in the lab were playing around creating. But what I am saying is, you and me and Doc have wasted—or lost—a lot of time. If I ever have a kid . . . I'm gonna be there, no matter what. Must have killed him not knowing about me, then finding out like he did . . . or knowing about you and having to love you without letting anybody know so they wouldn't put both you and him in a glass cage. Damn. It's no wonder we're all screwed up."

She could only nod; what her brother was saying was true, but right now she was so worn out emotionally that it was hard to process.

"Like . . . remember when the Vamps snatched me and kept me hostage, hooked up to their frickin' blood machine?" Crow Shadow was leaning forward with his hands clasped together, and Sasha covered his hands with her own.

"Oh, God, how could I forget?"

"I thought I was gonna die, but I could feel you searching for me. That's what gave me hope."

"I felt it," she said quietly. "I can't explain it, but I knew you were alive and that I had to find you."

"Right—that's what I mean. There's no explaining the wolf."

Sasha offered him a sad smile. "Now you sound like Hunter."

"Then you have to know that I know something between you guys isn't right."

Sasha slowly sat back and wrapped her arms around her waist.

"He didn't say anything to me, Sasha, so relax." Crow got up and came to sit on the bench beside her. "I could feel it as he talked about you, and I could sense it when I came up those steps and looked into your eyes. Something isn't right. Whatever is going on, don't do this. He loves you, you love him. I can say it to you, because you won't bare fangs at me."

She gave him a wan smile. "You sure?"

A supportive arm came across her shoulders. Little by little she gave in to the pull of it and allowed Crow Shadow to hug her.

"You are such an alpha . . . I can feel you fighting the tears, Captain . . . can feel you fighting to keep that stiff upper lip. But I'm telling you it's cool—I'm your brother, okay. It's safe with me, Sasha. I don't know what happened, and it isn't my business . . . but I can tell you that something built up inside that man—he's wounded."

She couldn't answer, could only squeeze her eyes shut more tightly and nod, breathing in short, anguished bursts.

"You can let down your guard and I'll have your back just like you had mine." Crow Shadow hugged her tighter until she rested her forehead on his shoulder. "If this is all I can do for my baby sister, let me, all right? You saved my life, came in there with another huge alpha, Hunter's brother, and kicked ass when it would have been so easy to just leave me. You didn't even know I was part of you, then, but you wouldn't leave me."

"We don't leave our own," Sasha said in a muffled voice, her voice beginning to quake. She drew in another deep breath to steady herself and then fisted her hands at Crow's back. "I am just so tired . . . of proving myself."

"With us, you don't have to," he said quietly. "Just be you—that's good enough."

Elder Vlad stood at the edge of Lake Pontchartrain eagerly awaiting the uncustomary icy breeze that would announce the arrival of Queen Blatand of Hecate. She was an Unseelie masterpiece. The ancient Vampire felt his fangs begin to lengthen as frost covered the blades of grass beneath his feet, even in New Orleans in July. Within moments his sight was rewarded as the fragile, porcelain beauty materialized out of an icy mist. A wash of blue-white moonlight sparkled in the tiny, sequin-like icicles that crusted her pale blue gown. Penetrating pale blue eyes arrested him, and her frosted blue lips quirked up in a half smile. Tonight she'd left her long platinum hair down as though to tease him, and he studied how it spilled over her shoulders and petite, perfect breasts.

"Cerridwen," Elder Vlad murmured.

"You have summoned me," she said, quietly coming to him and placing a cold hand against his cheek.

He turned his face into her palm and kissed the center of her hand. "Yes . . . it is done."

"The creature has a body?"

Elder Vlad smiled a toothy grin. "Indeed." But his smile faded as Cerridwen backed away.

"Witches and warlocks can be . . . how shall we say . . . sometimes unreliable. They are, after all, human."

"True," he said, with confidence, taking up her hand for a moment. "But given your opposition to Sir Rodney, and all that you have to gain from taking his place at the UCE when this plays out . . . your hands must be clean." He stared into her eyes and then kissed the back of her chilly hand.

"I am slightly uncomfortable with some of the logistics associated with this plan, but I do trust you implicitly."

Colonel Madison looked down the jump-seat row at his men. The engine drone of the aircraft felt like it was drilling a hole in his temple. Two more innocent humans had been found in that supernatural cesspool called New Orleans? He'd clean it out, would eviscerate any wolf dens down there—then would come back to Denver and address the dual wolf threat that was too close to the base. There had to be more of them locally; he could feel it. They traveled in packs, clans, Trudeau's report had said. She'd tried to blame things on so-called Vampires. *Bullshit.* These were wolf killings. Vampires would be next on their target-of-value list. Right now, Vampires weren't active, weren't draining human beings of blood and snatching bodies.

Pure hatred burned within him as he thought back on how the two wolves had bested them over at Ronnie's Road Hog Tavern. And the brass had let one of those beasts in the U.S. Army? She'd scammed the brass, had lied! There was no difference between a fucking Werewolf and a Shadow Wolf, except that the former was vulnerable to silver and the latter was not! He'd seen them slip in and out of shadows using stealth, and something that agile, that strong, and that dangerous *had* to be eliminated. A beast like that moved humans down a notch on the food chain, which was unacceptable.

Talking about wolves that were demon-infected versus those that were not was splitting hairs; they were all rabid dogs, as far as he was concerned. He'd frag that bitch Trudeau as soon as look at her if he got a chance— and there would be a chance, one night, somehow. The fact that she was allowed to even wear the same uniform and claim to be of service to *his* country was a slap in the face. Affirmative action had gone too far!

Worse yet, his own command had allowed her to pass off information from her animal lover as intel? As far as he was concerned, anything that wasn't 100 percent pure human needed to be exterminated—wiped off the face of the planet.

The thought of it made him grind his teeth with unspent rage. The huge male wolf had toyed with him and probably given three of his best men concussions. But this time they'd be ready. They could heal later; they were warriors. Right now it was time to rock and roll. The two-hour-and-thirty-six-minute flight from Denver to New Orleans was the only thing standing between him and monster killing.

Madison glimpsed out of the window, glad that it was still dark. A full moon would hang around for at least two nights, long enough for them to kick in some doors, blow up some bayou hideouts, and come out with a wolf hide.

"Juarez, you good?" Madison said, glancing at the flank man who'd taken the first blow to the head in the tavern's parking lot.

"Never better, sir," Juarez shouted over the din of the airplane motor.

"Good man," Madison shouted back. "McPherson, Johnson, you good?"

"Roger that, sir," McPherson said with a hard nod, returning a steely, blue-eyed gaze.

"Locked and loaded, sir," Johnson said, his dark eyes set hard within the ebony frame of his face.

"Pho?"

"They never laid a hand on me, sir—but I've got an early Christmas present for 'em," Pho said, patting his weapon.

Colonel Madison nodded toward his men and then sat back in his seat. "Hoo-rah!"

"Wait, brother!" Shogun called out to Hunter, leaving Sir Rodney and his retinue behind.

"Just howl and we will guide you to the sidhe," Sir Rodney shouted toward the retreating wolves. "You have safe haven there."

Moving quickly to catch up to Hunter, Shogun simply waved and kept running.

"Brother, we are one clan! Do not go into the shadows where I cannot follow you!" Frustration turned

Shogun's gait into a flat-out dash until he caught up with Hunter, rounded him, and stopped his retreat by body-blocking him. "Stop and talk to me!"

"There is nothing to discuss. We must find your aunt and put her out of her misery before she does more harm." Hunter sidestepped Shogun and kept walking.

Again Shogun caught up to him, but this time grabbed his arm. "No, there is more than that!"

Hunter snarled as he looked down at Shogun's hand, but Shogun didn't remove it from his bulging bicep.

"There is nothing more than that!"

"Now I know your wolf isn't thinking clearly," Shogun said, slowly letting go of his hold on his brother. "There is evidence to gather."

Hunter glared at Shogun but didn't move.

"Yes, brother," Shogun said firmly. "We must stop Lady Jung Suk, but we must find out who embodied her . . . this will take investigative work. We must fan out our forces, get to covens—the only source strong enough to cast such a spell, or prove that the Unseelie acted on this—and then we must find the benefactor."

"We already know it was probably Vampires."

Shogun nodded. "This is truth. However, that is also how we have arrived at this political dilemma. We knew it was them, but we didn't have evidence before we acted. This time we must arrive at the UCE with hard evidence, or there will be an open license for retaliation against us. Sir Rodney could also be sanctioned, which would give his ex-wife, Cerridwen—Queen Blatand of Hecate—his seat." When Hunter turned to fully look at him, Shogun stepped back and relaxed. "The ruling power that comes from the bench is something I do not have to review with you, yes?"

Hunter released a quick breath of frustration. "I am aware."

"Then what happens if the Unseelie queen and the Vampires take control of the United Council of Entities? How long do you think it will be before the other supernatural parliaments fold and brutal rule returns? Then . . . what happens to our wolf Federations—whether they are Werewolf or Shadow Wolf, we face certain extinction, as that is the goal, and always has been for the Vampires. It doesn't matter that the Unseelie only care about annexing power from Sir Rodney's Seelie court. *They will exterminate us, brother.* Wolves will be no more—only those who have been demon-infected and living behind the demon doors." Shogun slapped his chest hard with emotion, making his long spill of jet-black hair sway and shimmer in the moonlight. "Your kind, my kind, our clans living peacefully amid humans will be a thing of the past!"

Silence stood between them for what seemed like a long time.

"This is how I know you are distracted," Shogun said carefully. His tone was nonjudgmental and weighted with compassion. "We have come to know each other well . . . we have battled side by side, even though we were raised to adulthood never knowing about the other until recently. But there is a bond. You have saved my life, I have saved yours . . . we are not each other's enemy."

"You are indeed my brother," Hunter said after a moment. "Yes. What you say is true. Forgive me."

"I am going to risk my life by telling you the truth . . . since the one thing that is constant with Shadow Wolves is that you are no liars." Shogun smirked and stepped back out of Hunter's swing range and then dragged his fingers through his hair, his calm, almond-shaped eyes focused on Hunter's stoic expression. "We Werewolves do not have that same code of honor . . . we will lie, our value system is a little less rigid. But we do have our own code of honor."

Hunter nodded, his expression unreadable as he folded his arms over his chest and waited.

"You cannot think like this," Shogun said bluntly. "You will be a detriment to any investigation—because if you find the perpetrator, you will kill it on sight. That may not be what is required."

"I have restraint," Hunter said, his canines breaking through his gums as he spoke.

"No. You don't," Shogun said flatly. "Run your tongue over your teeth. The evidence speaks for itself."

"I do not have to justify myself to anyone!" Hunter shouted, pointing with a hard snap at Shogun.

"Then let me tell you the truth," he replied calmly, beginning to circle Hunter. "You need to go back to the North Country and rectify whatever has gone awry with your mate."

"What!"

Shogun leaned against a tree. "You heard me."

Again the two brothers stared at each other and allowed a brief silence to become the referee between them.

"It is understandable," Shogun said in a compassionate tone. "I have never said this to you, but it is time."

"Speak!" Hunter shouted, beginning to circle Shogun, who now remained still.

"I love her, too . . . If you were ever to die in combat, I would go to her and stay with her until she would have me." Shogun held up his hands before his chest in a slow, calm motion when Hunter's eyes changed. "However, as my brother, as long as you live, I would not cross that line out of pure respect for you and for her. I don't have to explain myself . . . do not listen to my words, look at my deeds. You have seen me save your life and fight beside you—I am not hoping for your sudden death and would give my life for you. Do not be a fool and allow anger or pride to throw away such a gift as Sasha."

Hunter turned away, and Shogun rounded on him. "I do not know what has happened between you. That is not my business. I can only judge by the result of your attention to this very pressing matter that it must have been profound."

When Hunter didn't answer and looked away, Shogun stepped into his line of vision again, pressing his point.

"I know this, brother—she loves you. The way I know is too painful for one man to disclose to another, but she is faithful. Trust me."

This time Hunter looked at his brother and onetime rival.

"Yes," Shogun said, nodding. "To even discuss this is my silver bullet," he added, covering his heart with a broad palm. "But as your brother I would be remiss if I didn't implore you to go home for one night, fix this, and then return. I can gather leads with my men and will report all to you. We have a fallback position in the sidhe and have Sir Rodney's forces on the ground and in the trees to provide us cover. You are no good like this to us."

"I am—"

"No good to us right now," Shogun repeated firmly. "And as your brother, being as honest as one man can be to another, if you let this break, if you throw away your gift, I have no honor . . . I will go after what you have cast away without shame."

CHAPTER 8

A lonely howl made her stand up and go to the porch rail. Crow Shadow was long gone; it wasn't him. She'd know that forlorn call that haunted the night anywhere. It knocked the wind out of her.

Sasha touched her amulet, nervously fingering it as she stared into the night. Initially seeing nothing, she took a deep breath to steady herself, set her gaze on the horizon, and then scanned the dark tree line until she heard movement in the shed.

He loped out of the folds of darkness wearing only his jeans and amulet, his eyes capturing hers. He didn't say a word. She gripped the railing tighter, not trusting her emotions, not trusting what would leap out of her mouth. Anger fought with worry fought with relief as she watched him stop at the foot of the stairs. His mood was impossible to judge. She just prayed he hadn't returned to argue.

"I came to report on what I found in the bayou," Hunter said quietly.

Sasha didn't immediately reply; she let the evasive comment stand between them for a moment before offering one of her own. "I was hoping you would let me know what was going on down there."

He didn't blink, just stared at her with those intense amber eyes that made her want to go to him.

"I can't do this without you," she finally said in a quiet rush.

"You know that I will always help you with your missions, Sasha—"

"No," she said, cutting him off as she moved to the top of the stairs. She shook her head, her voice becoming fragile. "That's not what I meant . . . what I just said before wasn't honest—we're dancing around the subject, but it's there, Hunter. It hasn't gone away. What I'm trying to tell you is that I can't do this life without you. I just can't. And I've never made that clear to you before . . ."

He mounted the steps and met her at the top of them. A pair of warm hands caressed her shoulders gently before she was enveloped in the heat of his sure embrace. She could feel his heart slamming against his chest as he breathed into her damp hair. Their amulets touched, radiating an additional prism of heat where they met. The familiarity, the rightness of his body against hers melted her bones into his stone-cut torso. Her palms slid up his naked back, splaying in search of more of his glorious skin.

"I cannot stand by and watch them hurt you," he murmured against her scalp. "Don't ask me to do what is beyond my capacity . . . Sasha, when they disrespect you, it kills me. That bastard drew a weapon on you, and my wolf needed to butcher him—it was only for you that I didn't."

She hugged Hunter tighter and then pressed her lips against his amulet before she moved it to caress the place over his heart.

"I just want you to be safe," he said in a low rumble that she felt inside her womb. "It was never about me versus the human military . . . I have no problems with your career or your rank—I'm proud of that . . . I'm proud of you. But I do have a problem with the humans who would attempt to abuse you simply because they know what you are. Don't hate me for that, Sasha."

"It's not possible to hate you for loving me." She squeezed her eyes shut tighter and simply nodded against Hunter's bare chest. His confession made her inwardly cringe. She'd been fighting the wrong war . . . had dug in and held her position because she'd thought it was about her role, her position—she'd been filtering his actions through her human cultural lens . . . the one where who made more in the male–female dynamic, who had more status, and who was so-called on top mattered so very much. That was her baggage claimed from years of fighting in a male-dominated profession. But Hunter was a Shadow . . . and the man was no liar.

"Sasha, I have to know that they won't take you away and lock you up and try to dissect you . . . or to steal your eggs to try to make lab experiments of what should be our children. Your commanding officer said that you were *their property* and I lost it . . . Can you understand what that did to me to hear something like that?"

His voice had become a plaintive rumble as his grip on her tightened. Until this moment she hadn't realized just how worried he was for her safety in the hands of humans.

"Oh, God, Hunter . . . they won't—"

"They will!" he shouted, breaking their embrace and holding her away from him with both hands. "Sasha, baby, our kind have lived for centuries in hiding from human invaders, and there are historical facts—we've seen the beast called man." Before she could respond, he clutched her to his chest again. "Don't you understand what drives me, what makes my wolf insane?"

His hands sought her hair as his lips pressed hard against her scalp. "If I lose you to them, I would go against every honor that I owned. The dark wolf would have me as though I'd gone through a demon door . . . and I would not rest until I destroyed the men who harmed you—and after that, there would be no returning to myself."

"I won't let that happen," she said, leaning up to send her promise into his mouth. "I won't."

Only touch could convey her intentions. Words failed so miserably now. That had always been the great failing between them—words. Knowing that, she allowed her hands to speak, reverently tracing the sinew-carved expanse of his back as her tongue swept his. Arms then encircling his neck, her fingers laced through his hair, she pressed full statements into his mind, her pelvis translating meaning into feeling. How did a woman say she was sorry when words had been her undoing?

Admitting error was simply not enough when there were so many wrongs to right. This recent struggle was just the last in a long line of incidents, and that awareness shook her to her core. Until now, until she was near ready to release all that she'd known, she couldn't see what she'd been doing to the person who loved her most. Surrender had never been an option for her as a soldier or as a warrior . . . but Hunter had surrendered to her on sight, and unlike her, he had never been conflicted about where he stood.

That basic truth crackled in his silvery aura. The deep heat emanating from his massive hands against her back and sliding over her backside explained it all. His words were always direct and uncomplicated, just like his touch. That had everything to do with his pure view of who she was and what she meant to him . . . if she'd only been able to give him the same.

For so long she'd offered him her body but never her full mind, and absolutely none of her spirit, yet he'd gone completely bankrupt for her. She'd known that from the start. But fear of loving too hard, too fast, too recklessly had allowed her to rob him of the totality he deserved. The man who held her was the salt of the earth, and she'd held him to a standard that was beneath his dignity.

Tears stung the back of her throat as she climbed up his body and wrapped her legs around his waist. "I was so afraid to let go," she whispered in an urgent rush against his temple. "I was fighting me, not you."

He nodded and pulled back to gaze at her in the moonlight. "I know," he said quietly. "But I was willing to wait for this."

Terror became enmeshed in desire as she stared at him, looking into his soul. He held nothing back in his gaze, and she'd never been so lost to another being in her life. He'd once told her "*mine*" while loving her hard, and tonight he seemed determined to make good on his claim. Holding back and not giving him her all was impossible.

"You own my heart, Sasha," he admitted in a deep murmur. "What more can I give you to make you trust me?"

She slowly shook her head to try to convey there was no greater gift and nothing more that he could give. Her damp lashes brushed his nose as she tilted her head and took his mouth, and then deepened their kiss. Instantly his grip tightened on her backside and her legs clamped tighter around his waist as though they were inextricably linked, one body joined at the heart. She caught his moan and swallowed it as he began to walk, helping him to manage the screen door so that he didn't have to put her down.

What had started as a long, sensual kiss had become a series of impassioned kisses between shortened breaths, between finding the sofa and stumbling until they came to rest in a pulsing heap. Their shadows danced across the moonlit cabin wall, moving separately from their bodies, undressing them faster than their hands could negotiate fabric and form. The skin-on-skin burn they felt before her bare breasts slid against his chest made them both cry out, made him yank harder on her jeans to free her.

But her giving to him in return made her slow him down, her cheek against his hot abdomen causing his hands to tremble as they sought her shoulders. He sucked in air between his teeth as she managed his button and zipper and caressed his navel with her tongue. He stepped out of his jeans, and she stepped out of her fears. Desire flared in his expression as she stared up and drank it into her soul. Surrender was imminent. This time it would be hers. He had already done so; tonight was about laying down arms and becoming one. The prospect was terrifying; she would give him everything within her.

Taking her time, she allowed the texture of his skin to play against her palms as they slid up his naked thighs and over his hips to finally find anchor over the tight swell of his magnificent ass. With her eyes closed she lolled her head from side to side, allowing her cheeks to graze the length of his shaft, reveling in the changes in texture from his wide base up the thick, throbbing member that was crisscrossed with a network of veins until her lips met the smooth, wet skin that made her finally stare up at him.

For a moment she watched his stomach tremble, each inhale he took through his nose a clear attempt to remain in control. But she had so much to give that her shadow mounted his as her lips parted. The combination of a shadow dance and the tight sheath of her mouth wrenched a moan from his depths.

Her spiraling tongue issued the first in a series of apologies working in concert with her hands that pulled him deeply into her mouth until she couldn't breathe. She didn't care. It was a matter of principle that became a matter of rhythm, inhales and exhales taken in through her nose on each withdrawal, fingers gripping the tight lobes of flesh in her palms until his taste became saltier, his breaths shorter like his strokes. That was when she abandoned his shaft to find his sac, her hands covering the slick wetness, pumping in unbroken glides, her lips gently pulling at the most fragile part of him with her tongue, only to return to give him more mouthed warmth.

A hard contraction made her grip him tightly just under the head and suck at it quickly, lapping the ooze until his voice broke her down.

"Sasha . . ."

He said her name like a plea the moment his knees buckled. Staccato breaths pelted her damp scalp as he bent trying to hold her, trying not to break her stride as his fingers sought to make contact with her skin. Her body was on fire, but tonight she was the giver. Her breasts ached as she watched pleasure consume him, heard it embedded deep within his moans. Each earthy response bottomed out in her swollen labia; every lick against his taut skin soon felt like sweet suckles teasing her engorged bud. Her tongue found the groove of his head, laving it, paying homage to it until her slit frothed and spilled, anticipation making her tremble and open her thighs wider. That was when she realized his shadow had not abandoned her.

It didn't matter that she was physically giving to him; his shadow had found her sweet spot, suckling her from behind. She leaned into the phantom sensation with a groan, unable to resist. The expression on his face, head back, mouth open, hands cradling her crown while his shadow continued to eat her alive, blew her mind. Even swathed in his own pleasure, giving to her turned him out. Being his witness nearly made her come.

Crazed, she needed to feel him everywhere at once. Her nipples sent shards of stinging want between her legs until she released him from her mouth and captured him between her breasts. The change in texture and temperature put canines in his mouth and a dip in his spine as he furiously pumped against her. Then her name devolved in fragments from *Sasha*, to *baby*, to *oh . . . God.*

It was too intense. The feel of his hot, wet shaft quickly rubbing her swollen breasts; his head thrusting against her tender lobes as her mouth eagerly sought to kiss it on each pass. Slick, salty essence flowed, making each thrust faster in the viscous fluid, driving them both to the brink while his shadow caresses made her strain against air, tears streaming down her face.

Unable to stand it, he grabbed her by her shoulders; limp, she complied with total surrender, climbing up his body as he put her down on her back hard. The joining was instant and soul shattering. He entered her like a hot knife cleaving butter, and cried out like a man who'd been shot. Her wail rent the living room, but he cradled her face with one hand while holding himself up with the other to look into her spirit. She nodded, tears flowing, clutching his back; his lids lowered slowly but not before she saw his eyes cross.

He immediately dropped down and enveloped her like a man possessed. The pleasure from his thrusts were almost paralyzing, each hard return threatening the stability of the furniture, the stability of her sanity, and she felt it the moment he lost all control. His shadow on the wall literally howled . . . never in her life had she witnessed such a thing.

It was as though his spirit pulled everything that was within him up his spinal column to explode colors behind her lids and pour all that he had from his body into hers. Devastating pleasure stole her breath as her nails raked his back, her arch becoming a shuddering plea for more that his convulsions answered.

Wrecking orgasms sent her into seizure. Fisting her hair, he gazed at her for a moment, his pupils dilating, agony etched across his handsome face, and then the next convulsion struck him. He turned away as though gut-punched and heaved; she caught him as he collapsed, climaxes ebbing with breathless shudders.

For a long while they lay like that, joined, his breath and hers the only sounds of the night. Crickets and night fauna were now so distant. There was only his heartbeat and hers. Only his breath and hers. Only his skin touching hers. Sweat, love essence, no dividing line between the two. Her palm lazily stroked his back as his lungs expanded and contracted with effort. She'd given him everything she could, had the intention of uniting with him completely set in her soul . . . and could only hope that he'd felt it.

"I did," he murmured between deep breaths.

Startled, she tensed. "How did you know what I was thinking?"

"You let me in," he said quietly and then swallowed hard, burying his face against her hair.

She didn't understand, but continued to send healing touch into his shoulders and sweat-slicked back.

"I don't know about this part of being a wolf," she said softly, trying to understand.

His breaths were shallow, his emotion too full to allow him to speak, so he just held her tighter for a moment. She could feel him battling for composure, and that made her struggle with her own. Something profound had just happened, but she wasn't exactly sure what it was. Yet she didn't want to ruin the moment by overanalyzing it. Then he began to rock her, stroking her hair, nuzzling her as though she were the most precious gift in the entire world.

"You finally allowed me to become your mate," he said in a thick, garbled whisper. "You willed your spirit to dance with mine."

"I love you," she said. "I told you that before."

He shook his head and let out a long, satisfied breath. "That was intellect talking . . . your mind. Maybe some of your heart . . . your body. But there was always a part that you disallowed me to share . . . and I so wanted to earn that right."

"Oh, my God, Hunter . . . I just didn't understand. I've never let anyone get that close—I didn't know how to begin to open that door . . . but with you, I wanted to with all my heart."

He leaned up so that he could look at her. His disheveled hair covered his face in a dark curtain, but the blue-white moon allowed her to see the tears that were shimmering in his intense amber eyes.

"We are empaths to each other," he said in a quiet rumble. "When connected. Family is . . . but when two not of the same blood are joined like this . . . connected by the same heart, I can hear your mind whisper to me."

She traced his cheek with the pad of her thumb and when she found his eyebrows and the bridge of his nose, the tears spilled over his black velvety lashes. Their lovemaking had put a rough layer of five o'clock shadow on his jawline, and she couldn't stop touching his face, reading it with her fingers as her eyes studied his.

"Sasha . . . if you want me to marry you in the human tradition, I will. I don't fully claim to know their customs, but I will honor any that are important to you . . . because I love you with the whole of my spirit."

"And I love you with the whole of mine," she murmured, tracing his lush mouth with her fingertip before gently kissing him. "I want your spirit to always touch mine, and I want to never hurt you by closing you out of it. Teach me everything you want me to know tonight."

CHAPTER 9

It had come in the window to stab into the bathroom wall of the cabin beside her. Sir Rodney had delivered; his Fae glamour would create a body-double image for the cameras in her apartment. But it would only hold until dawn. Sasha crept to the darkened doorway between the cabin's bathroom and the bedroom, watching Hunter's deep, restful breaths as he slept. She had to go. She needed to go to the scene of the crime and not have him possibly spotted by humans who would try to hunt him.

Gathering her clothes, she slipped them on, found a shadow to slip into, and was gone.

Silver Hawk took a deep breath, and the sudden motion gave Bear Shadow a start. The elderly shaman had been in trance for hours, sitting before the fire as though his body were just a vacant shell while his spirit ventured to places Hunter's lieutenant could never fathom. But the sound and movement, along with the instant crackle of the fire between them, made Bear know the clan's advisor had returned from the unknown realms.

Slowly Silver Hawk's grip tightened on his rattles, and he began the somber chant of the warrior spirit's return. The fire dipped and swayed as though dancing. Bear Shadow sat motionless on guard, his huge, hulking frame at the ready and his senses keened for any eventuality. Then just as suddenly as the old man had begun, he stopped and opened his eyes to stare at Bear Shadow through the fire.

"The evil of many has become one," Silver Hawk said, his wolf eyes gleaming. "Carry this message to my grandson on the next moon."

It was all so very interesting to him as he sat in the hotel bar and stared out the window. Patrons could not be on the streets, but as long as they were inside the restaurant or bar of their hotel establishment, so far, the government wasn't telling people when they had to go to bed. The beleaguered establishments were all too happy to extend service hours all night long to make up for the patronage they were losing to the strict curfew. An unexpected side effect was that it created a strangely festive atmosphere among the ghost hunters, journalists, and embedded media types.

Russell Conway sipped his beer slowly as he watched a military Humvee go by. Maybe this time they would believe. Maybe this time they'd know that people like him weren't crazy.

"The authorities confirmed that the bodies had been moved. The kill site of both victims was out here in the bayou, judging from the dirt and marsh residue on what was left. So while the local authorities are looking for any homes or establishments out here that have missing loved ones or employees, our mission is to see if we can get some traction in deep. When these beasts snatched their victims, they had to feed somewhere. If there's been no reports of busted-up houses or bayou bars being rampaged, then there's gotta be an abandoned car on the road, something we can look to as our tracking lead. I say we return to the scene of the original crime—this burned-down Bayou House that took out several state troopers and was in Trudeau's report as infested with Werewolves."

Colonel Madison glanced around his small squad, gaining nods of silent agreement before continuing. He looked out into the darkness at the burned-out hull of the building that was once an active brothel and backwater still, and then spit on the ground. The full moon cast an eerie shimmer over the broken trees and blackened structure; the parking lot was deserted save for several abandoned cars.

"Rest assured, these wolves are fucking with us. They could have left the remains out here in the swamp, where they probably ate them. Bringing them back into town to throw them in an alley is a dare, a challenge, like they were sending us a warning. So I say we send them a few warning shots to let 'em know we are not to be jacked with!"

A rowdy *hoo-rah* echoed through the small glen as the squad lowered their night-vision goggles and raised their weapons. Using the Humvees as cover, Colonel Madison accepted a shoulder cannon from Juarez with a hard smile.

"Let's see what we can smoke out, gentlemen."

The rocket-propelled grenade hit the already deci-mated structure dead-on. An instant orange glow flashed with the boom that rocked the ground. Madison's men slapped five hunkered down behind the vehicles while the colonel peered up to check his handiwork.

"If that doesn't smoke 'em out, then . . ."

A low growl in the tree line made Madison hold up his fist. Using two fingers, he silently motioned for Juarez and Johnson to head in one direction while he, McPherson, and Pho got around to the other possible attack position. Like synchronized swimmers, his men quickly fanned out, taking cover in a way that they could open fire without hitting their own men.

But as Juarez was making a run across the lot to take a deeper position in, something moving in a black blur cut him off. A machine-gun burst lit the night just as his scream reverberated off the trees.

"Juarez!" Madison rushed in, yelling to his men to get them repositioned. "Go, go, go!"

Sasha came out of the shadows and into the midst of the firefight. She hit the ground to avoid getting shot. But the moment she got her bearings, she knew the men around her were doomed.

"Hold your fire and get out of here!" she shouted. "Fall back! Fall back!"

But instead of hearing the order repeated, suddenly shells were coming at her following the sound of her voice.

"I'm a friendly!" she shouted, dodging in and out of the shadows to avoid sudden death.

Machine-gun fire covered the colonel as he went to

check the status of his downed man. But he briefly turned away in horror at the sight. Juarez's entire face had been ripped off. His goggles were gone, his helmet crushed. His body lay on the ground twitching, each limb jerking in a gruesome death struggle. Blood gurgled up from his throat, and the sounds of a man drowning in his own blood made the colonel lower his weapon and fire a single shot into Juarez's skull. Sasha whirled out of a shadow, startling him. His instant reaction was to train his weapon on her, but she sideslapped it away.

"Fall back, Colonel! Get your men out of here! I don't know what the hell this entity is, but it's not a wolf."

"You've violated a direct order, Captain!" he shouted back, training the weapon on her again. "You are hereby—"

A soldier cried out, the sound of his death horrific. Sasha fled toward the sound, trying to get between the man and whatever was savaging him. But it was gone in a flash, a black blur of nothingness. Then there was only chaos.

Colonel Madison heard it, but couldn't see it. His men were yelling, bursts of ammunition rent the air, then the yelling became screaming. He could hear Captain Trudeau yelling for them to fall back, but he knew in his soul it was too late. She'd been right, God help him . . . God help them all!

A grenade went off and he couldn't get in close enough to help his men. Captain Trudeau was on the wrong side of the line of fire, and his men were as afraid of her as they were of what was butchering them. They were firing blindly. One of the Humvees was ablaze. Then all was silent.

She came to him dirty-faced, panting, fury in her wolf-gray eyes. "It was too fast and your men wouldn't let me near them to help them." She walked in a tight circle. "Damn! This didn't have to happen like this. Get in the vehicle, sir, and go back to base!"

"You defied a direct order!" he shouted, his nerves shattered.

"Yeah, I know. But you're alive because I did—so let's just say you owe me." Sasha walked away from him toward the shadow of a large tree.

"Come back here! That is an order, Captain."

She didn't turn around, but kept walking and held up her middle finger when he hoisted up his weapon and cocked the hammer.

"Save your ammo, Colonel. You're gonna need it."

Then she was gone.

Hours passed and he held his position until dawn broke . . . suddenly realizing that he'd been spared, had been left alive for one purpose—to take back the warning to the others who might come. Sasha Trudeau was going down!

Hunter awakened to Sasha's smile. She was leaning on her elbow gazing down at him, her big gray eyes filled with an expression so tender that he held his breath for a moment, thinking he was dreaming. He'd never seen Sasha so free, so unencumbered by duty, and his hand floated up on its own accord to stroke her soft cheek, all while he wished they could simply leave the troubled world behind. But in the cold light of day, he knew that wasn't an option.

"I know," she murmured.

Just her saying that, reading him so completely, woke up the rest of his body.

"Mine . . . for now, anyway," he murmured, pulling her on top of him, and then brushed her mouth with a kiss. He could still taste her essence on his tongue and smell their lovemaking in his sheets. That aromatic reminder and her beautiful sunlit smile was all it took to get him going again.

"Yours," she said, giving him a gentle kiss as her body slowly devoured his with a groan.

He knew she had to go back to her apartment and make herself seen around town in order to keep the peace, just as he had to go back to New Orleans to begin a full-fledged investigation. But to his way of thinking, half an hour more or less to say good morning and then say good-bye wasn't going to change the course of history.

They came to a stop at the border between a bright swath of sunlight and the looming shadows cast from a stand of summer-red maple trees. Despite the fantastic night they'd shared and the glorious morning, now, as he stood before Sasha, looking at how the sun caught in her dark hair, his spirit was more disquieted than it had ever felt in his life. He touched her hair, saying nothing, and watching how individual strands of red and golden brown made up the silky thicket that played through his fingers. He smiled sadly as her wistful expression turned into a pout, and he kissed her again for good measure.

"I hate this," he said.

"Me, too." She released a little sigh and then leaned her head back, closed her eyes, and breathed in deeply. "Why can't everything just be like this? Smell the forest . . . it's gorgeous."

"You're gorgeous," he said, placing a palm over her amulet. When she opened her eyes he breathed her in, allowing the scent of her freshly washed hair to roll over his palate.

"I have to go . . ."

She cradled his cheek with her palm for a moment, and he turned his mouth into the creamy surface of it.

"They aren't so bad," she said with a smile. "Just a few bad apples along the way, but ninety-nine percent of the people I served with were decent and honorable."

He captured her hand and held it over his amulet. "When we met, I tried to tell you that about the Wolf Clans, yes?"

"Yes," she said, nodding and closing the small space between them.

"You didn't believe me at first—rightfully so, because a few dangerous rogues changed the landscape . . . no one was safe while they were around, and we fought together, Sasha—you and I—to eradicate them before they could do damage. Tell me what's different about self-policing our Wolf Clans and self-policing your human military when it's gone rogue?"

"You're right," she said carefully, "but it's a cultural problem."

He cocked his head to the side, waiting on a plausible explanation.

"General Donald Wilkerson was a crazy bastard who set up the Sirius Project under Operation Dog Star . . . and now Colonel Madison seems equally a cowboy. But," Sasha said with a hard sigh as she fingered Hunter's amulet, "the human process of routing out bad guys is as complicated when you reach the higher branches of the military and government as some of the Vamp politics. Things get messy, political, and are extremely time consuming. Besides . . . uhm . . . when I get back, I'll probably really be in trouble."

"That is not the way of the wolf," he said, sending his gaze toward the tree line.

"No, it's not," she said calmly. "If everything got dealt with honorably and straightforwardly, we could put a lid on all the nukes and everybody could just go home."

"Perhaps that is why the humans fear us more than the Vampires," he said in a sullen tone. "They are both duplicitous creatures capable of extreme violence and sociopathic behavior, easily justified by whatever unconscionable reason they can come up with."

"Hey!" she said with a wide smile. "I'm half human on my mother's side."

"Forgive me," he said, growing more morose by the minute. "I meant no slander against your mother or your mother's people, you know that. Some humans are capable of great acts of kindness and are evolved. But they typically don't get to positions of power in your culture . . . or if they manage to get through the maze of the walking spiritually dead, they are surrounded by those who seek to destroy them—thus making them ineffective."

A gentle kiss stopped his rant. He looked down at Sasha to see her eyes filled with mischief.

"I thought I'd woken you up on the right side of bed this morning? Damn . . . I really must be losing my touch."

Her wry comment made a half smile tug at his cheek. "You're not losing your touch . . . I'm just . . . I just don't feel good about this, Sasha."

"I know," she said, dropping her shoulders with defeat as her smile faded. "But if I seem like I've disappeared, that will cause issues. I want to keep my record clean . . . This is all new for the human world. Think of it this way," she added, beginning to gesture with her hands. "What must it have been like when the first demon-infected wolf showed up on the scene? I can only imagine that the Shadows and the Weres freaked out."

Hunter nodded, conceding to her point. "In a word, yes."

"Okay, then . . . and there must have been all sorts of martial law, the wrong leaders pointing fingers, pure chaos until the clans could figure out how that all worked."

"And that's my point, Sasha. During that chaotic era, a lot of mistakes were made. Clan elders were jumpy, quick to go to war, and quick to cull the ranks through exterminations. I see that same unsettled energy among your leadership. A man like General Westford, who is honorable, may not be able to protect you if things go badly."

"Point well taken," she said, staring at him.

It made him feel better that she'd heard him—finally heard what he was saying in context. This wasn't an idle rant about her human military pack that she loved; this was about the fact that frightened men who didn't understand the nuances of supernatural life might inadvertently go after one of their own.

"You call me when you get back to your apartment," he said, tapping the cell phone on his belt. "I'm serious, Sasha. You and I need to stay in constant communication."

"Okay, okay," she said, sounding like a scolded teenager.

He had to laugh. "I'm serious."

"All right. I get it."

He eyed her and she stuck out her tongue at him.

"But here's the problem—we have to talk in code." She shrugged and began walking toward the shadows. "They have my apartment monitored—I can tell, and they did it before. Doc never talks straight on an open line, because with the big eye in the sky, they can intercept cell phone transmissions and—"

"Okay, okay, I get it," he said, holding up his hands and cutting her off.

"I'm not supposed to be involved in any investigations . . . directly . . . per se," she said with a sheepish grin. "I may have done something to, uhm . . . set them off—but I covered my tracks, so I won't be directly in the line of fire, I think. It's Madison's word against mine and the cameras don't lie so—"

Hunter frowned. "Baby, what are you talking about?"

"Nothing, really, I just want you to understand that

and I don't want you to be worried about the political stuff going down with the military. All right?"

I won't be as long as you're not caged," he said carefully. "They should have no reason to take away any more of your freedom, especially if your contact will be feeding you valuable intel about the happenings that the asshole with a coupla bars on his chest wouldn't be able to get in a million years."

"That could work," she said, laughing, and then looked away with mischief blazing in her eyes.

"Then I'll come pull you into a shadow, ravish you in the way of the wolf, and you can claim that some rogue just had his way."

He grinned a wide grin, and she laughed harder.

"What's an unarmed soldier to do," she said with a wink. "Travel well."

She blew him a kiss and stepped into a shadow. He remained watching the spot where she'd been and then closed his eyes to draw in her lingering sweet scent.

Great Spirit help him, if anything happened to her.

"This sucks!" Sasha walked out of the closet to see her bed flipped over and all her dresser drawers on the floor.

Seeing this in the morning just pissed her off all over again. Before she called Hunter, she needed to calm down. Stepping over the mess, she glanced into the bathroom, only to see her medicine cabinet flung wide open and over-the-counter meds on the floor and sink. Tampons were flung everywhere, and a crushed box had a boot mark on it. She counted to ten as she went into the living room and just stood there. The wall unit was down, and the flat-screen television hadn't survived. Good thing Mrs. Baker had taken in her goldfish, Fred, who'd happily died of overfeeding at her hands—most likely beat suffocating on the floor.

"I don't like you, either, you butt-wipe," she said, beginning to right furniture. "But was all this necessary?"

She reached out and touched her silvery image, which was sitting in the only chair in the room that wasn't completely destroyed and watched it quickly merge with her body, hoping like hell that anyone watching would think the flicker was just a digital transmission distortion.

But Sasha just shook her head as she stared down at the boot print on her sofa cushion. When she glanced at her small kitchen pass-though, it was obvious that any glass dish she owned was probably shattered. Small appliances, like her microwave and coffeemaker, were hammered on the floor. Every cabinet door was open and of course the neighbors probably hadn't heard a thing. All this because some guy got his ass waxed in a parking lot. What a bitch.

A knock at the door gave her a start, and she was glad to have an eyewitness to this travesty. Only her guys or Doc would come over after something like this went down, and they were good company to have at a time like this. The pounding got louder and she hurried to open the door.

"Yeah, yeah, I'm coming." She threw open the door and froze, not expecting to see MPs.

"Captain Sasha Trudeau?"

She looked from one pair of mirrored aviator sunglasses to the other. "Yes."

"You are hereby remanded to the custody of the United States Army."

CHAPTER 10

She remained extremely calm on the entire ride to the base. Okay, admittedly it was a bad plan, and she had this coming. But there was information she'd wanted to try to get while down there in New Orleans, plus she knew in her soul that an entire squad had been sent on a suicide mission. If she could have saved them, she would have. Getting Hunter involved in all of that would have put a target on the man's forehead or possibly gotten him killed. And had he known she'd gone, the fight would have lasted all night long when there wasn't time for that. The only good thing she'd learned while away was that whatever had come for Sir Rodney had passed through his system, and he swore an oath that he'd send his best purge specialists to check out Clarissa.

A hundred postbattle rationalizations fought inside Sasha's head on the very silent ride to the base. What the hell had she been thinking?

The poor MPs who had come to collect her seemed as though they were ready to jump out of their skins. The scent of fear and adrenaline soaked their clothing, even though she'd come out of her apartment and gotten into the jeep like a model citizen. Still, she knew it wouldn't take much provocation for a man to get skittish and draw. Then that would get complicated, unnecessarily so. Therefore the best thing to do would be to chill until she could figure out what had happened. She was sure Colonel Madison didn't appreciate the save, rat bastard.

As the MPs processed her in at the base, the grim faces around her seemed as though they wanted a reason, any reason, to frag her on the spot. Then she realized she wasn't headed for the Situation Room—but rather a cell? Holy Christ . . . she hadn't called Hunter, and he'd have a cow.

"Can I speak to Doc—I mean, Doctor Xavier Holland, who was originally on the—"

"Ma'am, we are not authorized to bring any visitors or have any discussion about your incarceration."

The MP had cut her off and abruptly left. But *ma'am* . . . not *Captain*. WTF? Oh, so now that the word was out about her being a supernatural, she was no longer one of them? No longer had rank in uniform that she'd earned? Even more importantly, *incarceration*? Okay, now it was time for some answers. Yeah, she had violated an order, but she'd also come to the aid of men under fire, and had kept her commanding officer's ass alive.

Sasha sat down on the cot and stared at the floor. After about an hour, judging from the drips of water beating the metal sink and fraying her nerves, General Westford arrived at the bars with Doc and Colonel

Madison. Two armed military police escorts stood in the background. Sasha immediately got to her feet.

"I have only allowed you to talk to this animal as a courtesy," Colonel Madison said, pointing at Sasha.

"Now, wait just a minute," Doc countered, glaring at the colonel.

"This is a fine officer, not an animal. Have you lost your mind?" General Westbrook shouted. "You have no evidence!"

"I lost four good men in ways you don't want to imagine down there in the bayou!" Colonel Madison shouted. "I was there! She was there!"

General Westford and Doc looked at Sasha hard.

"You violated a direct order, Captain?" General Westford spoke through his teeth.

Doc closed his eyes.

"You lost *four* men because you wouldn't fall back when I told you the entity out there wasn't anything we'd cataloged yet!" Sasha shouted, looking at Colonel Madison, clutching the bars. "We definitely need to talk, sir."

"Where were you last night?" General Westford said, anger burning in his eyes as he approached the bars.

"Trying to keep Colonel Madison and his men alive," Sasha said, her gaze steady on the colonel. "I knew they were walking into an ambush and—"

"Tell me how you knew?" Colonel Madison shouted. "She ate my men, she butchered them!"

Sasha shook her head in disbelief as General Westford walked away from the bars and dragged his fingers through his hair.

"What do you have to say for yourself, Captain?" Colonel Madison yelled. "Is that how you planned to get back your command, by murdering my men!"

Sasha just stared at him for a moment, unable to answer such a ludicrous charge.

"What are you going to do, waterboard her if she doesn't answer you?" Doc said, and then turned away to look at Sasha.

"If we have to, that's an affirmative, sir," Madison said, his voice dripping with hatred.

"I know you don't believe that," General Westford said, but his voice had much less force in it than Sasha had hoped it would.

Disbelief filled Doc's eyes and resonated in his tone. "Don't you speak until you get legal counsel, Sasha. This is bullshit."

"This visit is over," Colonel Madison said. "General, you were relieved of duty yesterday by the secretary of defense—this is my post now. I was the one who saw men butchered, and after this suspect is interrogated under the laws sealed by the Patriot Act, as well as sanctioned by the Department of Justice—"

"Look at the tapes from my apartment, sir," Sasha said quickly. Her gaze shot from Doc to General Westford. "I know I've been under surveillance, but I bet he didn't know to what extent. I have nothing to hide and will fully cooperate. He is the one who would do anything to pin some horrific crime on me. This man trashed my apartment, came to a civilian location wearing a sidearm off post! Bring in a military tribunal, pronto. Get someone to take my statement. I'll submit to a polygraph test, sodium pentothal, you name it, because I *did not* go after *anyone*. I did not savage his squad, I went down there to save them and to gather vital intel that he'd never get in a million years. Eating people? The thought is abhorrent, and I want out of here so I can help find who took out our men."

When Colonel Madison didn't immediately respond but glared at her with hatred, Sasha looked from him to the general.

"Whatever happened last night, I can account for being up in North Country and then, yeah, I slipped into a shadow and went down to New Orleans—but fell headfirst into a firefight. Before I even left to head north, though, and way before I even went to New Orleans, I stopped back at my apartment only to find Colonel Madison and one of his lieutenants trashing it."

"That's a lie!" Colonel Madison shouted, rushing the bars. "We were looking for evidence that would—"

"You were angry, sir, because you baited a fight with a civilian—my Shadow Wolf contact at Ronnie's Road Hog, where I bet I can give you a dozen eyewitnesses." Sasha turned to the general and continued speaking. "Colonel Madison then took the fight outside with an armed squad, he and four of his men. When the fight did not go as he'd obviously planned between him and the civilian, he drew on not only me but also my team, which consisted of two unarmed soldiers, Lieutenants Woods and Fisher, as well as three unarmed civilians." Sasha's gaze narrowed on Colonel Madison. "Therefore, if I am being held and charged with some unknown offense, I'd like to enter a formal complaint in the records."

"And that's why I know you killed my men in

retaliation!" Colonel Madison shouted. "You followed us to New Orleans to butcher us!"

"That's a lie! I went down there to help you, because I knew by the way you led them against us in the parking lot that, if you took them to live action against supernaturals as unprepared as you were, people were gonna die. And they did!"

"What!" General Westford bellowed. "Open this goddamned cell this minute, Colonel, or I'll have you sitting in a cell beside Captain Trudeau until we get to the bottom of this."

"Have you seen the remains that were flown back?" Colonel Madison shouted, spittle flying. "Let's go take a walk to the morgue, sir, and then you decide. And if she knew we had come to search her apartment for evidence of consorting with known targets of value, then she had reason to be further enraged and to ambush us! If she didn't do it, then she knows who did! There's also the career aspect of this—to take out a squad before they've served one night would put her back in command as the most knowledgeable on the subject. This was sabotage—treason!"

"In my professional opinion, General," Doc said loudly with a narrowed gaze, "I think this man is having a psychotic break and needs a sedative along with a thorough psychiatric eval for post-traumatic stress syndrome. Then again . . . as the project leader for Operation Dog Star, I've seen men in combat who've hunted Werewolves—seen them come back nicked, scratched, bitten, and acting erratic." Doc smiled a hard half smile as the MPs behind Colonel Madison backed up quietly and took the safeties off their weapons. "You might need to be quarantined—testing could take at least a month to see how you respond under the next full moon . . . it takes that long for the virus to set in."

"I wasn't nicked, and you know it, Holland!" Colonel Madison shouted.

"I don't know anything," Doc countered. "You were never examined to my knowledge."

"No, siree," General Westford said with a smirk. "But that does need to be added to the emergency report to the Joint Chiefs."

"This is bull," Colonel Madison said, wheeling around. "I'm clean!"

"You were the sole survivor of a brutal wolf attack," Doc said evenly, rage burning in his eyes. "Every man with you went down and was eaten, and only you . . . for some strange reason . . . lived—with a full magazine of ammo still left. Interesting . . . curious, actually. We can test the contents of Captain Trudeau's digestive tract to find out if she ate one of your men . . . that might only take a day. But you'll need at least a month of quarantine. Care to wager a—"

"You know I wasn't scratched or bitten! We can go to the labs right now and I'll strip!"

"Doesn't matter. The infected generally heal immediately, the initial wounds are hidden, they have increased metabolic rates and—"

"Enough! I know what you're trying to do and it won't work!"

Doc Holland moved in close to Madison and spoke quietly enough that the MPs standing by couldn't hear him. "I've been in the military a long time, and I worked through all the bureaucracy long before your ass was out of diapers—so don't fuck with me, son. And if you ever pull a stunt like this against Captain Trudeau again, I swear you'll find yourself in a padded cell baying at the goddamned moon."

Once tempers cooled, she was glad to be back in the Situation Room. It beat a jail cell. More important than any career jockeying or grandstanding, four men in uniform had died, along with two civilians. In the weeks to come, after all the forensic testing and PR damage control, there would be memorials, and families would finally have a chance to say good-bye. It didn't matter that Madison's men had trashed her apartment. They were still somebody's sons, husbands, and possibly fathers. Someone would grieve.

In the grand scheme of things, the offense of vandalism could have been taken outside and handled the old-fashioned way, and it truly hurt her soul that Colonel Madison actually thought she'd slaughter any human being. And for what, something as stupid as disrespect, trashing some furniture—things easily replaceable? Didn't he think she had enough humanity within her to respect life, all life? That was the part of it that simply blew her away, his complete incomprehension. Prejudice had blinded him, and the man had lost his grip on one core fundamental: No one deserved what had happened, especially not given the brutal nature of the killings.

A cool shiver ran down Sasha's spine. She sat back from the gruesome forensic pictures for a moment. All eyes were on her, except Colonel Madison's. But this time she addressed him with respect in her tone. Fear did strange things to people, and after what the man had been through, she was willing to extend a little compassion in his direction.

"Colonel," she said in a firm but gentle manner. "Maybe we got off on the wrong foot. We both have a job to do and love this country and want to protect the people in it. For what it's worth, I am very sorry for what happened to your men. I might not have had a chance to meet them under the best of circumstances, but they were ours. They stood up for the same flag. So I want you to know that, no matter what you may think of me personally, I will help you in whatever way you allow me to find out who did this. There are things crawling around down there in that swamp that deserve our respect—"

"Our respect?" Colonel Madison said, leaning forward.

"Our respect, sir, as vicious killing machines that know no bounds. I came in contact with the enemy on several occasions . . . once, unfortunately, it was one of ours. My commanding officer, then, Captain Rod Butler—and I had to put him down."

"Are you threatening me, Captain?" Colonel Madison said, eyes wild with a combination of rage and disbelief.

"No, sir, not at all. And I mean that, sir. I am just saying that I know what it's like to lose members of your unit. I know what this beast can do when it goes up against human flesh and bone. Your men were not prepared for that eventuality, sir—in my humble opinion.

If you would allow me to share my expertise with you, I can possibly keep your replacement team out of harm's way . . . but you have to allow me to do my job, sir."

"And just *what* is your job? You are so far out of line and out of order, Captain, that it is stupefying. You plan to sit here and tell me what *your job* is after you've been relieved of duty because of a failed mission—of all the arrogance . . ." Colonel Madison shook his head and folded his arms over his chest. "You are so amazingly beyond redemption on this, I actually want to hear what you have to say, Captain," he added with a sneer, and then glanced down the table at Doc and General Westford.

"My job has always been to find and eliminate any threat to humanity, especially to the citizens of the United States of America, sir." Sasha didn't blink or stutter as she held Colonel Madison's gaze. "I know this enemy, sir. I know how it feeds, know how to track it. I have Native American contacts that have kept this predator at bay for centuries. I also know the political nuances among the various supernatural factions and nations. The regional dynamics are more complicated than those in the Middle East, if I may speak freely, sir . . . and if you go mucking around down there without a guide or without understanding the different species and how they attack, you will jeopardize your mission, your men, and possibly your life."

General Westford folded his beefy hands in front of him. "I think this recent development, along with *all* of its nuances, as the captain so aptly put it, needs to be reported to the Joint Chiefs."

* * *

Change within the military was an agonizingly slow process. Sasha sat with her team in their old offices at NORAD waiting on word from General Westford's meeting. As the old project leader with twenty-five-plus years of experience, Doc was able to sit in, at least. But the morale damage to her Paranormal Containment Unit had already been done.

Speaking in hushed tones, her team strategized career options while she watched the clock. She had to get a call off to Hunter soon or else he'd wig. Then there was the not-so-distant worry about his safety tugging at the back of her mind. They'd all seen their share of demon-infected Weres. If a rogue like Lady Jung Suk was on the loose or in attack mode, even a seasoned Shadow Wolf warrior had to be on guard.

"Screw it," Winters whispered. "If we all send in our resignations on the same day, what can they do? Nobody has our level of expertise on the subject. Then I can set up a company just like that on Legalboom dot-com," he added, snapping his fingers. "It would be an LLC, a limited liability corp, and we could hub out of Denver, or better yet out of New Orleans, ya know. Properties are going for real cheap down there now—and we'd better hurry before all this paranormal media blitz drives the rentals through the roof. Soon everybody'll be trying to get an office set up down there."

"Right," Fisher said, pounding Winters's fist. "Me and Woods got the backup and security for clients—you know we come locked and loaded . . .'Rissa and Bradley can do the forensics, since they know all that dark arts crap . . . same with Doc. Like, we so do *not* have to take this shit."

"Yeah, and what about the fact that they've got our apartments under surveillance," Woods muttered. "As a private citizen, I'd have my rights."

"In your dreams," Bradley said, slumping with his head in his hands. "The Patriot Act killed that . . . heard NSA even has some journalists on their list—plus guys serving overseas. Remember that big scandal that broke on MSNBC where they were listening in on people's private conversations with their wives and girlfriends? They've got phone sex on tape just for grins, as though that would produce any terrorist leads. So you know the boys in Homeland Security would tail us, given what we do."

"I am *so* screwed, man," Fisher said, dragging his fingers through his hair. "Like, dude, they really listen in on *those* conversations?"

"You should watch the news more often," Clarissa said with a sigh. "Or maybe read a few serious articles from time to time, Fish."

"That's what I have you guys for in my life—who wants to sit up late nights watching talking heads, 'Rissa? You're the researcher, not me," Fisher complained.

"Yeah, well, speaking of research—as much as this government gig pisses me off with the way they've just shunted us aside, this is the resource mother lode." Clarissa blew out a breath in frustration, making a stray wisp of blond hair from her bangs float off her forehead. "Hello . . . labs, ammo, the best research environment and technology a geek like me could ever dream of. That ain't gonna happen in a shack in New Orleans, guys. Any of you got investment capital? Do you have any idea what a *real* microscope costs, not to mention all the sexy stuff we get to work with for free? We are in a recession, last I checked. And I haven't even begun talking about medical and dental. Face it, we're lifers."

"Stop being so negative, 'Rissa. You're giving me a case of the hives. We own expertise . . . like how many times do people quit their gig on a Friday and go back to work at the same desk for ten times what they made on a Monday? You have to negotiate a contract, take risks. Hell, if Blackwater can do it, we sure can."

"Bad case study, dude," Bradley said, sprawling in a chair. "They're getting indicted."

"Again, my point being, watch the news," Clarissa said, shaking her head.

"Okay, okay," Winters argued. "Maybe I don't have all the angles worked out, but I'm not taking this smelly pile lying down!"

"Guys, knock it off. Heads up," Sasha said, standing. "Brass, incoming."

"Love how you do that, Captain," Woods said, getting to his feet.

Hunter looked at his cell phone again and then slipped it back into its holder. The only call he'd had was from Bear Shadow giving him an update on his grandfather's vision. This was unlike Sasha. Something wasn't right, and she hadn't answered his voice mail or texts. But he couldn't focus on that now. The information his brother and Sir Rodney were sharing was chilling.

"The poor bastards never got fifty yards from their vehicles," Sir Rodney said in a low, conspiratorial murmur as he glanced around The Fair Lady tavern. He took a sip of Fae ale and shook his head. "Our archers were on bayou detail, heard the machine-gun report. By the time they got there, only bodies remained. The first thing they saw was an arm still attached to an M16 . . . after that they pretty much knew what they'd see. However, what they never expected to find was one guy left alive, clinging to his weapon and huddled in the mud against a burned-out car. We couldn't go to him, given his mental state. He would have shot first, asked questions later. Couldn't blame 'im."

"Damn." Hunter looked off into the distance for a moment, hoping that's what had delayed Sasha. If human military personnel had been attacked, no doubt they'd have her in war room meetings. Slowly, he relaxed, and then returned his focus to the table.

"The area is crawling with human military," Shogun said. "Rodney is right, we can't get in close enough to be effective without detection. The entire site is hot."

Hunter released a hard breath. "The humans have *got* to get out of that area. They are screwing up the tracking, walking through scent trails . . . damn it!"

"I know. That's why we laid low," Shogun said, "hoping the lone survivor would just be freaked out enough to get in his vehicle and drive off to give us a few minutes to case the area, to do some tracking. But he called in reinforcements and held his position. Gotta give him that, the man had balls. Next thing we know, a bunch of guys from the local naval air station came over and began sealing off the area, picking up bodies . . . jeeps and Humvees where everywhere—boots on the ground. The site is practically worthless now. We tried."

"Hey, there's nothing you or any of us could have done about that without putting a bull's-eye on your foreheads." Hunter pushed what was left of his burger away from him and polished off his beer. "Brother, I know you're not going to like what I've got to say but, I think you and your men should stay in the sidhe at night until this is all over." Hunter held up a hand to stop the objection he could already see forming in Shogun's eyes. "Last night you gave me a piece of advice," he added, locking gazes with his brother. "I didn't like hearing it, but it was sound."

Hunter waited until Shogun leaned back in his seat and looked away, unable for the moment to address Sir Rodney's glance of confusion. This was between wolves, this was between brothers.

"I listened to you," Hunter pressed on, keeping his voice low and modulated. "You were right. And you told me things because you were concerned for my welfare. Now I'm only doing the same." He waited until Shogun's gaze returned to his. "At night, under the full moon in wolf form, you and your men will be sitting ducks. You do not have the shadows as an added defense mechanism. The humans are frightened. They will fire on you if they even get a glimpse."

"What Hunter says is true," Sir Rodney chimed in, glancing at Shogun and then Hunter. "My men report that they have the forest lit up like Christmas in July. They've even got dogs out there barking their bloody heads off. Forensics crews are combing the area. Military helicopters above have the area sectioned off as a no-fly zone. My Fae archers could only get close enough using the glamour, but even that was risky because they've got so many hounds out there that can still smell what they can't see. You mix a Werewolf on a full-moon shape-shift, who cannot hide in the shadows, with skittish humans who've got weapons we've never seen before, and I call that a not-very-bright idea, my friend. Take my two pence for what it's wcrth."

Hunter simply opened his arms and shrugged. "There you have it—an impartial source who also loves you like a brother, man."

"Then, what of you?" Shogun sat forward and grabbed his brother's forearm. "Am I to abandon you? Don't ask me to do that."

"By day, we hunt as one. By night, you lay low," Hunter said. "I'm leaving my own men back in the North Country for this very reason. This area is too hot right now, and I want to be sure that my local pack has strong lieutenants guarding it while I'm gone. In the sidhe, Sir Rodney could use reinforcement against potential Vampire incursion or whatever else they've got cooked up. By day, we can go lean on the sorcerers; maybe Rodney's men can help with a little glamour, until we smoke out the source or get some witnesses."

Seeming unconvinced, Shogun looked at Hunter hard. "I will send my men to help guard your local pack in the North Country, as you advise. It is possible that an attack could be launched against the closest wolf Federation, and I am already well fortified in Asia. But you are not invincible, brother. If their dogs pick up your scent, if—"

"Don't worry, man. Dogs can't go through the shadow lands, last I checked."

CHAPTER 11

His worst fears had been realized as he held his cell phone to his ear and listened to Crow Shadow's breathless account. Sasha's apartment had been trashed?

"Was there blood?" Hunter waited, his gaze locked with Shogun's and Sir Rodney's.

"No," Crow Shadow replied. "But when I went to find her team, they were all gone, too. Then I began asking their neighbors stuff, playing like I was family . . . well, technically I am, by way of Sasha. People said that military police had rounded them all up. I thought she was with you . . . I'm so sorry, man. I backed off my detail when I heard you howl for her last night. I knew you were headed to the cabin and I waited till noon to just check in, I—"

"It wasn't your fault," Hunter said, closing his eyes. "You did what was right, what I had asked. Stay there in North Country with Bear to protect Silver Hawk and the rest of the pack. But do not, I repeat, *do not* engage the humans. There has been a situation down here that could have possibly changed everything. I will fill you in later. If I do not hear from Sasha soon, I'll go in and get her myself."

"But—"

"Do not disobey me on this, Crow. It is critical that you listen!" Hunter lowered his voice as his canines crested, ignoring the concerned stares from Shogun and Sir Rodney. "You can only shadow-jump in quick evasive moves without an alpha or an amulet. You cannot shadow-travel long distances or stay within a shadow too long, *you know this*. The demon doors will claim you and you have no idea if they've stripped her of her amulet yet. I don't need to have to go searching for you *and* her. If she's in mortal danger from the humans, I will go in. Are we clear?"

She looked around the teahouse with delight. Chaya was beautiful . . . The manicured gardens offered lush balm to her senses as she stared out the window admiring the mirror-like carp pool. Lady Jung Suk lifted a tiny, porcelain cup to her lips with a delicate hand and sipped the fragrant white tea. It had been so long since she'd enjoyed a body . . . so long since she'd felt youthful and exquisite. And now she'd been immortalized.

Stroking her own cheek, she relished the softness of her new skin. It was supple yet fragile, just like the pretty rice paper screen that hid her within her private room. She ran her graceful fingers through her spill of onyx hair, allowing the silky strands to fall through them, and then sighed. Every feature of her heart-shaped face was lovely; her feet were tiny and possessed perfect little toes painted in a sheer cherry-blossom pink. Her figure was daintily alluring . . . oh, how she would enjoy seducing men again with it. Elder Vlad had chosen well. Elder Vlad had done well.

"Heal, Sir Rodney. Heal, Clarissa McGill." Queen Cerridwen reached out her hand and drew the poisonous black possession into her icy grip, seething. With a quick bolt of ice lightning from the end of her frozen wand, she watched it die a screaming death on the floor of her private chambers.

"So, you did not trust me and sought to go between husband and ex-wife, and then attacked the frail human female to also set the wolves against me . . . all so that I would have no choice but to side with you? And this is your offer of a trusting alliance—to go behind my back and make sure that I am blamed for that which you claim I should be exempted from? Duplicitous bastards, the lot of you."

She strode away from the smoldering green ash on the floor and clucked her tongue. "Silly Vampire. Don't you know that even according to human laws, possession is always nine-tenths of the law!"

"Captain Trudeau, your personal possessions have been cleared for return, and we will need you to sign for them," an MP said. "We will also need each of your team members to follow us and to claim their possessions so that we can process you out, and then the colonel will see you, along with General Westgate and Doctor Xavier Holland."

She gathered her disgruntled team, and they all followed the MP down a series of long corridors to an empty interrogation room, where plastic bags containing wallets and cell phones were distributed on a metal desk and thick stacks of in-triplicate paperwork were handed out. Sasha signed her name at the bottoms of the proffered forms without even looking at what the legalese said. It didn't matter anyway—it was sign or stay cooped up without her stuff, and she was so out of here.

The moment he left the group and locked them in the interrogation room, Sasha went to Clarissa.

"How are you feeling?" she asked, checking her friend's eyes and her brow for signs of fever.

"Really way better, which doesn't make sense, given where we all are right now," Clarissa said, glancing around.

"Why?" Bradley said, stepping to Clarissa's side to stare at Sasha. "What happened to her? What aren't you telling us?"

Sasha let out a hard breath. "Somebody picked up the tail end of that possession spell that hit us from the Unseelie court last month, and tried to boomerang it back on Sir Rodney and Clarissa. He was a target because he's still the Fae monarch, and obviously his ex-wife is in cahoots with the Vamps, and she's not happy about his reign. They hit Clarissa to give us a wake-up call that, if my Shadow Clan sides with the Seelie Fae, then our team is vulnerable. But Garth, Sir Rodney's man, caught it in time." Sasha ruffled her hair up off her neck and let out a long breath. "But that's why we're in here. I had to head down to New Orleans after I got the Fae missive, but that's all I know. I didn't really have a lot of time to learn more before things sorta got insane."

"I knew something was wrong," Bradley said, holding Clarissa by both arms. "Next time I ask you to, humor me!"

"Okay, okay, just everybody fall back," Sasha said, too weary for any additional emotional turmoil. "She's fine now, we're ninety percent sure. So keep an eye on her, but I suggest you keep your voice down unless you want her to be kept here for testing."

Bradley simply hugged Clarissa, crushing her against him as the others went to find chairs.

Every second that ticked by on the huge wall clock in the barren room made her feel like she was about to scream. Sasha began pacing; it was a nervous habit that couldn't be helped. The waiting was torture enough. Right now she felt trapped, and the last thing wolves could stand was being trapped. It also still didn't matter that she finally had her cell phone on her. Down in the bowels of NORAD's underground city, it did her no good—reception didn't exist.

Rather than make herself crazier than she'd already become, Sasha turned her mind to solving the puzzle of how to get evidence to clear the wolf Federations' record.

They'd already lost a precious twenty-four hours— partly due to military politics, but the rest of it was personal. That was the part that was kicking her ass; it was probably kicking Hunter's, too.

Had they not gotten into a dispute and then had to work all that out, they both could have been in New Orleans going over the old hunting grounds where they'd encountered rogue wolf activity before. There was also some sort of possession thing going on that had tried to get its icy claws into Sir Rodney and her team member Clarissa. She was pretty sure who'd sent it, but the hard issue was always gathering evidence among a community that had magic spells, potions, body doubles, and whatever. Regular identity thieves were bad enough in the human world. It was ridiculous in the supernatural underground.

Then again, going to New Orleans last night was a direct violation of her commanding officer's order. That had probably not been a good idea, though at least she'd been able to keep one man alive. The one who was causing her the most grief. But a part of her wished she'd just followed his orders and stayed in Colorado. It also would have made things cleaner. She immediately jettisoned the thought. As much as she hated Madison, he was still one of her own, a man in uniform, and bringing him back alive was part of her job—even if the guy was a jerk. Some things were ingrained.

Last night she wasn't ready to just up and tender her resignation; this afternoon was a wholly different matter.

But she was still trying to rein in the rebellious wolf clawing to get out of her. Worse yet, she'd have to explain to Hunter that she'd left his bed to go on a fool's errand, gotten Sir Rodney to body-double her image in front of the surveillance cameras . . . and still wasn't able to get a direct bead on what had attacked him or possibly her teammate Clarissa. If she had been able to save Madison's squad, it would have been worth it. She wondered if Hunter would consider her not mentioning what happened as a lie of omission, already knowing the answer.

Sasha released a hard sigh and sought a chair at the

far side of the room, needing space. Turning it around backward, she flopped down and stared at the blank wall. She was glad that her team had stopped bickering about Clarissa's need to stay out of all future psychic surveillance and the unfairness of Madison's reaction to being spared. And after the forensic photos she'd seen, they were staying in Denver. That much she was clear on. She'd never forgive herself if she had to look at Winters or 'Rissa or any of the guys in the kinds of pictures that turned her stomach. She couldn't blame Madison for flipping out; if she'd been there with her team and thought she knew who'd slaughtered them, she would have probably behaved the same way . . . maybe worse.

Instinct told her that this case was different than those she'd investigated before. Although the killer was bold and feeding heavily on human flesh, this didn't have the feel of one or two innocent humans who just happened to get caught in the midst of a supernatural dispute or killings contained to the paranormal community. This was a Were on the loose feeding at will. And based upon what she'd learned from Madison's report, there was also something taunting them. It had left a survivor to bring back word to the human world. As a rule, demon-infected flesh-eaters didn't have that level of strategic restraint. They killed and ate until everything in their wake was savaged. It should have circled back for Madison, or eaten another human nearby. But it didn't. It stopped feeding and went away.

Hunter had said that he and Shogun had scented Lady Jung Suk on the scene, and it was true she'd never been caught. It made sense that it would be her. But trying to catch a being as old and crafty as that Were Leopard was, in Sasha's opinion, futile. It would take longer than the two weeks they had, that was for sure. And if the Vampires were behind all this, it was clear that everything had been strategically made to look like a wolf attack. Not to mention, the Vamps had made sure humans and the military got involved so they'd screw up any tracking ability the wolf Federations had on the ground.

Sasha rubbed her chin, deep in thought. But there was more than one way to skin a cat. This old chick now had a body, and she had to have gotten that from somewhere. So the only way to out her would be to backtrack to missing persons—and she was pretty sure that Lady Jung Suk was vain enough to want a young, nubile body, not one from some old homeless hag who might not be missed. But given all the focus on deaths in the area, and the mysterious military activities in the bayou, it would be days before the missing girl showed up in the news, if she made it to the headlines at all.

It was all a giant jigsaw puzzle in her brain. The right approach to solving this new crisis in New Orleans was becoming clearer as she sat waiting for release. The entity that had snatched some young girl to get a body would no doubt lead her to whoever had an agenda, just as the movement of the half-eaten civilians from the bayou floor to an alley in town had to be done by someone other than the feeding Were. Generally when demon-infected Weres went in for a kill, there was plenty of blood, and they normally didn't pick up entire carcasses to deposit by a Dumpster. They just weren't that environmentally concerned.

An absence of blood at the original abduction scenes would tell her something, too—just as *when* the missing person had gone missing would bear critical clues. Hopefully the human authorities hadn't screwed up that evidence trail as well.

One thing was for sure: putting Lady Jung Suk into a body required two elements. First, a body; second, someone who had a soul that could deliver a serious spell. A little digging in the sorcery community might shed light on the process, which would give her more direction about where to look for additional evidence. Plus, someone had fed Lady Jung Suk at least two people, if there was no blood at the abduction scenes for the first two civilian victims.

The door opened and Sasha's attention snapped toward it. She and her team stood. Colonel Madison entered, seeming much worse for the wear. General Westford and Doc had dour expressions but didn't seem cowed in the least.

"Captain," Colonel Madison said. "Your team is free to go, but you have been reassigned to the mission as the unit expert."

The last place she wanted to be was on a military flight to New Orleans seated across from Colonel Madison. Not only was the mode of transportation slow, but she'd only been able to send Hunter a quick text that said: *I'm OK, will talk later.* That would go over big after all these hours.

The only upside was that Madison was going to take her to the scene of the military killings in the bayou. If there was any shred of evidence left, she could also get her team involved in doing some of the analysis. They'd grumbled about being left behind in Denver but felt a little better when she'd told them that they'd be in the labs on this one and still a part of the mission.

Sasha just stared out of the window, wishing she could time-jump as well as she could shadow-jump.

Hunter just stared at his cell phone and stood. If Sasha had been abducted by the human military, they would have stripped her of her cell phone. Anyone could have answered his texts by simply hitting REPLY and texting him back. Until he had actual voice confirmation, as far as he was concerned, she was in mortal jeopardy.

"What are you going to do, brother?" Shogun slowly rose from his seat with Sir Rodney.

Hunter placed his palm over his amulet. "She is not in the shadow lands. I cannot sense her on the ground."

"Then maybe they've taken her down into that place . . . that fortress," Sir Rodney said with a frown.

"NORAD," Hunter muttered, looking out the window.

"Brother, promise me you will not try to go into a military citadel like that alone," Shogun warned. "If she sent you a text, send her another requesting voice confirmation that she is all right. Do that before you act."

He knew it was insane before he even did it, but if they had harmed her, it was all over. Hunter came out of the shadows inside Sasha's apartment and looked around in disbelief. There had been a struggle of this magnitude? *Madison's* scent was there? *He'd* done this?

Gone in an instant, Hunter emerged in a long corridor beneath the ground and then followed his nose, slipping past NORAD guards and then dead-ending in a jail cell.

They'd caged her? They had caged his woman?

Incredulous, he slipped into another shadow, now on the hunt and losing more of his human as his wolf-self took over. He could feel the electricity of Sasha's outrage. An argument had taken place on the other side of the bars. Doc's scent was there, Westford's, *and Madison's.*

A low growl rumbled in Hunter's throat as he followed Sasha's scent, and then tracked her to the airfield. Turning in circles, he was claimed by frustration. Hunter briefly closed his eyes and held his amulet in his fist.

"Tell me where you are, baby . . . I won't let them do this to you. I'll find you."

It was good to be back on the ground and back on the move, but the hair at the nape of her neck was standing up. Sasha pulled out her cell phone as Colonel Madison drove.

"What are you doing, Captain?"

She glanced at him. "Making sure that my on-the-ground contact is aware of—"

"Put it away, Captain," he said, almost swerving the vehicle into another lane. "This is a classified mission. Only those with top military clearance are to be communicated with. Do you read me, Captain?"

"Yes, sir, but—"

"No buts, Captain. That is a direct order!"

"Yes, sir." Sasha sat back in her seat, frustration making her ears ring. This guy hadn't learned yet.

The moment he stopped the vehicle, she was out. She had to get away from him and view the scene, lest she turn around and lose her career over rank insubordination. But the stench of rotting flesh and blood mixed with the faint hint of sulfur ratcheted her fury down a notch. It was awful.

The humid air held the reek of broken bowels, old blood, and carnage. Human authorities were combing every inch of the area. She strode quickly to keep ahead of Colonel Madison, who was heading for the yellow caution tape line. That's when she saw them . . . the dogs.

Initially she'd been downwind from them, but a change in direction caused immediate canine panic. Forensics German shepherds, bloodhounds, and black search Labradors turned toward her and went nuts. Straining at their leads, the dogs instantly bonded against a perceived wolf threat and became a hunting pack, dragging their human masters along in an attack frenzy until their leashes popped. Military personnel lowered weapons in her direction, only hesitating to avoid shooting the colonel behind her. Fear was resident in every pair of eyes that stared at her, and now she'd probably have to show them some shadow-disappearing shit that was really gonna freak them out.

The moment Sasha's feet hit the ground, he felt her in his soul. Hunter moved through the shadow lands at full velocity, his human shedding and giving way to his wolf. Panic echoed from her spirit into his; she was under attack! He bounded out of the shadows, jaws open to land between her and baying hounds.

They'd set dogs upon his mate—his wife! Insanity

blurred his vision. Her voice was a bleating refrain in the distance. He heard her shout no, saw the dogs skid to a stop as he lunged to take a shepherd down. In the back of his mind there was a burst of machine-gun fire . . . and her wolf emerged to make sure that a dog was out of harm's way?

The small animal's yelp confused him. Sasha hadn't killed it, but had allowed the dog to scurry to safety. Why? He didn't understand her fighting strategy. His gorgeous silver wolf had sailed over the dogs and flattened him on the ground—that didn't make sense. In the next moment she was in her human form, naked and trying to grasp the thick fur at his neck. Guns were drawn, Madison was on the ground. He didn't understand and shifted back into his human form to shove Sasha behind him, eyes glowing.

"Hold your fire!" a soldier yelled over the din of agitated but frightened dogs. "You'll hit the colonel—snipers on your mark!"

"No, stand down! Stand down!" Sasha shouted. "Hold your fire!"

Colonel Madison got up slowly and backed away from Hunter and Sasha. She turned quickly as she watched marksmen get in position to deliver single shots to take her and Hunter out.

"It was the dogs, sir!" Sasha yelled quickly, as Hunter slowly got up. "Tell them to put down their weapons and hold their fire. As long as you're threatening me, he will use deadly force! Look at me, I'm unarmed!"

"Stand down," Colonel Madison said slowly, his tone unsure and grudging as he brushed himself off. His eyes never left Hunter's.

Sasha held Hunter's arm. "Call off the dogs," she yelled to the surrounding soldiers, who stood mesmerized, clutching their weapons. "We are the property of the U.S. government, the ultimate fighting machines created and designed to combat this enemy threat. We are *not* the enemy!"

"We, *hell* . . ." Hunter muttered.

Hunter spit on the ground, his furious gaze following Colonel Madison. When none of the soldiers moved he turned and growled at the pack of dogs; they yelped and scurried back toward their masters.

"She said to call the animals off!" Hunter shouted, eyes blazing. He lolled his neck and then sent an angry gaze back toward Colonel Madison. "You abducted her from her apartment and put her in a cage!"

"No—"

"I smelled him there, Sasha! Do not protect this bastard any longer!"

"Okay, he was there, but it was all a big misunderstanding. True, he trashed my apartment and there was a little dispute at the base," Sasha said quickly, coming between Hunter and Madison with her eye constantly on the snipers' positions. She flat-palmed Hunter's bare chest. "But, baby, can we talk about all of this after we both put on some clothes?"

CHAPTER 12

"Risky . . . unorthodox," Sasha said, teasing Hunter as they walked through the burned-out Bayou House, "but effective. Done with a certain theatrical flair." She didn't want to razz the man too badly, but he had to know that the stunt he'd just pulled could have cost him his life. Maybe it was sheer relief that was now making her giddy.

"I said I was sorry," he rumbled in a sullen tone, walking past her.

"Hey," she replied, putting both hands up in front of her chest and trying hard not to laugh. "It got a response, so who's mad?"

"I thought they were after you," he said, growing more peevish. "It was an honest mistake."

Sasha jogged to catch up to Hunter, and she held his arm for a second. "Battlefield humor, I'm sorry. You could have been shot—a single shell to the head." She touched his face and gentled her tone. "Those boys out there are quick and accurate, Hunter. The only reason we're both still standing is because Madison was in the way and they'd never seen anything like that before. That gave us maybe five seconds."

"I thought . . ."

"I know. That was my fault—I couldn't get in touch with you, though. When I got back and saw my apartment, it was only minutes before MPs came and said that the brass back at the base wanted to have a word with me." She blew out a hard breath. "And yeah, it was fucked up, but I wasn't in mortal danger . . . so from here on out, you've gotta trust me, okay? Our human politics are as messy as supernatural politics— but I'm not a damsel in distress. I'm not going to stand around and let them put me in front of a firing squad or something equally archaic, that I promise you."

When he sent his gaze out of one of the shattered windows, she leaned in and kissed his cheek. "It was kinda sweet, really . . . it's not often that a girl who carries a sidearm gets to have somebody go Old World for her, ya know."

He cut her a glare and she smiled.

"I'm not teasing you or being sarcastic. I meant that."

"I will trust you in the future, but it's hard not to follow my instincts around you." Hunter sent his gaze toward the window again. "They're just standing there, staring at the building. What do they want? The colonel said that we could collect our clothes and dress, and could come in here to see if we could gain intel from any scent trail that might be lingering."

"They're probably trying to decide whether to hit the building with a rocket-propelled grenade or call in a frickin' missile air strike or something," she said, chuckling, but then held Hunter's arm when he growled.

"Just joking." She shook her head. "It's freaked-out human—that's what you're witnessing. First we were people in their minds . . . but you did a Houdini and came out of a shadow. Then, presto-chango, we transformed into wolves—always a good thing to get the human heart and adrenaline pumping. Not to mention you being a three-hundred-pounder on four legs that moved like black lightning and probably ruined every dog out there. Then we turned into naked people right in front of everybody, *embarrassing,* but I digress. However, the upside of that is, if the colonel had any questions about whose dick was bigger in a pissing contest . . . uh . . . I'd say he's now been thoroughly briefed."

Staring at Hunter's profile, Sasha placed a finger to her lips with a wide smile behind it for a moment, watching a sly half smile finally come out of hiding on Hunter's face. "The boys in uniform back there are just a little worse for the wear emotionally. Plus, don't forget, this was the scene of a mauling, and whatever did it came out of this building. So, yeah, they're watching the building really, really hard."

She tugged Hunter's arm so he'd follow her. "I wouldn't stand too close to the windows right now while they're jumpy."

Although the building yielded nothing, the afternoon wasn't a complete loss. Something remotely close to respect had been established now that Madison finally got to see with his own eyes, along with about fifty other specialized personnel, what had always been kept on a need-to-know basis. Reading it in a report was definitely a different experience from seeing it live. Another real plus was that Colonel Madison now saw her and Hunter as true experts and was giving some ground, allowing them to suss out any evidence leads and no longer barring them from crime scenes.

The only thing was that the man insisted on a private debrief in his Humvee, which meant she had to leave Hunter out there waiting for her with extremely jumpy soldiers giving him wide berth. This little impromptu meeting was burning valuable daylight, but if it got Madison to stop acting like an asshole, she'd endure it.

"I, uh, had a few questions, Captain," Madison said nervously as they both climbed into the vehicle and shut the doors. He glanced at the two soldiers who stood not far off at the ready.

She glanced at Hunter and gave him a nod that it was all right.

"Sir?" she said, turning to the colonel.

"They're personal in nature, some of my questions . . . off the record, just as one soldier to another."

"Sure, sir," Sasha said, relaxing, finally beginning to see the man behind the bluster.

"What does it feel like?"

"Sir?"

Colonel Madison chewed his bottom lip. "To be able to change into something that powerful at will."

"Oh, the wolf thing," she said with a weary sigh. "At first, it scared me—sorta like being a new driver and somebody sits you behind the wheel of a Porsche on the Autobahn. The first time I changed . . . man . . . I freaked out, sir."

"Your partner—or contact—had to stand three feet at the shoulders . . ." Colonel Madison rubbed his palms down his face. "Jesus H. Christ."

"Yeah, well, Hunter is a little special, sir."

Colonel Madison glanced out the window. "Are they all that huge? There's more?"

"No, and yes. No, they aren't all that huge—Hunter is a pack alpha, sir. Until there's one who can take him, he rules North America. And yes, sir, there are a lot of them. Hundreds."

"How did we survive, as humans?" Colonel Madison's eyes were wide as he glanced from Sasha to Hunter, standing off in the distance. "They could have eaten us all by now, right?"

No," she said, shaking her head, becoming annoyed. The brass were as bad as Congress; nobody read the full reports. "Normal Werewolves and Shadow Wolves, just like regular wolves, have a complete aversion to human flesh. Yeah, they'll give cattle ranchers a run for their money, but they don't go after human beings unless those wolves that attack are demon-infected."

The colonel nodded, but she could tell by his stricken expression that her comment hadn't made him feel better.

"And . . . along with demons, then, there's Vampires, right?"

"Affirmative, sir." Sasha gently touched his arm to steady him. "And there are Unicorns and Elves, Dragons, and pretty much everything else that you heard about as a child in so-called mythology and fairy tales."

She watched sweat bead on the colonel's brow. He nervously wiped at it with his forearm. She removed her hand after feeling dozens of questions brimming under his skin; some he'd ask her now, some would come out over time and a beer, if things ever got that relaxed between them. But it was nothing she hadn't heard before. Hell, Winters had asked her if she-Shadows had litters of puppies versus one human-looking baby, and even a swift kick from Clarissa hadn't dissuaded him.

"I read most of your reports and initially thought a lot of it was bullshit . . . ," Colonel Madison finally stammered. "I thought—I don't know."

"It is a lot to take in at one time, sir."

"I'll never be able to sleep at night without meds after this—after knowing."

"If it's any consolation, sir, General Westford said the same thing when he first took over our unit. It is a mental paradigm shift that takes some getting used to."

Colonel Madison stared at her for a moment with a pained expression. "But how do we win against this, Captain?"

"You coexist with it, you can't wipe it out. It's been around too long. What I've been trying to get across to the Joint Chiefs is that, if we elect to go to war, go into direct confrontation . . . well, the ramifications could be catastrophic. Each group of entities—which prefer to be called *beings*, if you want to be politically correct—considers itself a sovereign nation that was here on this land first, just like the Native Americans were, and they will fight to the last being to protect their boundaries, populations, cultures, and borders. So rather than behaving like exterminators, we have to be in the mindset that we're supernatural cops . . . patrol officers or, better yet, peace officers that kinda keep the lid on things when one of the species gets out of hand—and eating us is getting out of hand. No one from the supernatural community is going to blame us for retaliating against what just happened back there with you and your men. They'd do no less."

"But how do we guard against such attacks . . . I mean, I saw what a wolf can do. Captain, no offense, but I saw you and Hunter, and I'm glad you're on our side. I've gotta tell you, though, my men are freaked out . . . I'm trying to be sure not to make any sudden moves while talking to you in this vehicle so I don't seem like I'm threatening you in any way. I don't know how to read this. How in the hell do we keep the human population safe if the supernaturals pick us off like cattle to eat us whenever they want?"

"Generally, that doesn't happen, unless something is going wrong. But they have their serial killers from time to time just like we have ours—and the supernaturals hate their nut jobs just as much as we hate ours, because letting them roam loose causes chaos and draws undue attention to their otherwise quiet, off-the-human-grid existence."

"You keep saying 'us' and 'we' when referring to humans, Captain . . . and I mean no disrespect, but how can you say 'us' when you're technically not human?"

For a moment Sasha just stared at him, but then nodded to make him know that no offense had been taken. The last thing she wanted to do was scare the poor man by delaying her reply, but his statement had taken her aback. He was right. Until he'd pointed that out to her, she hadn't thought of it that way.

"I . . . sir . . . you're right," she said, now looking out of the window. "I'm a hybrid . . . half human." She returned her conflicted gaze to his. "I was·raised as a human, conditioned as a soldier, and love the uniform I wear and represent. But you're right. I walk a fine line. When I speak of humans, my mind says 'we' and 'us.' But when I'm with my wolf pack and the den leaders, the Shadows, I also say 'we' and 'us.' I guess that's something anyone who is half of one thing and half of another goes through? You claim, and are claimed by, both. But rest assured, Shadow Wolves don't eat people and I've never, *ever* in my life fed on a person. Nor has Hunter."

The colonel nodded, seeming to understand and seeming equally relieved by her assurance. "But what about the Vampires?" he asked after a moment, new strain lacing his voice. "Okay, I can see how the wolves and whatever can eat other things besides people, but the entities that survive on human blood—what do they do, go to blood banks?"

"Well, there's the rub, sir," she said, trying not to smile. "Vampires prefer their blood warm from the vein with a little adrenaline fear kick mixed with some sexual desire in a cocktail served right off the neck—but there are enough kinky donors to keep down the attacks on humans who don't want to play."

"Who in *the hell* would knowingly give their neck up to a bloodsucker?" Colonel Madison leaned forward, eyes bulging.

"They tell me those beings are really good in bed. I can't give you perspective from direct contact . . . but they definitely have a cult following of humans—plus they're rich as all get-out. Then, of course, they have their own private-label bottles, hideaway blood banks for emergencies, et cetera."

Colonel Madison sat back as though he'd been sucker-punched. He stared out the window toward Hunter and spoke to Sasha without looking at her. "Can I ask you something, Captain, that's really personal . . . you don't have to answer, but I'm trying to wrap my mind around so much in the last twenty-four hours that . . ."

"It's okay, Colonel."

"Hunter, as you call him . . . he's not just a subject-matter guide, he's a paramour, right?"

She swallowed a smile. "Uh, yeah . . . sir . . . and he's also a head of state in the wolf world, like I am." She waited until he looked at her full-on. "Trashing my apartment, locking me up, pointing weapons at me, stuff like that, sir, would be like going into the White House and treating the POTUS's wife like that . . . it would cause Secret Service to come running from fifteen directions to put you down hard, sir. Not a threat, just a fact that you should know, sir."

"Okay," Colonel Madison said, glancing from where Hunter stood outside then back to Sasha. "I hadn't really put all that together in quite that way before."

"Not a problem, sir . . . just know that we have a vested interest in keeping a lid on this current problem and finding out who did it."

"That's good to know, Captain," Colonel Madison said with a genuine nod of respect. "Thank you for that."

"I may have been made in a lab, but we wear the same uniform, sir. I know your men meant a lot to you . . . I know they meant a lot to their families. We'll find who did it . . . but you have to let me work unencumbered, sir. You have to get our people to stop shooting at me and Hunter and stop delaying us during the investigation." She nodded toward the crime scene. "The scent trail is worthless to us now, just like your dogs out there are walking in circles because there's been so much human contamination to the site."

Colonel Madison nodded. "We'll stand down and just keep a scene containment squad. We can be at your ready."

"Sir," she said glancing at the late-afternoon sky. "Please take my advice when I tell you that in all honesty, since it'll be getting dark soon, the safest place for all your men is back at the base. You leave a unit of young soldiers out here in the bayou at night to protect a crime scene that's as good as worthless, and you'll just be asking for their funerals."

She'd gotten out of the Humvee mentally drained. The colonel's innocent questions had given her a lot to think about regarding her personal life. How did she identify, human or wolf? And that analogy to the POTUS's wife? Sheesh!

However, the nature of her identity—wolf or human—was a truly haunting question that would linger at the back of her mind for a long time to come. It was the crux of the issue that Hunter wanted resolved within her once and for all. She was just glad that Hunter was completely ready to get out of there. Sir Rodney and Shogun were waiting on his return in town, and they were all losing precious daylight.

It was odd to see everyone gather around her and Hunter with curious gazes. But it was good that as long as she announced how they were going to leave by way of shadow—with everyone looking on in awe at the spectacle—thankfully no one would get nervous and shoot.

CHAPTER 13

Diner patrons craned their necks to watch the television on the wall as the waitress turned up the volume with the remote. Even the fry chef leaned through the kitchen partition to hear the breaking news. The cable news anchor's voice blared through the now silent eatery before announcing Colonel Madison.

"The U.S. military is calling off its investigation of paranormal activity in the New Orleans area, citing insufficient evidence. In a news conference expected to take place in the next few minutes, West Point graduate Colonel Keith J. Madison, who had been appointed to a special investigatory unit by the Pentagon's Joint Chiefs in Washington, will take the podium."

Russell Conway stared at the screen in disbelief as the diner began to murmur with disgruntled comments. But a hush fell over the establishment once again as soon as the images on the screen cut away to a live shot at the NAS base.

"Good afternoon," Colonel Madison said, reading from a prepared statement. "We have combed the area with the best forensics teams and technology, as well as employing some more traditional techniques such as tracking dogs. Based upon what we've been able to view with boots on the ground, we believe at this time that the incidents that have occurred and have unfortunately taken human lives were the result of catastrophic drug wars that played out on American streets. As you are aware, the Mexican drug cartels are brutal, using heavy body armor and assault weapons like AK-47s, et cetera. When seeking revenge, it is also characteristic of those illegal organizations to take hostages and dismember victims of their kidnappings in order to strike terror into the hearts of those they seek to leverage. Therefore, our units will reinforce the border and place additional pressure on these cartels by assisting the efforts of American law enforcement, which has been stretched thin."

Reporters at the press conference went wild, shouting questions toward the colonel. The governor at the podium had to regain order.

"Colonel Madison will answer a few questions only and then he must return to more pressing matters," the governor said crisply, and then waited for a nod from Colonel Madison to choose a journalist.

"What was going on in the bayou last night, Colonel? Why was there a no-fly zone over the old Bayou House? Some say there was an incident out there involving heavy gunplay? Were any military personnel or civilians hurt?"

Colonel Madison cleared his throat. "Although that was more than one question, I will be happy to answer."

Nervous laughter filtered through the television crowd, and Russell leaned forward to hear better.

"Local law enforcement as well as the FBI have been doing a fine job combing the residential areas and business districts. Therefore, the military went back to the original scene of the horrific shoot-out that occurred at the location. The Bayou House was our AO, area of operation—and we did not want news helicopters flying overhead and possibly prematurely broadcasting any potentially sensitive data that could help us in the investigation. Now that we know there was no additional evidence to be found, we have removed our restriction. However, the area is still dangerous, the building out there is unstable—hence it is still off limits. We do not want civilians going out there scavenging or doing amateur investigations until all rubbish can be removed from the site."

"But what about the reports of gunfire, Colonel?" another reporter shouted.

"We have no knowledge of that in the area." Colonel Madison looked away. "Next question."

"Ambulances went down the road, Colonel. So you're saying there were no fatalities or injuries out there?"

"No." Colonel Madison lifted his chin, ignoring the new barrage of questions. He gave the governor a look, who stepped in front of him at the podium.

"Martial law will continue in New Orleans for another week at least until the local law enforcement and FBI can ensure that the violent activity surrounding this most recent drug war outburst has been contained."

"But, Governor, what about the two civilians found—"

"We cannot comment further on an ongoing investigation." The governor turned to Colonel Madison.

"Thank you for your time today, Colonel. The people of the great state of Louisiana appreciate your service to our country."

Russell pushed back from the table with disgust. It was the worst cover-up he'd ever seen, and he'd seen plenty. He fingered the Blood Oasis membership card in his khaki pocket. Vampires were as good as bloodhounds. They hated Werewolves probably as much as he did, and could lead him to their dens.

Sasha nodded and turned away from the bar television mounted at The Fair Lady. "Damn, he's good." She was surprised when Hunter quietly agreed with her.

"Is that the colonel who was giving you a ration of dung?" Sir Rodney asked frowning.

"One and the same," Hunter muttered.

"Well, either the man is blind or he's a quick study," Shogun said carefully, glancing between Sasha and Hunter. "Which is it?"

"He's a quick study," Sasha said, oddly feeling protective of the colonel now that she knew him a little better. "He's a good man . . . just got screwed up by the fear. But he's cool now."

Hunter cleared his throat. Shogun just sat back.

" 'Fraid you're selling to a tough crowd. I take it that wolves don't get a bad scent out of their noses easily, especially if their noses have been put out of joint."

"So I've noticed," Sasha said with a hard sigh and then quirked a half smile. "But gotta love 'em anyway, Sir Rod."

"Ah . . . the forgiving heart of a lady," he said with a small bow from where he sat.

Sasha laughed. "Chauvinist to the end."

"Too old to change my ways," Sir Rodney said with a casual shrug. "But I'm not generalizing about the female species. Remember, I was married to one who had held a grudge for at least two hundred years with no end in sight. So, lassie, you are special—one of the good ones."

Sir Rodney's wry comment finally made Shogun laugh and brought a smile out on Hunter's face. The more he fought it, the wider it got, until he stopped being so morose and just gave in and laughed.

"See, I could be like her," Sasha said, raising an eyebrow.

"Okay, okay," Hunter said, waving her off. "I can live with you forgiving Madison."

"Thank you," she said, "Sheesh, you guys are rough." Then she looked at Sir Rodney. "Thanks so much for having Garth make sure Clarissa was all right."

"Aye, now how could I allow an innocent who is like family to you remain bewitched by an Unseelie spell? That would be unfair."

Sasha leaned over and hugged Sir Rodney. "I won't ever complain about public displays of chivalry again."

Bodies relaxed, smiles merged with Fae ale and more burgers, and sudden peace came over Sasha. Even though she knew there was a tough few weeks ahead of her, the camaraderie that permeated the small table of leaders soaked into her bones. For just this moment in time, there was no conflict between her dual roles as a military person and a wolf. There was no conflict between rival brothers, and Shogun looked good . . . his eyes were merry and his color was good;

he didn't seem like a man wallowing in what could have been. Hunter had eased up at the table and wasn't on guard, tensing at his brother's presence and listening too hard to every inflection in every comment Shogun threw her way. And Sir Rodney was Sir Rodney—funny, droll, an Old World trip.

Stuffed and sated, she pushed her clean burger basket away from her and then stretched. "All right, so we're all good on the plan? We've got like three hours until it gets dark, when you two head back to the sidhe."

Shogun nodded. "I'm good with that. It also makes sense that I cover ground in the Asian community . . . it's very closed to outsiders, in general, and I think I can break through faster if they think I'm a Korean American cop or FBI guy that can speak the various languages in that community. My father, before he died, insisted that his children learn as many regional languages as possible—Mandarin being one of them. If I know my aunt, she probably snatched a young Chinese girl . . . and if she's coed-age with all that's going on, they haven't even taken a missing persons report on her yet."

"This is where a little Fae glamour can help." Sir Rodney discreetly summoned several books of matches from the bar to their table with a wide smile, folded them into his hand, and began distributing FBI badges.

"Where were you when I was in high school?" Sasha said, laughing.

Sir Rodney bowed and then wagged his finger at her with a broad grin. "I would not have been party to corrupting the morals of a minor, even if it was just to get her a fake ID."

"What can ya do?" Sasha said, marveling at her badge. "This is really pretty cool."

"Fades at midnight, as most quickie Faery charms do . . . but on the morrow, I can make more."

One day she'd have to ask Sir Rodney if Cinderella was truth or legend, but she needed to stay focused.

"I've got Tulane," Sasha said. "It'd probably be better if a female cop or FBI type went in there and checked around the dorms looking for any students who've gone missing. One of the victims was a student, so it's likely Shogun's aunt got a body and then fed from the same hunting source—the university."

"Sounds like a plan," Sir Rodney said, polishing off the last of his Fae ale. "But I won't be needing a badge for where I'm going. Visiting the local ladies of witchery by definition requires that one be anythin' *but* a human cop."

"No argument there," Hunter said, glancing around the establishment. "While you charm the ladies, Rodney, I'll just hug the shadows out by the baron's old burned-out manor house. If she attacked out in the bayou and the military went in there full-force, she'll find a safe fallback position . . . one heavily guarded by Vampires, if that's who she's allied with now. Their human helpers by day are no problem to evade. I'll be out of there before any Vamps wake up and take issue with me snooping around on the premises."

"I'm not so much worried about Vampires as I am worried about her," Sasha admitted, now staring at Hunter without a smile. "We're still within that couple-of-days window where the moon is full enough for a Were transformation, and if Lady Jung Suk is trailing sulfur, then that means she's demon-infected. So, just be careful."

"Demon-infected?" Shogun leaned forward and gave Hunter a glance. "When we went to the location of the second victim in the bayou, there was no sulfur trail."

"That's true," Hunter said, dropping his voice even lower as he sat forward at the table, leaning on his forearms.

"Yeah, but we picked it up out there in the bayou," Sasha said, sending her gaze around the group. "It was thick inside the old Bayou House, as well as out by the kill locations."

"But it definitely wasn't at the site of the second victim or even near where the first one was thrown in the alley in the French Quarter," Hunter insisted.

"Maybe the sulfur you guys picked up at the Bayou House was from the past and not fresh. There was all sorts of insanity going on at that house—and you said yourselves that humans had mucked up the scent trail." Sir Rodney glanced around the table to see if his theory had any takers, then pressed on. "What if an infected Were came out of the demon doors through that house during all the hullaballoo that took place out there before or something?"

"It could have been old scents that lingered from a time past," Hunter said. "The scent was so mild, so dissipated, I couldn't tell."

"Neither could I," Sasha admitted. "If it was a brand-new Were who'd just come through the demon doors, I'd still be tasting sulfur at the back of my throat."

Shogun nodded. "It takes days to get that pungent

sickness out of our sinuses, Rodney. If my aunt was recently infected, she would have left a reeking trail, not a faint one. That had to be old."

"All right," Sir Rodney conceded. "But we do know for a fact that, based on what you guys sniffed, Lady Jung Suk killed those first two humans. My curiosity is that she actually ate her victims—two females and four men." He glanced at Shogun and held his gaze. "I thought Weres of any kind abhorred human flesh unless they were infected?"

Shogun nodded and let out a long breath before pushing back from the table. "Normally, we do. But my aunt is Old World and enjoys forbidden things . . . to her human flesh is probably a delicacy—not to mention that she's one really twisted bitch."

"Aw, come on Esmeralda, have a heart." Sir Rodney leaned against the living room arch and smiled at the distraught woman before him.

Esmeralda was gorgeous, and it was hard to separate his mission to get information from her voluptuous form and Creole face. Her hair was a natural, stunning auburn: a lush thicket of deep red tresses that seemed so satiny, men yearned to touch it. She'd formed her kissable pink mouth into a defiant pout and had folded her graceful arms over her ample breasts. Not giving an inch, her hazel eyes stared at him directly as she spoke in a hushed, sensual southern drawl.

"I am so not about to get in between anything going on with the Vampires, Rodney, you know that. Why would you even try to put me in a position like that?"

"Because you're my favorite girl," he said smiling, pushing off the wall of her antebellum town house. "And because you are the best at what you do."

"With friends like you, who needs enemies?" she fussed as his hands lightly rested on her shoulders.

"I'm not asking you to get involved, I'm asking for information—basic information."

She turned her face away. "Yeah, right. Don't even try to glamour me, I'm immune."

"And I am hurt, shocked, and appalled that you would think I'd do something like that to you, love."

She smirked. "Uh-huh . . . I can tell the time of the month by you—isn't it every three weeks you want to come by and talk, and that winds up being the last thing we do?"

"Ah, now I am truly wounded," he said, smiling broadly and covering his heart with a palm. He theatrically hung his head. "It's just that every so many weeks, just at the new moon, I am captured anew by your spell, milady."

She laughed and then entered his embrace. "Go away, you horny man."

"I just want a little information that could keep me in my glamour."

"Okay, what?" she said with an exasperated sigh.

"If there was, say, a disembodied spirit that wanted to enter a body . . . who around here has the expertise to allow that to happen? Could the Vampires do that alone?"

"No."

"Oh, come on, love. Please relent from the one-word answers. You've now cleared the Vampires of being able to do this deed and I trust you. My own advisors said as much, too."

"Then why are you asking me?"

Sir Rodney clucked his tongue. "Woman, thou art as fickle as the wind, and now my crime against this is consulting my advisors . . . Oh, the shame of it all."

Esmeralda laughed and looked up into Sir Rodney's multihued gaze, giving in to his attempt to glamour her. "They can't do it without help because they don't have souls, and they need one stronger spirit to be able to overtake the victim's and essentially duke it out inside the new body, just as that body's life force and will are weakest."

"Sounds diabolical," he murmured, sobering as he listened.

"It is, and a lot of people can't do it because you've got to be willing to play with your own soul, to roll the dice, so to speak. If there's a moment of hesitation, the victim's spirit can fight off the taker's spirit and leave it in limbo while the body dies . . . but then the two that have been joined, when the taker was trying to pattern over the new spirit, start heading toward the Light where all innocents go. Problem is, a taker isn't going in that direction—so they scorch on impact with the Light. That's why a lot of witches don't do those types of spells. It's very advanced, very risky, and just isn't worth it."

"So nobody around here is actually qualified or predisposed, even for a grand amount of money, to take that risk?"

"Hell no, sugah. In all honesty, what you're talking

about is a very old and complicated spell. It needs a victim—but that's the easy part . . . the delicate part is making the transfer at the exact moment the victim expires." She shook her head. "I don't know anybody locally with that know-how. You might have to travel up to Salem, Massachusetts, or head to London to some of the older covens. That's the best advice I can give you."

It was the last thing he'd expected to see when he came out of the shadows at the baron's old manor house. Rather than it being eerily abandoned and burned out, and the perimeter surrounded by armed human henchmen, there were construction bulldozers and normal work crews going about the business of razing the old house with the obvious intent of rebuilding. This was not the quiet lair of a demon-infected Were Leopard in hiding. Hunter sniffed the air. Not even the mildest hint of sulfur came to him.

Finding the Chens had been a stroke of dumb luck, but he'd gladly take leads from any source he could get. Shogun entered the small convenience store that had a pretty young girl's picture in the window with an urgent parental message written above it in neat Chinese calligraphy. The request for help to find their missing daughter was heartrending; other locals had pointed him toward the herbal apothecary, who'd sent him on a zigzag mission through the fish market, whose proprietors pointed him to a boutique owner, who remembered seeing a small sign about a lost girl at a convenience store next to a take-out joint.

It would have been so much easier and would have saved time if there were signs posted all over. But Shogun censored himself and let go of the frustration, knowing that was not the Chinese way. The law-abiding citizenry believed in following the rules. If the police said to wait several days before a true missing persons report could be filed, they would accept that fate. They were also very private, and so it was only logical that their pleas for help would be a small cry done in a dignified way. But that did not diminish their pain.

Shogun stood outside for a moment, looking at the young woman's face, her smile, assessing her delicate features. He steeled himself before he entered the store, knowing that her parents' pain would carve a hole in his soul. If he had a child, losing her like this would be unbearable. The many losses he'd already endured began to awaken within him as he pushed on the door and heard the light chime.

A weary-looking man peered at him from behind a counter that was surrounded with bulletproof glass. His tired wife shuffled out to stand at the register, waiting on his purchase decision.

"Lottery?" she asked in a flat tone, observing that he hadn't brought any grocery items to the counter. "We close soon. Curfew."

Shogun hesitated, almost hating to use the phony badge as a ruse now, because he knew it would only inspire hope in the distraught couple. "I have a few questions about your daughter, Mr. and Mrs. Chen. I am so sorry for your loss." Shogun produced the badge, and immediately the owners ran to the side door beside the glass and unlatched it.

"Come in, come in," Mr. Chen said eagerly and then ran to the front door, bolted it, and flipped over the CLOSED sign. "You have news?"

His wife clutched her hands to her chest as though in prayer, and then squeezed her eyes shut. Two big tears rolled down her weathered cheeks and she spoke quickly in broken English. "My daughter is good girl— she no out at parties! She no have boyfriend! She study hard, work hard!"

Mrs. Chen's sob drew Shogun to her as he tried to comfort her and usher her to the back room with her husband. "I know, ma'am, I know," he said, and then lapsed into Mandarin to ease communications.

"Have you found her?" Mr. Chen asked, his voice hesitant and unsure. "Alive . . . please, say alive."

Mrs. Chen released a bloodcurdling wail, her pain like claws against Shogun's conscience. "I keep the incense lit for her soul," she wailed, pounding her chest with her clasped fists. "My only child, I will call the ancestors, I will make medicine. I will call the ghosts . . . I will beg the Dragons, but my only child cannot be taken away from me like this!"

"We thank God that the authorities sent you— someone from our people," Mr. Chen said, beginning to tear. "Someone who knows our community, who *cares* about one missing girl and knows that she matters to us, even if she does not matter to others."

Shogun covered Mrs. Chen's hands with his own, almost unable to look into the poor woman's face as he spoke to the couple. "I care, sir. I . . . my heart goes out to you both. We have not found her yet, but we will look for her until we do. Please, if I can ask you questions about the last time you saw her, about where she was and who she was with . . . what her normal patterns were . . . then we will start from there."

CHAPTER 14

She hated dead ends worse than she hated demon doors. Sasha clicked off the cell phone call with Hunter and stashed it in her back jeans pocket. This was so not what she'd wanted to hear. Sir Rodney's message wasn't much better. Two damned bars left and she needed to find a charger, or else by the time Shogun tried her, her phone would be dead.

Mentally crossing another name off her list, she glanced at the sky. In less than an hour it would be dark. Shogun would have to be headed into the sidhe with Sir Rodney. She wanted to kick herself for all the precious time that had been squandered today. The news had finally released the names of the two victims, a young blond co-ed and her Goth boyfriend . . . couldn't have been more than twenty years old. Sasha shook her head. What a waste. Somebody's parents were probably laid out prostrate with grief over this and couldn't even tell their child good-bye—this was a definite closed-casket scenario.

But at least a diligent journalist had given her a name trail. With the sun going down, any student who lived on campus or in the surrounding apartment areas would be home. The curfew was a blessing, in that regard. Wouldn't be too hard to find the friends who had commented on the news. Walking across the rolling expanse of the campus, Sasha whipped out her cell phone and called Winters. He picked up on the second ring.

"Hey, dude—can you go on Facebook and tell me the names of all the people who sent in RIP stuff for the two kids from Tulane who got killed?"

Sasha had to pull the phone away from her ear as Winters's excited voice assaulted her sensitive hearing.

"When are you gonna let me strap you with a Crack-Berry or like an iPhone, Captain? Or I could get you a Palm Pre, if you wanted to go light . . . Do you know how many apps are out there these days—stuff that can solve almost every issue you have in the field—but nooo. Oh, my God, tell me you did not call me to do an FB search—like, that is so—"

"Winters, my phone is dying. I left my charger because I didn't expect to be gone all day. The stores are all pulling down their grates because of the curfew, and—"

"So do your shadow thing and go get a new charger from Radio Shack, c'mon."

His comment annoyed her, but she had to smile. She hadn't thought of that. Somehow stealing stuff was always a remote thought . . . Now, blowing stuff up, that she was good at. "Okay," she finally said in a huff.

"You sure you don't want us to investigate something sexier than that for you—like I could hack into the Pentagon—"

"Noooo," Sasha said, shaking her head. "Just a nice, clean, legal search, thank you very much."

"Fine. Gimme a coupla minutes. Go find a charger, juice up, and I'll call you back."

"Oh, man, here we go." The local police officer wiped the sweat from his brow as he spoke to his partner. "I get so tired of this stupid shit, Dwayne, I'm about to turn in my badge."

"Yeah, it isn't even dark and the crazies are out. What is it about screwing with mausoleums, huh, Leroy? Why desecrate the dead? That is so disgusting." He peered in and held his nose. "Man, the bodies ain't even in the caskets."

"What? Don't tell me some old maggoty bones were left on the ground for stray dogs to yank all over the place—that is so nasty!"

"Naw, man. The bodies ain't in there."

"You think we should bother calling this in, with all the hell that's been breaking loose here lately?"

"Do you wanna be standing in a graveyard all night on vandalism detail all because a couple of punks turned over some old-ass graves and flung ashes everywhere? Because the bodies are missing, you and I both know that's a lot of paperwork for felonious acts, taking it up from just being a stupid pledge prank. So you tell me, partner, if that's what you wanna do tonight."

"Hell to the no, partner. Put it in the report tomorrow morning . . . we could say we had to respond to a more immediate situation, but we'll report it so the family can get their insurance claim. You know, tell the truth all way up till the last part . . . we got the anonymous tip that something was going on over here, we came, we saw, and then we had to leave to provide backup to another officer."

He whipped out his cell phone and called their buddies in another squad car. As soon as the call picked up, he hit SPEAKER. "Yo, Jeff, we got us a bullshit detail here, wanna ask for some backup? No, not you coming to us, us coming to you. Isn't there a curfew violator that's getting a little rowdy?"

Laughter filled the cell phone and the officers pounded each other's fists.

"Cool."

They both looked at each other as their NOPD patrol car radio squawked.

"Like I said, we had to pursue another incident of higher priority."

Sasha tapped her foot as she waited for her phone to charge while sitting in the back of the darkened electronics store. Everything seemed to be *hurry up and wait,* and she was glad to at least be able to write down a list of names provided by Winters.

"Slow down, slow down, Sparky," she said, writing the names down quickly on the back of some receipt paper she'd pilfered. "Can you give me a sublist—like kids they went to school with from around here." She let her breath out hard. "I know there are hundreds of condolence notes on there. Well, if you're gonna whine, put Clarissa on the phone."

All her old contacts were still in hiding in the sidhe, including Ethan McGregor and his family. It would have been a big help to have his wife, Margaret, a nurse from Tulane Hospital, on the scene. But who could blame the couple for going on hiatus until every evil being involved in that last big debacle was brought to justice? The McGregors had kids to worry about; in their position she'd be locked away in the sidhe, too. Then there was the little Pixie who lived in the tea-house gardens, or used to, anyway . . . it would have been great to ask her if she'd experienced any more Were invasions on the grounds, but she was long gone, too.

Sasha kept walking. Most of the kids on the FB pages that Winters had hacked lived in off-campus apartments. There was a common theme, though: It seemed to be a Goth crowd, based on what he'd told her. The couple of pics he'd sent confirmed it, and she was sure if the police and FBI were diligently doing their jobs like she assumed, none of these kids would want to talk to anybody with a badge. On the other hand, after having interviewed the first five very tear-ful teens, even the sublist of twenty-five students to talk to seemed daunting.

She took out her cell phone again and looked at the pics. Maybe she was going about this all wrong. The FB comments from some of the friends of the victims had a decidedly Vampire-like theme. Zeroing in on the angrier responses, she studied Fanglegnd4eva. *You guys were supposed to live 4ever—this sux.*

Okaaaay . . . Sasha quickly called Winters back. "Dude," she said, beginning to jog. "Can you get into Fanglegnd4eva's page? This guy seems really ticked about their deaths."

"A lot of people process their grief by getting pissed off, Trudeau. My two seconds of pop psych for the trouble."

"Yeah, I know," she said, listening to Winters's fingers click the keyboard. "But he made your top twenty-five list because he kept posting and posting, asking them if they'd 'come back,' and then challenged them to not forget their friends, right?"

"Kinda freaky, kinda sad—but yeah . . . and bingo, got an address with a regular name. Dude is Lawrence DeWitt. He just posted, too, saying screw the police, tomorrow night there's gonna be a rave in honor of their friends that got suckered by suckers."

"You're the man, Winters," Sasha said, memorizing the location.

"My kung fu is strong," he said, laughing, and then clicked off the call.

In and out of a shadow, she arrived under a street lamp in front of a run-down apartment building that still seemed to have flood damage stains on the crumbling outer walls. All the lights in the building were on, but in a place like this there was always a closet shadow.

Sasha stared up at the fourth floor where Lawrence DeWitt lived. There were no names on any of the doorbells, and she wasn't inclined to hang outside and ring, anyway. A hunch tugged at her gut. This guy's posts sounded like someone who had a real axe to grind . . . like a person who might have been promised one thing and then something totally screwed up happened. Plus, it was a young couple in the Goth scene—and she wondered now if they might also have been in the Vamp rave scene. Coincidence that they both ended up dead? Not.

Boldly playing that hunch, Sasha left her fake badge in her back pocket and entered the building with ease. The hallway smelled like burnt microwave popcorn, bug spray, mold, old cheese, and weed. She made a face and took the stairs two at a time all the way to the fourth floor. Oh, yeah, the marijuana was coming from DeWitt's place. But when she got to the front door, she stopped and sniffed harder. Why in the world was garlic stinging her nose?

Listening closely through the blaring heavy metal, she could hear DeWitt moving around in his apartment. Small moves. Someone-seated moves. Sasha went to the end of the hall, entered a shadow, came out in a coat closet, and then opened the door.

"Hey, Lawrence," she said, allowing her inner wolf to help make her eyes glow. It was the first time in her life she'd intentionally scared a human with her supernatural ability, but she needed answers, and time didn't allow for finesse.

He shrieked and leaped out of his chair, his chubby rolls jiggling as he grabbed a gallon jug of water and brandished it in front of him. "How did you get in here! You can't cross without an invitation. I have Holy Water. Get back!"

"Wow . . ." Sasha was at a momentary loss for words. This poor kid actually did think she was a Vampire. So her little ruse had struck a nerve. Somehow she suspected that if she showed him canines, he might have a coronary. Rather than have a medical emergency, she stayed still to allow him to calm down. "I just want to talk."

"I didn't do it. Yeah, we were all pissed, but we didn't do the graveyard thing. We wouldn't be that stupid."

"Okay," Sasha said leaning against the wall. "Who did?"

"I don't know. A bunch of us were gonna go out there later tonight to find our mentors and ask what happened to Jim and Tanya, but when Mouse rode by there on his bike, he saw the mausoleum trashed and was like, we are so screwed, because it'll seem like we're involved when we aren't!"

"All right, all right," Sasha said, holding up a hand. "Relax."

She sighed as Lawrence started crying. Huge tears rolled down his fat face; his mascara was running. Every few seconds he'd wipe his cheeks, flashing her black nail polish, and she focused on the big, dime-size holes in his ears that the black steel disks made.

"Can I at least finish my joint before you rip out my heart? I know you don't believe me . . . I know this is the part where you say I'm not going to hurt you but then you make me scream like a little bitch."

Sasha shook her head. "Some of my colleagues might be inclined to do that, but tonight is your lucky night. All I want to know is what happened." She pulled her cell phone out of her pocket and pushed the video button. "Tell me."

"Oh, God, oh, God, I'm going to be in a Vamp snuff video! I mean, not oh God—I'm sorry, I didn't mean to say that word. Oh, Jesus, please . . ."

"Gimme a break," Sasha snarled. "I'm not going to snuff you—but I do need your version of what happened for the record so that nobody else decides to. Now *talk!*"

"Jim did everything he was supposed to do," DeWitt said, sniffing. He clutched the plastic jug of Holy Water to his chest as though still not convinced he wouldn't die. "He'd gotten all the way up there . . . brought plenty of donors, worked at the club as a human helper. He was even tattooed and ready to descend . . . all he had to do was bring them a body and he'd get the bite."

"And he brought them their sacrifice?"

"Yeah. A virgin. Some Asian chick in Tanya's lab."

Sasha coolly nodded to remain in character, even though sickened to her stomach. "So what went wrong?"

"Can I have my joint?" DeWitt looked at the smoldering roach in his ashtray.

Sasha motioned to the Marlboro reds on the kitchen counter. "Try those, stay lucid at least while you're talking to me."

"Oh, shit, oh, shit, I knew it . . . you guys don't like pollutants in the blood and—"

"I'm not going to bite you or kill you, and I'm not worrying about you making me high off a couple of tokes." Sasha walked over to the kitchen counter, tossed DeWitt his smokes, then went to the ashtray and crushed out his roach. "But I want you to clearly remember what happened so I can try to save your life, you little shit . . . even though you didn't give a damn about that poor girl you guys gave to the . . . community." She put one hand on her hip and tried to steady her cell phone as she clamped her mouth shut, glad that she'd stopped her rant just short of calling Vampires, which she was supposed to be, *Vamps*—a slur in their world.

"Me and Jim got her on campus . . . Tanya called her and said she wanted to study late to go over her part of the project—so getting to her was easy. She was really tiny, you know, fragile, so it was easy to grab her and tie her up—smash some duct tape on her mouth. Then Jim took her in his trunk to the club."

"The Blood Oasis," Sasha said flatly, trying not to bare canines.

"Yeah, where else. That's where he always met his mentor. Ariel was really excited, said he'd done good because they wanted the Asian chick for some big event going down in the bayou. Told Jim to get his girl-friend and stand by—later that night was gonna be it." DeWitt's hands shook as he managed a cigarette and lit it without letting go of the Holy Water. "But, see, that's where things got all fucked up. My tight never came back. He and his girl were gone all night and we were all celebrating our asses off, because one of our own had descended, had become an undead. We were like waiting on the next night—it was gonna be glorious. I knew Jimmy would come back and make me first . . . that's what was supposed to happen. Our whole crew would be in with him and Tanya."

DeWitt took an unsteady drag on his cigarette with a trembling hand as new tears welled up in his bloodshot hazel eyes. "But they came back in a fucking Dumpster in pieces like they were an appetizer or some really whack shit. It just wasn't right."

"Disappointing, I'm sure," Sasha said in a flat tone,

eyeing DeWitt. "But probably no more disappointing than what the family of that girl is experiencing."

"I mean, c'mon," DeWitt said, dragging hard on his cigarette. "She was a nobody, not even into the dark side. Besides, how many Asian chicks are there in the—"

Sasha had crossed the room so quickly that DeWitt never even got to scream. She held him by the throat and pressed the Holy Water in his arms hard with her torso until it seemed like he couldn't breathe. Furious, she angled the cell phone camera over his head, close to biting his face off, but instead crushed his fallen butt under her heel to avoid an apartment fire on the cheap rug.

"What was her name!"

"I don't know," DeWitt stammered, glimpsing down at the Holy Water that separated them. "Wait, wait," he said, choking as Sasha's grip tightened. "Amy Chen, I think."

She stepped away from Lawrence DeWitt and wiped off the hand she'd held him with on her jeans back pocket. She snatched the Holy Water from him, set it down on the coffee table, and glared at the foolish student in front of her.

"That girl was *a human being,* which is more than I'd call you—you little turd. She had to have a family, had to have people who loved her—people who are waiting and wondering when she'll come home . . . lighting candles and praying . . . and you gave her up for your own personal games? I oughta rip your heart out myself, but you'll find a way to allow the Vampires to do that one night, I'm so sure." She pointed to the Holy Water. "That only works if you believe in the power of the Light over the darkness." Then she walked around the room and snatched down hanging garlic cloves. "This will only piss a Vampire off. While you're jerking off on Internet porn tonight, I suggest you do some real research and keep your dumb ass alive."

Sasha flung open the smelly closet door and was gone. Despair and fury collided in the center of her chest. How had the Vamps seduced so many when what they did was so foul? She came out in the middle of the street in a car shadow so angry that she was nearly in tears. Amy Chen was as good as dead, but she'd call Winters to get a pic as soon as she calmed down. Now that she knew what body had been used, it might be easier to flash around a photo to see if anybody in the supernatural communities had seen Lady Jung Suk. The sick thing was, she was going to have to try to keep Lawrence DeWitt alive long enough to haul his fat ass in as a possible witness.

Working quickly, Sasha uploaded the video to Winters for safekeeping at NORAD. After all that she'd been through in dealing with Vamps, she knew Murphy's Law followed her around like a little black rain cloud. It would be all that she needed to lose her freaking cell phone during a clothing shed or a ground fight, and she really didn't have it in her to go back and get another confession from DeWitt without killing him. As soon as the transmission went through, she sent Winters a quick text: *Lock it up tight. This might save my ass one night. Thx.* She shoved the unit back into her jeans pocket and headed toward a series of shadows across the street.

A hard vibration thrummed against Sasha's back-side and she whipped out her cell phone again quickly, thinking it was Winters responding. Instead a quick confirmation text popped up from him while Shogun's sad voice filled the receiver. Sasha simply closed her eyes as Shogun spoke.

"Thanks, Shogun. I can't even imagine how her parents reacted," Sasha murmured. "I got a confirmation on the name . . . yeah, same girl. Just get back to the sidhe, okay . . . it's a real bad moon out here tonight."

CHAPTER 15

Sasha released a long, mournful howl, and within minutes Hunter met her in the graveyard. She pointed at
the desecrated mausoleum. "Ariel Beauchamp and a
couple of his lady friends apparently used to live here."

"Did you do that this afternoon?" Hunter said with a
sly smile. "I thought we were supposed to take the
subtle approach, but nice work."

"Nah. Wish I did, though." She let out a hard breath
and placed both hands on her hips. "Kids claimed they
didn't do it, either. But it doesn't make sense for Lady
Jung Suk to have done this—unless the Vamps reneged
on some deal she'd made with them?"

"Kids?" Hunter's expression instantly sobered.

She stared at Hunter, becoming nauseous again at
the thought. "Yeah . . . you'll never believe some immortality seekers on campus kidnapped an innocent
girl and gave her over to those bloodsuckers, and in
exchange one of their friends was supposed to get the
permanent life bite. From there, their little plan was to
infect all their friends and have a great ol' time forever
at the Blood Oasis."

"You have *got* to be kidding me." Hunter raked his fingers through his hair.

"I wish I was," Sasha said, shaking her head as she sniffed the remnants of Vampire ash. "Amy Chen was her name . . . Shogun called me and I could tell just by the sound of his voice that her parents are destroyed. I don't think I've ever heard Shogun sound so upset."

Hunter nodded. "Given the circumstances, he had the toughest detail in the group. Where is he now?"

"On his way back to the sidhe with Sir Rodney."

"Good." Hunter walked closer to the mausoleum and made a face as he peered in and then jogged back to where Sasha stood. "If they had anything to do with that, they won't live very long and I'm not sure there's much we can do about it."

Sasha nodded and pulled out her cell phone. "Get a load of this." She replayed DeWitt's interrogation.

"Send it to Sir Rodney. Even if he's in the sidhe now and the transmission can't go through until he exits, the message will be stored and waiting for him."

"Yeah, can't have too many copies of this floating around," Sasha said, manipulating her phone as they began walking. "But it's just the beginning. All this shows is that the vamps had an Asian girl abducted, whom we have to presume is dead or inhabited . . . and that they most likely killed the two students who were once in their employ. But it still doesn't definitively link them to aiding and abetting a fugitive—Lady Jung Suk."

"We'll definitely need something harder to go on in order to show Vamp wrongdoing," Hunter said in a low rumble. "But now that we have a face . . ."

"Great minds think alike." Sasha stared at him, enjoying the fullness of the moon for a few seconds.

Hunter reached out and caressed her cheek. "We're going to beat this together."

"How sweet," a light male voice said, making Sasha and Hunter whirl on the sound.

Within seconds, blurs surrounded them to quickly materialize into Vampires.

"Adding to your offenses tonight?" a tall platinum-blond male said with a sneer. His onyx eyes held cold fury, and his black leather coat billowed out behind him as he looked at the destruction of Ariel Beauchamp's mausoleum.

"We didn't do this," Hunter said. "But I so wish we had."

Vampires hissed and levitated two inches above the ground. Sasha counted them quickly. Ten seasoned warriors against the two of them did not make for good odds. For a moment she considered the cell phone evidence in her pocket, but then thought better of it. DeWitt would have a target on his scruffy neck. She couldn't sentence a nineteen-year-old to Vampire retaliation, no matter how much he deserved it.

"Let us pass and there will be no bloodshed," Hunter said evenly, his eyes already glowing.

"But we love bloodshed," the group leader said and then flew at Hunter, claws extended.

His wolf savaged a limb, tearing at flesh and bone as the attacker screeched and yanked away to lob a solid blow. Vampires flew up, circled, and then dove in again. Sasha went airborne, catching the first attacker in the throat as Hunter shook off the punch and disemboweled him. Rolling out of the way of extended claws, Sasha missed a swipe just as another Vampire leaped onto Hunter's back. But a third wolf hurdled over a gravestone, ripping out that Vampire's spinal column. Shogun threw his head back and howled. From a shadow, Crow exited with a thick tree branch in hand and staked through the back the Vampire who was headed toward Sasha.

Coalescing into an angry funnel cloud of bats, the seven survivors swept away. Breathing heavily, Crow Shadow jogged over to where Sasha, Hunter, and Shogun had transformed back into their human forms.

"I thought I gave you a direct order to stay in Denver," Hunter growled, out of breath, as he began tugging on his pants.

"My sister . . . family emergency rules apply, man," Crow Shadow said, resting his hands on his knees as he bent to suck in huge gulps of air. "Good to see you, too."

"And you were on your way to the sidhe," Sasha said, pulling on her T-shirt, giving Shogun a sidelong look.

"Heard your howl, knew it was war—we don't leave our own." Shogun pounded Hunter's fist as he picked up his pants.

"The humans haven't taken the bait," Cerridwen said coolly as she swept past Elder Vlad's long, onyx table.

She touched the surface of it, watching glimpses of the human news report as it iced over. He sat back and lifted his golden goblet of warm blood before it froze.

"That is of no matter . . . right now they are frightened and do what humans always do—put their heads in the sand for a period."

Cerridwen placed an icy finger against her blue lips. "Odd that after two maulings they are not calling for a wolf hunt."

"They made one in their very own laboratory," Elder Vlad said through his fangs. "Sasha Trudeau. This was nothing more than a cover-up! But rest assured they are looking for their rabid dog and we shall help them find her with blood on her hands."

"While that may be so," Cerridwen said coolly, her gaze becoming distant as her mind engaged the problem, "I think it could not hurt to send out additional spies to be sure that our plot is not discovered. Lady Jung Suk worries me . . . she is, for lack of a better description, primitive."

"And her sorcery skills are amazing," Elder Vlad said, taking a slow sip of blood.

"But why do you need her when you could avail yourself of Unseelie magic?"

Elder Vlad smiled into his goblet and considered Cerridwen over the rim of it while taking a sip. "Because, my dear, she has a soul at present, and you and I don't. That allows her to perform some of the most exquisite spells."

"And you have the dark covens at your behest," Cerridwen snapped.

"As do you," Elder Vlad said with a toothy grin. "That would make us evenly matched in power bases . . . except that I have one additional entity under my *sole* control. Is that what disturbs you? This slight advantage?"

"Certainly not. It has nothing to do with that."

"Then come, come, my darling . . . let us enjoy each other's company tonight. You seem so unsettled."

"You should come out with our investigation team. We'll get on tape what the mainstream media is afraid to show, dude."

Russell nodded. "Thanks, Bob. Maybe you're right. I'm sick of sitting around here; wanna get in on some of the action."

The small ghost-hunting team raised their beers toward Russell.

"Hey, we need an embedded journalist."

Excitement ripped through Russell as he reached into his wallet and produced the Blood Oasis card. Murmurs of awe tore around the table as the three men and one woman who made up Ghost Finders, Inc., leaned in to finger the coveted access card.

"You ever kill an entity?" Russell asked the group leader.

"Uh, no, not really," Bob said. "We just sorta monitor activity and tell people if their home or institution is haunted. Like, dude, it ain't that serious."

"It is that serious," Russell said, and then moved to stand. John placed a hand on his forearm, staying his leave.

"Hey, hey, wait a minute. Just because we haven't done that before doesn't mean we can't—if something attacked us, I'm sure we'd all fight."

Russell sat back down and leaned in. "That's all I'm saying. I'm not about to go into the Blood Oasis with a bunch of amateurs and get sucked dry by Vampires. But I've been researching supernaturals for years, and the one thing I know is that Vampires and Werewolves are mortal enemies. From the little bit of truth that's leaking out in the regular media, I'm pretty sure that the killings were done by Werewolves. The Vampires in the area are not gonna take kindly to having a rogue feeding on humans in their backyard. If we stir the pot a little, maybe go to a Vampire arbiter and offer ourselves as bait for a chance to get a real Werewolf attempted attack on tape so the Vampires can bag it and tag it . . . we might make some history."

"That is so fucking outrageous, dude," Bob said, shaking his head as he dragged his fingers through his hair. He looked around at his team. "John . . . Ralph, Sally, you in?"

"That's crazy, but yeah," John said, gaining nods.

"No time like the present," Russell said with a half smile. "First off, we hit the club and make the offer. If they accept, we go to the location where all the military scoured. I *know* something happened out there, and it's still a full moon."

"Your proposal is bold, innovative . . . and completely insane, Mister, ahem . . ."

"Conway, Russell Conway," he repeated to the club manager. "But surely you don't believe in Vampires, do you?" Duval Hempstead rubbed his jaw and sat back, his large gold pinkie ring catching the pulsing red club lights.

"I believe that some humans are in denial, others ignorantly oblivious," Russell said flatly. "I want wolves seen for the monsters that they are, and I'd love to get an attack on tape. Once something that frightening is shown and the authorities can prove that it hasn't been digitally altered, maybe they'll send tanks down city streets to do a wolf hunt in earnest."

"And you are willing to be bait . . . you and your team of ghost finders, *oui*?"

Russell memorized every facet of the Vampire's café-au-lait face and watched his piercing green irises begin to be eclipsed by the expanding black pupils. "Yes," he said, feeling the magnetic pull of an attempted mind seduction.

Duval Hempstead smiled slyly, allowing a slight crest of fang to show. "Brave man. But I will have to take it up with my management."

"Of course. And while you mire yourself in bureaucracy, we'll be out at the Bayou House trapping a rogue Were. If you care to join us, please know that you're welcome. Under normal circumstances we would wait, but it's a full moon."

Duval nodded as Russell stood. "We'll be in touch."

"I've never been at a site this hot with paranormal activity in my life," Sally whispered, scanning the area and holding out a boom microphone.

"Where'd you get all these guns, man?" John said, holding a pump shotgun in one hand and a heat-sensitive digital camera in the other as they trudged along.

Russell kept his camera held high and a tight grip on his handheld automatic. "If you're going to do something like this, you can't be stupid. I collected this stuff over the years as I was doing my research."

"So the Vampires said they'd come?" Bob said eagerly, stopping every few steps to film the group in motion and to do a bit of narration.

"They were noncommittal," Russell said, not bothering to hide his disappointment. "But it doesn't matter. The main goal is to get an attempted attack on film." He looked back at Bob. "Keep up with the group, man."

"This place is so hot," Sally said quietly. "Look at the readings—they just spiked off the far end of the scanner. I don't feel good about this. The hair is standing up on the back of my neck."

"Mine, too," Russell said quietly.

That was the last thing said before they heard Bob scream.

"Did you hear that?" Sasha turned to the group. The four wolves remained still for a second.

"Humans under attack," Hunter said quickly, and instantly their group started running toward the sound.

Moving in and out of the shadows at breakneck velocity, Hunter, Sasha, and Crow Shadow arrived on the scene with Shogun skidding to a halt behind them. A burst of semi-automatic fire ripped through the trees in their direction. Hunter snatched Shogun out of a fatal path of gunfire, but not before Shogun's arm was grazed by a blistering silver bullet.

"Hold your fire," Sasha shouted. "We're here to help."

She stepped out of the shadows to find one lone human brandishing a weapon with a digital camera still running.

"Sir, you're going to be all right. We are here to help you."

"They're dead! They're all dead!"

Sasha didn't look down. She didn't have to; she could smell it. But when she stepped on something slippery, she looked down and cringed. It was a section of skull with long brunette hair still attached to it.

"This man is bleeding badly," Hunter said, glancing at Shogun. He hoisted his brother up. "I need to call Rodney and get him to the sidhe. We need to get there, too, for the night, judging by what's left this carnage."

"Sis, listen to the man . . ." Crow Shadow said, stepping forward but standing still when Russell brandished his weapon.

"If you make a wolf call now, I guarantee you this man is going to melt down and spray us," Sasha said carefully, ready to leap out of the line of fire. "Let me talk to him, all right?"

"Do it fast," Hunter said though his teeth. "We go to the sidhe; Rodney can have his guards take this man back to town and then disappear . . . maybe even glamour him till the shock wears off. But my brother must have healing attention *now*."

"I'm okay," Shogun argued and then winced. "Just need to get the silver to stop burning."

"Sir, what's your name?" Sasha said as quickly but as calmly as possible.

"Russell Conway—reporter," the traumatized man said.

"Okay," Sasha said quietly, walking forward. "But we can't leave you out here alone. You fired on one of our men and he's bad off. We're going to have to ask you to put the gun down so we can call our friends. We'll get an armed escort to take you back to wherever you're staying in town while we seek medical help. You can go to the police and have them help you, all right, Mister Conway?"

"I got it all on tape—I got it," he said, laughing and crying like a madman as he offered Sasha his weapon. "Wolves did it!"

CHAPTER 16

"This really looks bad," Sasha said with her head in her hands. "I almost wish your Fae archers hadn't made a quick duplicate with their magic. If I hadn't seen this, I would have felt a little better maybe."

Sir Rodney shook his head as Shogun, Hunter, and Crow Shadow gathered around the sidhe war room table. Ancient coats of armor remained at attention under vaulted ceilings, guarding the Old World luxury of the castle. But not even being ensconced in the hidden world of the Fae could make Sasha feel as though the danger was behind them; Colonel Madison was going to crap a kitten.

"The evidence is damning," Sir Rodney admitted. "All you can see is screams and shouts. Body parts go flying and you hear machine-gun reports; then you guys step out of the shadows, eyes gleaming and canines shown. Not good at all."

"Tell me about it," Hunter muttered.

Shogun rubbed his bandaged arm. "Run it back again."

"Dude, your aunt was moving too fast," Crow

Shadow said leaning against the high-back chair and closing his eyes. "All you could see was a black blur."

"And us," Sasha said with a groan.

"But in her Were state," Shogun argued as he looked around the group, "Lady Jung Suk is a white snow leopard with black spots. Run it again."

Sasha managed the technology as Sir Rodney's elderly magic advisors gathered more closely, their wrinkled bald heads and thick pointed ears turning subtly to watch and listen to the video replay with rapt attention.

"Slow it down," Sir Rodney commanded; his voice was distant and distracted as his senior advisor pulled out a wand from his brown monk-like robe sleeve. "There, there, stop it there."

"It's shaped like a wolf, but is almost transparent in a black blur . . ." Sasha frowned and stared hard, but then sat back in frustration as the digital camera disintegrated into a pile of leaves. "Great."

"Just kiss my ass!" Crow Shadow shouted and then pounded the table. "So what do we do now?"

"I take it that it's midnight," Shogun said sarcastically, closing his eyes.

"There's nothing more that can be done tonight, good lady and gents," Sir Rodney muttered in frustration. "I suggest a hot bath and strong ale and a good night's rest. On the morrow we can go find the inimitable Mister Conway and glamour his digital recording away from him."

"Just a question—not trying to cast aspersions on the archers who escorted him back to town safely," Crow

Shadow said. "But is there any reason your men let him walk with the real camera and gave us the bogus one?"

"Most assuredly that is a sound question," Sir Rodney said with a weary shrug. "But I'm pretty sure it had something to do with not wanting Mister Conway to rush to the human police, who are already somewhat wary of supernatural goings-on, and then have a camera turn into a pile of leaves right before their eyes. We, the Fae, have been in the human detection avoidance business for *thousands* of years."

Crow Shadow just nodded. "My bad."

Sasha dragged herself out of the plush velvet seating of the war room and pushed away from the round table. Sudden fatigue finally claimed her as she, Hunter, and their two brothers passed enchanted suits of armor that stood magical guard, saluting the wolf retinue as they passed. She loved Sir Rodney's sidhe, but the prospect of having to stay behind the walls of his Neverland-like fortress for the duration of her natural life span, all because they were being set up by Vampires, was not one she could tolerate.

It took everything within her to climb the huge stone stairs and follow Rupert, Sir Rodney's most efficient and ebullient valet, to their suite. No matter what time of night or outrageous time of morning, Rupert had the same hospitable disposition and a warm smile on his gaunt face.

"Milady," he said with a quiet bow. "Milord. Your baths have been drawn; all the toiletries and supplies you may need are in your suite. Just speak into the silver domed trays on your dining table and your menu choice will appear. The goose down in your bedding has already been bespelled to offer you a peaceful, healing sleep . . . and as you know from previous visits, just drop your soiled clothing in the hamper and it will be returned freshly laundered and folded in the morning. Good night, all."

"Good night, Rupert," Sasha murmured, giving him a quick hug.

She delighted in his smile. He was family, as far as she was concerned.

"I could truly get used to this," Hunter said once she'd shut the heavy wooden door and latched it.

"Man, no, you couldn't. Tonight, yeah. But after three nights of not being able to run free in the North Country—you'd be baying at the moon."

"Not if you were here," he said with a half smile and began shucking his clothes.

"Maybe . . . ," she said, loving the view of his back as he tugged his T-shirt over his head.

Every defined muscle in Hunter's back moved like cables beneath his skin, functioning as though they were brackets around his shoulder blades, cording his shoulders and biceps and along his spine . . . down to his deliciously muscled behind.

He glanced over his shoulder as he undid his jeans and kicked out of his boots. "You getting in the tub?"

"Yeah . . . just enjoying the view."

He smiled and stripped off his pants. "I hate to admit it, but after all this bull today, about all I have to offer you is a view."

She chuckled softly and began undressing. "Don't

mind me, I'm just talking trash. I'm so tired that I just want you to be sure I don't drown while we take a bath."

"Ditto," he replied with a deep yawn.

They'd slept like the dead . . . well, not quiet dead, but close to it, Sasha thought as she stirred awake. Sir Rodney had the best beds on the planet, sprinkled with a little Faery dust for a relaxing sleep no matter what the circumstances.

Opening her eyes slowly, Sasha glanced around the room. Sumptuous Old World luxury surrounded them, and it was going to be hard to go back to battling in the bayou. But dawn brought reality and she knew they had to get up.

Sunshine warmed her face as she stretched and pushed back deeper into the spoon of Hunter's embrace. Cool, soft cotton sheets that covered sensual goose down felt like a drug as she struggled to fully wake up. Add to that Hunter's steady breathing, the rhythm of his heartbeat against her spine, and his warmth coating her entire back and backside, it was enough to keep her in the mild coma she'd been in all night. Once they'd lain down, neither of them had moved. The possessive hold he had over her waist felt like a huge tree limb had captured her, pinning her to the bed.

But she had to move; they had to get up. There was much to accomplish . . . but damn, the man felt so good.

"Good morning, baby," she said, beginning the difficult task of untwining their bodies.

"Not yet," he said, releasing a deep rumble inside his chest.

She felt it through her back and felt his grip tighten. "C'mon, don't start."

His answer was simple and definitive and nonverbally male. He just flopped a heavy leg over her legs, holding her in place.

"Not fair . . . I don't have the energy to lift your leg, man." She relaxed back against him and kept her eyes closed as his hand stroked a lazy hypnotic pattern against her belly.

"Not trying to be fair."

She wanted to laugh, but only a groggy chuckle came out. "We have to get up."

"Why?"

He kissed the back of her head and slid his hand up to capture her left breast. His body was definitely awake and pressing against her backside, even though he was only semiconscious. Warmth radiated through her body and lingered between her legs as he gently kneaded a taut nipple until she moistened.

"I'm trying to remember," she said through a quiet moan. "Aw, c'mon, Hunter, don't do this—we've gotta get going."

"True," he murmured, leaning in to kiss her shoulder. "We've definitely gotta get going before we leave this room."

"Colonel Madison," the MP said, as soon as the call connected. "We have a civilian at the guard entrance checkpoint trying to enter the base to see you, sir. He has some sort of video—the same video that is breaking on the news. Should we detain him, sir, or bring him to your office?"

"What video breaking on the news?" Colonel Madison said, looking at the clock.

It was zero-six-hundred. He'd already been up since zero-five-hundred, unable to sleep.

"The news breaking on the local channels, sir," the MP exclaimed, clearly unable to keep the panic out of his voice.

"Bring the civilian to my office," Colonel Madison said, grabbing the remote and turning on the television.

Only three minutes passed and his direct line from the Pentagon rang.

"Good morning," Sasha said, greeting the small team assembled in Sir Rodney's war room.

Crow Shadow and Shogun grunted a reply as they ate, and she was glad that his arm had healed.

Sir Rodney lifted his coffee cup in salute. "Top of the morning to you. Breakfast?"

Rupert scurried over to pull out Sasha's chair as the men at the table stood.

"I'm good," Hunter said with a broad smile. "Already ate."

Sasha refused to look at him as she sat, and Sir Rodney gave him a wink.

"Coffee then?" Rupert said, trying unsuccessfully to swallow a smile.

"Thank you," she replied and gave Hunter a sidelong scowl before turning her attention to the group. "What time is it? My clock gets all messed up in the sidhe."

"This is a timeless place, that's why," Sir Rodney said with a gallant bow from where he sat. "But in human time, it is six A.M."

"Okay, then—thank you for the hospitality, but can we get that coffee to go?" Sasha looked around the group as everyone stopped eating. "The base starts reveille at zero-five-hundred. There are bodies in the woods, so even if Russell Conway couldn't get anyone out there in the dark, at daybreak he might get some action. I can't get a cell phone signal in here, and you don't have a TV."

"Whew . . . somebody got up on the wrong side of the bed this morning. Sis, you are seriously stressing," Crow Shadow said, slurping his coffee.

"I thought I'd rectified that," Hunter said under his breath, accepting a cup of coffee from Rupert.

Shogun chuckled into his cup. Sasha shot out of her chair as though a bee had stung her.

"Look," she said, now talking with her hands, "a feeling just came over me. I know you guys don't approve, but for better or worse I'm half human and I know how humans think . . . I'm connected to their energy, and when big stuff goes down the hair stands up on my neck—the same way it does when I get a wolf feeling. I respect both; I act on both . . . plus I have the advantage of a little feminine instinct that you guys in the magic kingdom still haven't been able to quantify."

She blew out a long breath and paced to the window and back when all they did was stare at her, chewing slowly and sipping their coffee slowly. "You guys have *got* to get up on the new technology and come into the human twenty-first century. Their technology makes them almost as formidable as you—it's their brand of magic, their brand of telepathy, all right? So stop looking at me like I've grown two heads. This is serious. I

need to check in—so can you just take me to the outside wall and drop the drawbridge so I can at least get
cell phone reception?"

It was worse than she'd thought. Her cell phone was
blowing up. Every member of her team had called
twice, and Colonel Madison beat Doc's three calls by
mere seconds. Starting at the top of the food chain, she
called Colonel Madison, then Doc, checked in with
Winters and told him to get back to Clarissa and company, all while half listening to the phone conversation
that Hunter and Crow were having with Silver Hawk
and Bear.

"Respect restored, lassie. I need to create a human
communications room in the sidhe somehow," Sir
Rodney said, looking at Rupert. "Who knew?"

"Definitely," Sasha said, terminating the last call
and shoving her phone in her pocket. "Okay, here's the
deal—I have to go to the base alone." She glanced at
Hunter, and he nodded. "Whatever any of you do, please
do not rush in there and freak people out. Things are
badly tense right now."

"You have my word," Hunter said. "I must go
through the shadow lands taking Crow with me. Silver
Hawk has seen much in new visions that could help our
cause."

"With a little glamour," Shogun said, nodding to Sir
Rodney, "I can work with Fae forces to try to track
down where Lady Jung Suk is resting by day. After all
her night hunting, she must be fatigued . . . and cats
sleep by day, anyway. If she's embedded in the Asian
community, my language skills there will help."

Sir Rodney nodded. "Summon my captain of the Fae guards, Rupert. I want an all-points bulletin out on this Lady Leopard, now that we have her image." He tapped his cell phone and tossed it to Rupert. "Make sure my men know what she looks like. We follow Shogun's lead, but we'll have to glamour him since his face was on that video the civilian took."

"We'll all meet back up at sundown at The Fair Lady," Sasha said. "But don't anybody get jumpy—call, use a cell, send a missive, whatever, but no crazy, sudden moves."

CHAPTER 17

The entire base was in a frenzy by the time she stepped out of the shadows. The only thing that kept her from getting shot was that she'd forewarned Madison and had simply shown up in his office.

"Why didn't you call as soon as you saw the bodies?" he said, not bothering with formalities after she'd given him a start.

"These don't work in the shadow lands or the sidhe, sir," she said, showing him her cell phone. "We were unarmed, save our ability to do hand-to-hand combat, sir. You saw how that predator moves and what it can do. Our first priority was survival and evasive tactics. We took a fallback position in the sidhe. One of our men was injured and we had to get him out of there. He's not a shadow-jumper, couldn't get out of harm's way other than to get him to the fortress."

Colonel Madison nodded. "Been there. That is what I will report to the Joint Chiefs."

Sasha relaxed even while remaining at attention.

"Course of action, Captain?"

For a moment, she just stared at him. Was he actually asking for her opinion? Wow . . .

"I need to get back to the scene of the crime before the scent trail gets too weak or is destroyed by human boots on the ground."

"We already have a team en route that will seal off the area and will not even touch the bodies until you and your trackers can make an assessment."

"Thank you, sir . . . thank you for not believing what you saw on that video."

Colonel Madison nodded. "It was jarring, initially, Captain. You looked dirty, clothes torn, looked like you'd been in a scrape. But based upon the amount of blood that was let . . ." He shook his head. "You all would have been splattered from head to toe, no matter how fast you were moving."

Again, she just stared at him for a moment, allowing new respect to dawn between them.

"I'd like to interview the civilian, sir, and then I want to take some samples from the bodies and have them sent to Doc in the lab. He's familiar with demon-infected Were saliva. If he could also have a sample from the remains of your men, sir," she added more gently. "We have to be sure that it was actually a Were and not a Vampire. They have different saliva tracers. We learned that when investigating the late General Donald Wilkerson's death."

"Consider it done."

"And we're definitely going to need ammo, sir. My weapons were stripped from me when I was detained at NORAD . . . but—"

"Say no more. You're locked and loaded, Captain—and you just tell me how many men you need to hunt this beast down."

"Thank you, sir. But before I put human lives in harm's way . . . let me assess the predator, find out where its lair or den is, then I promise you I'll come knocking."

Colonel Madison gave her a slow, respectful salute. "I know we don't generally do this indoors, but I owed you this."

"Thank you, sir."

He shook his head. "No, Captain. Thank you." His gaze locked with hers as he lifted his chin a little higher. "Never in my life have I seen anything like what this beast is or what it can do . . . and you were out there with it alone with a team of unarmed men . . . and you are ready to head right back into hell, going where angels fear to tread. As a fellow warrior—you have my utmost respect. *Hoo-rah.*"

"*Hoo-rah,* sir."

No one could have prepared her for the way Colonel Madison responded to her. That was the glorious and also unsettling thing about humans—you could never predict how they'd process any given situation.

Sasha's nervous system felt like it was on fire as she walked down the long corridor to a conference room, where two MPs stepped aside to let her and Colonel Madison enter.

Russell Conway looked up from his Styrofoam cup of coffee, his hazel eyes holding a slightly insane quality as sunlight shimmered in them. He was unshaven, his clothes rumpled and his hair mussed, like a man who'd slept on a park bench all night.

"They finally believe me. The world finally hears what I've been trying to tell them for decades."

Sasha listened to the unstable wobble in Russell Conway's voice and gave Colonel Madison a sidelong glance.

"Are you hungry, Mister Conway? Can we bring you some doughnuts or something?" Again, Sasha glimpsed the colonel, who nodded to an MP.

"No . . . no. I cannot eat food now. The ecstasy of discovery is far greater than you can know. They believed me!"

Sasha slowly moved to the table and sat down. An MP slid a yellow legal pad and a pen over to her as the colonel took a position in the back of the room.

"Mister Conway, can you go back to that night and tell us again in your own words what happened?"

He took a deep slurp of his coffee and then began toying with his cup. "My story won't change, you know. It's all on the videos. Those guards you called took me back to the hotel I was staying at, and it was loaded with journalists. I woke everybody up and showed them my camera. They ran with the feeds—let me give them copies and upload it everywhere. It's worldwide now—breaking news. I'm famous. They've tested it and they know it wasn't digitally altered or a hoax."

"We believe you," Sasha said carefully and slowly. "I was there, remember. We came up and got to you just in time, just before the predator got you."

"Yes, yes, you see, Colonel! One of your people saw it, too!"

The colonel just nodded. Sasha leaned forward and clasped Mr. Conway's hands, but then quickly drew back. The surge of insane energy made the hair stand up on her arms, and suddenly she felt nauseous.

"I'm sorry," she said, "I didn't mean to invade your personal space—you just seemed upset and it was reflex. I was out of line," she added, trying to recover.

"It's all right." He smiled and leaned close to her. "I now know you believe me and I also know what you are." He laughed insanely and shook his head. "You're one of them and they probably don't even know it."

"Sir, I'd like you to focus on last night. Let's go back to when you were walking in the woods to investigate the Bayou House with Ghost Finders, Inc. Did you hear any growls, any specific sounds . . . can you remember any smells?"

Russell Conway sat back in his chair with a smug expression and then stared at the wall. "I want a lawyer, if you're going to detain me . . . and I have an interview at ten A.M. on CNN. Can I go?"

"There's no reason to hold this man," Sasha said, still trying to shake off the willies Conway had given her.

The colonel called the MP over. "Process him for release from the base and give him an escort back to his hotel." He turned to Russell Conway and offered him a slight nod. "Thank you for making us aware of the situation."

Russell Conway just laughed the shrill, high-pitched laugh of the insane.

Sasha stood and waited until the man had been escorted out of the room before speaking to the colonel. "You might want to put a detail on him. He's thoroughly unstable. Something happened to him out there in the woods . . . might be a psychotic break, might be worse. But I'm concerned, sir."

"He knew you were a wolf. You could see that in his eyes. Maybe he saw what we saw out there when you and your guide came out of the shadows."

"Yeah . . . ," Sasha said, sounding distracted as she rubbed the nape of her neck. They'd come out of the shadows with eyes gleaming and canines presented, but hadn't shown Conway a full transformation. Still, he was into supernatural research; that might have been enough.

"You said 'might be worse,' Captain . . . what could be worse?" The colonel's eyes held quiet fear as he stared at Sasha. "I was out there under the same conditions—a sole survivor. Is the Werewolf virus airborne, catching?"

Sasha shook her head and extended her palm. "Let me shake your hand, Colonel."

He stared at her hand for a moment.

"I need to feel your aura, your vibe. It's sort of a wolf thing."

Complying, he nervously shook her hand.

"You're clean, sir. A little weary, but clean."

"And that guy wasn't?"

Sasha shook her head. "Not completely . . . but it wasn't Were contagion. Truthfully, I've never directly felt anything like it in my life."

* * *

This was the part of her job that she hated most, the aftermath forensics. A cloud of flies took to the air as she covered her nose and plowed through the swarm. Louisiana in July was no joke. Heat and death roiled the acid in her empty stomach, and she was glad that she only had half a cup of coffee in it.

Thick sulfur stench assaulted her nose as she stooped down to look at the claw marks on an arm and hand that was still attached to a camera. Carefully lifting the tissue by the open gashes along the bicep, she took a section of loose flesh off the limb with a pair of tweezers, dropped it on a petri dish, and covered it with the lid.

"Mark this claw tear sample," she said to the soldier beside her. "Watch where you step, it's gruesome out here. Ship that on dry ice to Doctor Xavier Holland at NORAD."

The soldier nodded and extended the cooler for her with his eyes watering from the fumes.

"Just one more, and then you guys can bag 'em and tag 'em," she said. "I need a bite site for saliva."

Sasha stood and allowed her gaze to scan the ground, looking for a gouged body part. But everything that she saw seemed as though giant claws had raked it. The torn-off limbs clearly had been removed by powerful swipes. So had most of the guttings. Then she spotted a crushed skull that had been shorn from the body and walked over to it.

The person's face was crushed flat as though each side of the head had been held in a vise-like grip. Brains had exploded out of the back; the eyes had obviously burst from their sockets given the sudden pressure. But to actually get the head off the shoulders required huge fangs.

Hurrying to the gruesome task, Sasha called over her assistant and got another lab evidence dish and several swabs. Green, slimy goo mixed with blackening blood stuck to the long swab and came away from the bite site in a tar-like string. Her assistant turned away and finally tossed his cookies.

"Sorry, ma'am," he said, panting and covering his mouth and nose with his forearm.

"Not a problem, soldier," Sasha said, stripping off her latex gloves and dropping them in the cooler with the last sample. "Just as long as you missed a body and didn't upchuck in the cooler, it's all good."

Fresh air never felt so good. She didn't care that it was close to ninety-eight degrees or that the humidity was probably 102; she just needed the downwind scents of the true outdoors to clean the filth out of her sinuses.

Every so often, Sasha leaned her head out of the Humvee window and took a deep breath. It would have been easier to shadow-jump, but after what she'd seen, she was bone-weary. A little normal human companionship, even by way of a silent MP, was better than going into the misty darkness alone.

She gave her driver the location of Lawrence DeWitt's apartment and jumped out of the vehicle when it came to a full stop on the street.

"Wait here," she told him. "I'll be ten minutes, tops."

It seemed like a simple thing. She just wanted to check on the kid and ask him a few more questions.

But when she came out of his closet, for a moment all she could do was stand there.

Blood and flesh were everywhere. Sulfur reeked so thickly in the room that it made her eyes water until she gagged. It was as though something had exploded DeWitt. A lone eyeball stared up at her from the rug. Green gook mixed with fat, muscle, bone, and flesh covered the walls and furniture, splattered his television and computer screens. The kitchen cabinets and counter were sprayed, and every few feet she could see chunks of flesh embedded in the blood-soaked rug.

"Shit . . ." Sasha backed into the closet and came out in the alley to begin casing the building for signs of how the attacker had gotten in.

If it was Were, it could have just crashed through the door, a wall, or a window, but the building was intact, just as DeWitt's doors and windows seemed to be. He was fortified against Vampires, since her little visit, unless he'd foolishly opened the door for one—which was very, very possible. But she'd never seen Vampires off somebody like this. Then again, they might have thought he and his crew had opened Ariel Beauchamp's coffin to daylight and been really pissed. Plus, he had ratted them out on cell phone video, which she'd sent over the airwaves to Winter's. "Damn, damn, damn!"

With a knife in her conscience, she walked back to the military vehicle. "Let the colonel know there's been another killing. One civilian, male, ID: Lawrence De-Witt. No need for a body bag, just an evidence cooler and a wet vac."

*   *   *

Elder Vlad opened his eyes in his lair and chuckled as his fangs lengthened. He breathed in deeply and then closed his eyes again, sending his thoughts to Cerridwen.

Have you watched the news, love?

She opened her eyes as her fingers curled around the icy armrests of her throne. "Yes," she murmured. "The butcherings leave nothing to the imagination. The humans are now fully engaged, I suspect."

Yes . . . you and I now have our wolf hunt. All that is left now is to bring it all to a vote.

Hunter sat before his grandfather, listening to his slow post-trance speech pattern while trying to understand the ancient wisdom embedded in the parables and images he conveyed.

"There is a twin evil slithering in the darkness. Two souls inside the same body . . . one is but a faint wisp of life—the other ferocious." Silver Hawk drew a labored breath, and Hunter placed a hand on his shoulder.

"Grandfather, you must rest. How deeply did you go into the shadow lands for this information?"

Bear Shadow and Crow Shadow glanced at each other when the elderly shaman didn't respond.

"He was in at least twenty-four hours without relenting," Bear Shadow confided. "There were times he seemed to be fighting something or wrestling something."

"Grandfather . . . why didn't you call me to you in the shadow lands? You went through the demon doors, didn't you!"

Hunted squatted down before his grandfather, who was seated on the cabin sofa.

"I am old; my life force is to be used for the future generations, not to cling to this world as though I am unaware that there is another side."

Hunter closed his eyes and hugged his grandfather for a moment before coming to sit beside him.

"I had to go in and seal the breach," Silver Hawk said in a rasp. "The sigils against each spirit in our clan that the Unseelie left from the earlier war—it weakened the veil between the worlds. The shadow lands were in peril. Something got out and had a grudge against the way of the wolf. This thing that is trapped cannot go back into our shadow lands or slither through by way of the demon doors. It is trapped in the world of the humans, hence it will continue feeding until it is destroyed."

Hunter pulled out his cell phone and showed him the image of Amy Chen that Shogun had given them all. "This girl, is she carrying the demon you speak of?"

Silver Hawk shook his head no. "She is the whisper of life and Light battling within her own body against a ferocious predator within. Her parents' prayers are keeping her light alive . . . but this other thing is stronger than what lies within her."

"Esmeralda, Esmeralda, please open the door!"

The locks to the town house quickly turned, and the witch opened the door for Sir Rodney, hustling him inside.

"This is a quiet neighborhood, Rodney, I've never—"

"Have you been watching the news?"

"No. Why?"

He yanked his cell phone out of his trouser pocket and opened it. "Have you seen this girl before?"

Esmeralda took the phone from him and studied the image hard. "Yes . . . she's new. She just came to our second night of full-moon rituals and was immediately invited to join our coven. Her energy was so strong, surprisingly so for a girl of so few years."

"How long did she attend?"

Esmeralda gave him a quizzical look. "Why?"

"It is of vital importance, love. Please do not be difficult."

"She came at sundown, as is customary," Esmeralda said, growing peevish. "She didn't come with an escort or a mentor. She just seemed to know where to find our meeting, which portends that her psychic abilities are extremely strong. She stayed until sunrise, when we all dispersed."

"You are sure about this?" he asked, now holding her by her upper arms.

"Yes, why? And you're hurting me." Esmeralda pulled out of his grasp. "I've never seen you like this, and you're scaring me."

"Do you know where she lives . . . where she sleeps by day?"

"Oh, come on," Esmeralda said with a smirk. "She's not a Vampire. That much we know for sure. She has a strong life force and knew all the rituals by heart."

"You said you trusted me, so I'll ask you again. Do you know where she sleeps by day?"

Esmeralda shook her head no. "But now that she's taken the coven ritual, I can consult my crystal ball and possibly find out."

* * *

Shogun sat under a wide yew tree in the teahouse garden watching the miasma of sparkling light dance about his head like dust motes. The Faeries had gotten Sir Rodney's Fae missive, and it was important to stay extremely still to hear what the tiny beings were saying. In his mind he blocked out distant traffic noise, becoming Zen—one with the peaceful oasis. This was the last place in the world he ever wanted to revisit . . . the place where he'd fallen so deeply in love with Sasha . . . the place where she'd allowed her shadow to dance with his.

For now, he couldn't think about that. He had to hear what the Faeries were whispering. They knew the girl in the picture. She'd been here just the day prior to have tea. He would not tell them that inside the beautiful face and delicate body lived a feline monster that could take their tiny lives.

They led him to the salon where she'd been and then dispersed. That was as much as they knew. Shogun entered it and tensed. He could smell her light signature scent, the new one she'd stolen from the innocent Amy Chen. But worse yet, his aunt was toying with him, knowing he would try to track her by traditional Were methods. She'd come to the same private room where he'd been with Sasha, where he'd tasted her mouth for the very first time.

His aunt was such a bitch.

Okay, now this shit was really getting on her nerves. Sasha stood by Doc's side in the lab as she handed the cooler to him and Clarissa. Waiting for a flight was out of the question; she needed immediate answers.

Her stomach did a weird flip-flop as she glanced at Bradley and Winters, who were on computers and ready for sample analysis to begin. Woods and Fisher hung back, waiting on Sasha to give them the go-ahead that they could join the fight. But first, she wanted to know what they were dealing with.

"I can't even begin to tell you what the scene looked like back at that kid's apartment. I've gotta know if Vamps did this or if this was from a rampaging Were Leopard." She set Russell Conway's digital camera down between Winters and Bradley. "I also need to know what that entity is that he captured on the vid. Shogun made an interesting point: Lady Jung Suk—our suspected predator—is white with black spots when in Were form. But what attacked that Ghost Finders, Inc., crew was transparent and black. Slow the frames down and you'll see what I mean."

"You okay, Sasha?" Clarissa asked as Sasha blotted her forehead. "You look flushed."

"I've just seen a lot of really horrific shit in the last twenty-four hours, and didn't really eat this morning."

"Get her some orange juice," Doc said to Fisher. "She looks like her blood sugar's dropping and she's about to pass out."

"I'm cool, I'm cool," Sasha said, weakly protesting.

Ignoring her, Fisher left the room as Clarissa opened the first cooler and then screamed. Everybody was on their feet, and the adrenaline spike instantly revived Sasha.

"Bradley, get a brick-dust circle going, stat!" Clarissa shouted, backing away from the cooler. "Demon essence in the house!"

Clarissa waited until Bradley was able to dig in the lab drawers and rush back to begin pouring the reddish dust into the floor from the hole he'd made in his fist. Then she put some on her hands and carried the cooler to the center of the circle, cautiously opened the lid, and jumped back.

Angry green slime hissed and popped and slithered over the edge of the cooler like a fast-moving cold fire. As soon as Sasha saw it, she vomited green bile, which Clarissa and Bradley hit with brick dust.

"Get a circle around her, people," Clarissa said, watching Bradley, Winters, and Doc jump into action. "You hold the line at the door, Woods; don't let it get out of the lab!"

"What am I supposed to do, 'Rissa?" he shouted, running toward the open drawer and grabbing a handful of dust.

"Make a line in front of the door!" she yelled back as Doc held Sasha up while Bradley began saying the Twenty-third Psalm in a very loud voice.

Just as suddenly as the fracas began, the essence in the middle of the circles quieted, turned from a vibrant green to a gooey black tar, and then torched.

"I don't think we need any analysis on the stuff in cooler number one. This was definitely a pure demon that took those folks," Bradley said.

"Bigger question is, how did Sasha get infected?" Doc peered at her with concern and helped her to a chair.

"I probably picked it up while mucking around at the kill sites," she said, wobbling to sit down.

"I want a full evaluation on her—she's not going

back through shadow lands in this state . . . there could still be some infection in her," Doc argued, folding his arms in front of her.

"As much as I appreciate the concern, no can do, Doc." Sasha offered him a wan smile. "There's a huge problem down in the Delta, obviously . . . whatever was in me for sure came out—my apologies to the team."

"Clarissa, can you scan her psychically, and at least make me feel better?"

"No!" Bradley shouted. "Just let Sasha step through some Holy Water or something."

Sasha nodded. "Clarissa's been through enough. Flash me with brick dust, the Twenty-third Psalm, Holy Water, whatever, but leave Clarissa out of any—"

"I'm okay, guys, no problem . . . but I think Sasha's all right. I'm not getting bad vibes now."

Bradley walked away from Clarissa, raking his hair in frustration.

"You're sure?" Doc said, looking at Clarissa hard. "And how are you feeling? You okay, McGill?"

"Yeah, and never better, sir," Clarissa replied, going to Bradley. "I'm all right." She placed a hand on his back.

"Then humor me and let me purge you, just in case," he muttered, slowly drawing her into a hug.

"Well, now that all the excitement is over, what the hell was that?" Winters looked at the cooler and ran his fingers through his hair just as Fisher came back in the door.

"Yo, what's wrong everybody?" Fisher said, glancing around. "What'd I miss?"

CHAPTER 18

Sasha sat across from Hunter and Silver Hawk, while Crow Shadow and Bear Shadow patrolled the perimeter of the leadership cabin. She felt a hundred times better, even though the information she'd gleaned so far really wouldn't help the wolf Federations fight the charges lobbed by the Vampires.

"It's a possession demon," she said calmly.

"A what?" Hunter stood. "And it tried to attach itself to you?"

"Yeah, pretty messed up what happened in the lab." She looked at Silver Hawk. "A piece of this same thing tried to get inside Sir Rodney and Clarissa, but the Fae blasted it before it could go full-blown. We've gotta get you cleaned out, just in case, all right?"

Hunter paced away from the table, seeming like he was ready to explode from frustration.

The elderly man nodded and released a long breath. "I do not feel like myself."

"Your silver aura is so strong that the thing is struggling within it, most likely," Sasha said in a quiet tone. "Did you touch anyone?"

Silver Hawk looked at Hunter. "Just my grandson."

"Why would a strong sorceress like Lady Jung Suk join a coven?" Sir Rodney said, staring at Esmeralda's crystal ball. "It doesn't make sense."

"It does if you want to amass even greater power," she said, watching the mist begin to part within the murky globe. "She could feed, like a Vampire, on all the souls in the group, sucking their magic from them, their life force . . . If she was given a body by the Vampires, as you say, beloved, then she would want to have a way to get strong enough to one day break their hold and control over her."

"That definitely fits the bill for her personality type." Sir Rodney sat back and rubbed his chin. "But how do we find her?"

"Patience . . ." Esmeralda sighed. "I'm trying to do a little remote viewing, and that requires concentration, all right?"

He held up a hand. "Sorry."

"Thank you," she said, and then gave him a sexy sidelong glance. "I want amnesty forever in the sidhe for this."

"You know that can be arranged," he said, leaning in close to her. "So, when we find this very bad little witch, how do we make sure her Were Leopard doesn't escape back out into disembodied form if we simply shoot her with a silver crossbow shot or something equally drastic?"

"Oh, no," Esmeralda said quickly, now turning to face him straight-on. "You must trap her in silver so her Were Leopard spirit cannot cross that plane. She will separate from the girl's body, pulling her spirit out of it to run from the silver. So mesh and then some sort of strong bars or energy field are required to actually trap her fleeing spirit. But if you want to save the girl, you'll have to pull her away quickly and try to resuscitate her terrified spirit. But to kill a disembodied means—"

A horrific scream left Esmeralda's throat as Sir Rodney grabbed her by the shoulders.

"What's wrong, love! What's wrong?"

Blood poured from Esmeralda's once lovely eyes, leaving dark holes in the sockets as she clawed at her face.

"I cannot see, help me, help me, she's blinded me!"

Lady Jung Suk slowly walked away from her kitchen sink and dropped the sharp knife into it with a clatter. Blood stained the white porcelain as a satisfied purr rumbled in her throat.

"That will teach you to spy on your elders," she mewed. She went outside in her garden to enjoy the late-morning sun.

Doc squinted as he peered into the microscope one last time and then sat back. "Lab analysis shows that the bites from victims one and two found on the first night the murders began are different from the others at the Bayou House, and the last victim, Lawrence DeWitt, wasn't bitten at all. That was more like some sort of protoplasmic depth charge, go figure. But those mauling victims prior to the ones found at the Bayou House didn't have any trace of that highly volatile demon virus resident in them. Now, why that cooler of tissue samples from there snapped, crackled, and popped like it did doesn't make sense to me. If it's the same contaminant in it as was in the bodies we brought back from Colonel Madison's first mission, then it should have reacted similarly."

"Unless an infected host, like Sasha, wasn't nearby," Bradley said, coming over to the now still samples.

"Bradley, my friend, you just may have a point."

Sasha put the cell phone down on the table and simply stared at it.

"What's wrong? What did Sir Rodney say?"

Sasha closed her eyes and ran her palms down her face. "Esmeralda, a friend of his, was attempting to locate Lady Jung Suk through opening up a remote viewing . . . she'd joined their coven so it was even easier than normal . . . and then something went wrong. Esmeralda's eyes got clawed out."

"Damn . . . ," Hunter murmured.

Silver Hawk nodded. "This is the powerful sorceress I spoke of. The predator within that is extinguishing the spirit of the girl's body she stole. In three days and nights, once the moon ceases to be full, the girl will float away and become an earthbound spirit. Lady Jung Suk is a being of darkness; she will never let the innocent girl find the Light . . . and she is so much stronger than that young girl."

"Rodney's going off the grid to take Esmeralda back to the sidhe for protection, but he told me what Esmeralda said about how to catch Lady Jung Suk. We owe it to Amy Chen's family to try to save their daughter, if we can." Sasha stood and went to the window.

"I know my brother is distraught about what he witnessed when he went to visit her parents while investigating," Hunter said quietly. "Shogun has not been himself since that time. His smile is slow, and it does not reach his eyes."

Sasha nodded and lifted the hair off the nape of her neck in frustration. "I almost don't care anymore that we only have shaky evidence to link the Vamps to unleashing an entity that killed two humans."

"I know how you feel, Sasha," Hunter said in a gentle tone. "According to UCE rules, they only care that the Vampires may have facilitated the embodiment of Lady Jung Suk—a treasonable offense, due to the fact that she was a criminal found guilty of crimes against the Seelie and was on the run. That would be enough to mitigate any claims they have against us, because under UCE law, thankfully, you cannot have blood on your hands and seek justice. You have to be clean. The Vampires are not."

"But they don't care about that poor girl, or even those stupid kids who thought they could bargain for immortality with the Vampires," Sasha said, waving her arms about. "Something's wrong with a system where any life or anyone is considered a second-class citizen."

"And as such," Hunter said slowly, "the UCE will not care about a possession demon on the loose. They only care to know that it is not wolves who have been doing the killings and thus giving the supernatural community undue exposure. They will call for a demon hunt, exterminate it, and then try to do damage control."

"Those are the twin evils that I spoke of," Silver Hawk said in a faraway tone. His gaze went beyond the window to a place they couldn't reach. "One strikes at the life force of an innocent, the other strikes at the life force of a community—and in order to bring balance back and clear the wolf Federations, you will have to solve a dilemma that will help others more than it may help yourselves."

"Before we do anything," Sasha said, going to Silver Hawk but not touching him, "we've got to get your aura cleaned."

After days of craziness, they had at least solved the first part of the jigsaw puzzle. They now knew what it was, but had run into the brick wall of trying to figure out where it was. Making things more complicated was the fact that they had to locate the predators but couldn't immediately engage them until they figured out how to stop them.

"That's right," Hunter said, speaking to Shogun in short bursts of information. "We've got like twenty-four more hours to find Lady Jung Suk before she completely patterns over that girl's soul, but if you do locate her, you can't kill her in the conventional manner or you'll hurt the victim."

Sasha watched Hunter as he paused. Both her eyes and Silver Hawk's were on him.

"Yes," Hunter finally replied. "Just scout her location and get back to the sidhe. Sir Rodney is conferring with his top magic advisors there about how to contain and destroy both types of entities. Esmeralda was severely injured because she wasn't clear about just how strong a force Lady Jung Suk is. So, brother, I repeat, do not engage the target. Wait for us at the sidhe."

They looked at Hunter as he disconnected the call. Crow Shadow and Bear Shadow had come into the cabin to stand at the ready for the cleansing of Silver Hawk. The elderly man stood slowly and nodded toward Hunter.

"Let us begin," he said quietly.

"They used brick dust in the lab," Sasha said, nervously glancing around.

"That will do in a pinch," Silver Hawk said. "But go to my desk, daughter, and extract the medicine box."

Sasha quickly moved to the handmade, antique rolltop desk and extracted an old silver tin.

"Bring this outside," Silver Hawk said calmly. He then walked past everyone onto the porch and down to the small clearing in front of the steps. "There is a pouch filled with silver shavings and herbs. Make a circle with this around Hunter and me, and then use the eagle feathers to draw another circle around that."

Working with unsteady hands, Sasha began to walk around the two men standing side by side in the front yard. Bear Shadow held the box; Crow Shadow held the eagle feathers. But as she neared the far side of the circle where she'd begun, nasty green ooze rose from Silver Hawk's back, flowed over his head, and tried to smother him.

Hunter grabbed his grandfather to keep him from

falling to the ground while trying to yank away the gooey toxin from his nose and mouth. "Close the circle!" he shouted to Sasha. "Quickly!"

Running backward, Sasha closed the circle, trying not to focus on the men who were gagging. Crow Shadow hurriedly brought her the eagle feathers and she raced around the circle, drawing a second perimeter in the dirt. The moment the second circle was drawn, the slime rose up like a giant serpent and began to slither around their bodies. In seconds Silver Hawk had become Silver Shadow, shedding his human form to become his wolf-self. The magnificent ancient being made a stunning vertical leap to go after the slimy head of the attacking entity before it could angrily whip around and go after his grandson.

Hunter doubled over, puked, and came up enraged, his wolf taking over his human so fast that his clothes hadn't hit the ground when he went airborne. Both wolves tackled the slime to the ground, decimating it, savaging it, until a piercing, shrill scream echoed in the glen.

The stench of sulfur made Sasha, Bear, and Crow cover their faces with their forearms. As soon as she saw the green pieces twitching like a severed worm on the ground, Sasha took a handful of silver dust and flung it toward the head; then she dusted both Silver Shadow and Hunter for good measure. Both men in the middle of the circle began chanting and walking around the slowly dying thing as it took on a dark, tar-like consistency and began to burn.

"Well done, daughter," Silver Hawk said, seeming much improved. "I will make you a shaman yet."

CHAPTER 19

Although she had a million questions swirling around in her mind, she only had time for a few before they left North Country by way of the shadow lands. At least now she knew how wicked both predators she was tracking could be. Silver Hawk had gotten a case of the nasties by going on a spirit walk without his amulet and tangling with the thing directly in his vision. Anybody else probably wouldn't have made it, so she was very glad that Silver Hawk decided to come back to New Orleans with her and Hunter, along with Bear and Crow. For this mission, they needed excellent trackers and a serious shaman. Bradley had his brick dust, but silver shavings, ground turquoise, bits of ancestor wolf bones, and white sage herbs was like C-4 next to a cherry bomb.

She and Hunter had also learned a very valuable lesson about how to supercharge their amulets before going into a demon battle, and just the fact that they were wearing them had everything to do with why the thing had only coated them and not penetrated as deeply as it could have.

Now the task was to create a lure. There were four sets of murders to be concerned about, and the killers each had their own signature and agendas, even if those weren't fully clear to her yet.

First, they were pretty damned sure Lady Jung Suk had taken out the two students, Tanya Mays and Jim Baton—plus she'd hijacked poor Amy Chen's body, and injured Esmeralda just for trying to look at her. Then the second set of murders came when something really wicked went after four marines as well as four members of Ghost Finders, Inc., out at the Bayou House, leaving an eyewitness each time, possibly for shock value.

The third murder set came by way of an unknown assailant who went after the students' Vampire mentor, Ariel Beauchamp, and a few of his lair kittens. Why was anybody's guess, but with it being so close in degrees of separation to the other murders, it had to be a related hit. Death by daylight was something done by someone who knew what they were doing, because Vamps generally didn't just lie there and play dead while one broke into their mausoleums and tried to fry them with the sun.

Then, last but not least, someone or something had killed poor Lawrence DeWitt—who'd arguably deserved it, but the murder still didn't sit right with Sasha. Doc said the green goo wasn't the same demon goo that had popped out of the cooler like a jack-in-the-box . . . it was more like some type of cold-water, slow-moving protoplasm, almost like cold algae. She couldn't even wrap her brain around that at the moment.

All of this notwithstanding, they were now stuck with solving four groups of murders when they'd only come down here to clear the wolf Federations of acting against the Vampires prematurely. These horrible events had nothing to do with wolves but everything to do with them. Regardless of politics, the wolf Federations had been thrust into the role of policing a supernatural community obviously gone wild.

Sasha stood in the bayou with the others waiting for Sir Rodney's archers to collect them. Frustration over the situation was clear in the group's body language and hard-set expressions. The familiar whistle in the trees couldn't come fast enough. As soon as the lithe archers appeared on high tree limbs, her group gave them a disgruntled greeting and trudged through the swamp.

It took a bit to get everyone settled in the war room. Sir Rodney was the last to appear.

"How is she?" Sasha said, monitoring the strain in Sir Rodney's expression.

He shook his head. "She will live, but she will never have her beautiful eyes again. It was a travesty . . . no one as good of heart as she should have to suffer so."

"I'm sorry," Hunter said, holding Sir Rodney's gaze. "I think I can speak for the group when I say that we were all deeply saddened to hear of her tragic injury."

"Yes . . . ," Sasha said. "What can we do? Is there anything we can do to make her more comfortable?"

"Thank you all, but no. She has been bespelled, healed as best we can, and the rest is just a matter of time. She is sleeping peacefully now."

Everyone looked down at their clasped hands. It was Shogun who spoke first.

"The only way to give this any meaning is to not

allow Lady Jung Suk to take another life. I sat with the parents of Amy Chen . . ." Shogun's voice trailed off as he shook his head. "For the first time in my life, I had no words. I did not know how to help those people or to comfort them."

Sir Rodney's most senior magic advisor stepped forward and drew his wand from his billowing sleeve. "We have conferred on the matter of grave consequence," the elderly Gnome said in a wheezing rasp. "Now that we know the life force of the young girl, as well as the energy pattern of Lady Jung Suk's coven, we can find her."

"But you saw what happened to Esmeralda," Sir Rodney said, quickly. "Garth, you may be my advisor, but you are also my eldest friend . . . since my father's rule."

"Unfortunately, Esmeralda is a young witch . . . impulsive and trusting. She was not aware of how dangerous this being was because she had seen her inside the body of the young girl. But we are not so naive." He swept his arm out to indicate the group of old wizards who would work with him. "We are formidable, and have set the crystal miasma to track her within a mirrored globe. This time she will blind herself. But we must work quickly."

"What do we need to do to assist you?" Shogun asked. "This case is a matter of principle. This abomination is of my distant family line, but Lady Jung Suk is of my blood, nonetheless. As much as I want to, I cannot deny the affiliation. Therefore, after having met the Chens and felt their pain enter my spirit, I must be at the forefront of this battle."

"And I will stand with you on this, brother," Hunter said, returning Shogun's slight bow.

Murmurs of agreement from the others followed Hunter's declaration. Garth, seeming satisfied, signaled to the four Gnomes standing at the perimeter of the room, and they extracted their wands in one synchronized move. They then lifted gnarled hands to catch what dropped down from thin air and brought forward a thick silver mesh the length and width of a king-size bedsheet that looked like silver chain mail. Immediately Shogun stood and went to the far side of the room.

"This is why it is good that your brother and the Shadow Wolves present will be there for your aid. Her body must be captured by this. We can glamour a camouflage in the bayou for it, and our archers can also help drive her into it. But that is where the delicate extraction must occur."

"Yes," another advisor warned. "We must hold the spirit that flees the body in a magic charge, while strong wolves drag the girl away. Someone with healing power must tend to the girl and speak to her frightened spirit, keeping her in the silver mail so as to disallow the soul predator from trying to reenter her."

"Hunter and I are healers, as is Silver Hawk," Sasha said.

"Then let your most seasoned healer work on the girl, while your most fierce spiritual warrior undertakes perhaps the most difficult aspect of this separation." Garth let out a weary breath. "As you know, true immortals have no souls . . . we have a different spirit being inside. But a human soul can call the angel Lights. That is what must happen. We can hold her as long as we can, but her disembodied spirit must be sent to the ultimate Light."

"Oh, I so can do that," Sasha said.

Hunter looked at Sasha and then at his brother. "If there needs to be one to pull the girl away from Lady Jung Suk's claws, I have that strength, and my grandfather is the most seasoned healer of our clan . . . He will be able to comfort the girl and to keep her weakened spirit light from going out."

"Then what of me?" Shogun said. "I cannot go near the mesh. How can I contribute?"

"Lure her, taunt her, and speak to her through the mirrored miasma that will track her. Tell her you want to have it out once and for all . . . use the years of family hatred to bring her to the trap." Garth looked around and pointed a crooked finger. "But beware. She will not come alone. There will be plenty of battle to be had by all. She will come with her constituents, we are so sure."

"I do have backup, you know," Sasha said. "If she comes with Vampires, it would be within the human military's right to make a retaliatory strike . . . They lost four marines, and by human standards also lost four students and four civilian adults."

"They'll have to be thoroughly briefed, then, Sasha," Hunter said carefully. "Not just for their safety, but for ours. If they freak out in a firefight when they see multiple entities or freeze at the trigger . . . I don't know. We really need to weigh that option."

"Okay, you make a valid point . . . but let's keep it on the table as a backup option. I have to brief Colonel Madison, anyway. I don't want anybody, human or supernatural, getting hurt who doesn't have to."

"All right," Hunter said, his tone still noncommittal. "As a plan B."

"When you send Lady Jung Suk to the Light, you will lose your evidence trail," Garth said, his tone measured and cautious.

"I don't care," Shogun said. "It is the right thing to do, and we know the truth of what happened before."

"Again, I stand with my brother in this," Hunter said.

"And I," Sasha said.

"And I," Bear Shadow chimed in with both Crow Shadow and Silver Hawk.

"Your honor is moving," Sir Rodney said, "but the alliance will crumble. They will still win, even if your honor is indisputable."

"They cannot stand up under the pen strike of the high court," Sasha said. "When we answer the charges and the book of truths opens to our testimony, our blood will not sizzle and burn, but will take to the book."

"Let us hope that you are correct," Sir Rodney said, seeming unsure. "It is a delicate game we play, with chess pieces not well placed on the board."

"Don't worry," Sasha said, holding his gaze. "Some things are just right."

"But there is also another predator that we must flush out of hiding," Hunter said, sending his gaze around the table. "That one may prove harder to track and trap than Lady Jung Suk. The possession demon that is feeding on humans and making it look as though it was wolf attacks."

"I have an idea," Sasha said. "But for this one I really am going to need Colonel Madison's help."

* * *

As insane as it was, Colonel Madison had her standing in front of a small classroom on the base, speaking to special forces guys. It was both an honor and one of the crazier things she'd decided to do in her life. But while Fisher and Woods were on a military flight to join her at the base, the two hours to give a small unit a heads-up that could possibly save their lives was the very least she could do.

"When Lieutenant Woods and Lieutenant Fisher arrive, they will be your point," Sasha said, holding a dry-erase marker. "They know the difference between a friendly supernatural and a deadly one. If you kill a friendly in a firefight, you significantly degrade your cover, understood? One friendly wolf can cover about ten human men, so the loss of one—especially if there's another Were on your ass—makes you dog meat. Literally."

Sasha turned to the whiteboard and began sketching a loose diagram of the Bayou House area and incoming gravel roads.

"I don't have to tell you, we lost four good Marines out there, four civilians, and it might have been the kill site for two or three missing students—two of whom were later found half eaten. Your task for this mission is to remain in a backup position only. There will be supernaturals deep in that bayou scrapping it out at velocities you cannot fathom. But they do fatigue and could get overrun by hostile forces. If you hear the howl, you come a-knockin' and let your weapon start a-rockin'. We clear?"

"The howl, sir?" one confused lieutenant asked, glancing around the classroom.

When others smirked at him, Sasha set down her dry-erase marker calmly. "It was a good question, Lieutenant Campbell. Under other circumstances, you wouldn't be able to trust the howl, because it could be coming from a demon-infected Were . . . that's why I'm bringing in Woods and Fisher. They have superior hearing, know the calls, and know all our voices." She threw her head back and howled, and then smiled as the stunned group of Marines simply stared at her. "Kinda cool, ain't it? Yeah . . . well, wolves can hear that for miles."

Another hand raised, and she motioned with her chin for the soldier to ask his question.

"Uh, Captain . . . you said to shoot by the color of the glow of their eyes. Red or shiny black for Vampires, and never go for the gold—your wolf company . . . but there's a hostile out there who might have green glowers . . . I mean, these are actual eye colors we're supposed to be looking for?"

"Yes, Lieutenant," Sasha said, looking at Colonel Madison for a moment. "Sir, it's going to be necessary for me to show these gentlemen what you saw, in order that they don't get jumpy and either freeze in a firefight or just frag one of us."

"That is exactly why I had everyone disarm before coming in to class," Colonel Madison said calmly, folding his arms. "Carry on . . . this is gonna be good."

Sasha chuckled. "All right, Lieutenant Peterson, this is what you are looking for." She closed her eyes for a moment, took a deep breath, and summoned a little of her inner wolf to the fore.

Instantly the front row of the class was out of their seats, having knocked into the rows behind them. Soldiers scrambled. She heard "Oh, shit" so many times that she almost laughed out loud.

"Now do you understand why it is vital that you get used to seeing this? I am a friendly. I'm your instructor. I'll be the one to save your ass from something really horrible that will eat you alive and make you wish you were never born." She turned to the colonel. "Sir, can you turn off the lights and have one of the men pull the shades. You think this is scary with the lights on, wait till you see it in the dark."

"Uh, Sasha—I mean, Captain . . . we don't have an EMT squad at the ready . . . one of these men will have a heart attack. Do you think this is wise?"

"I do, sir—because there'll be no ambulance out there in the bayou, that's for sure."

"Agreed," he said and nodded to a very nervous soldier who stood by the window seeming as though he was ready to leap out of it.

"Colonel, sir!" a squad commander from the back yelled. "This, this stuff really exists? All this stuff she was telling us about and what we were taught about in the unit . . . it's, it's not hypothetical, sir?"

"She can show you better than I can tell you," Colonel Madison said with his hand on the light switch as the shades lowered. "I lost four good men out there in the bayou because I thought this was some sort of joke . . . that the researchers were talking about the *potential* of supernatural activity, and my job was just to go out there and debunk it. Not so. Whatever you've heard in the general media press conferences is to keep the civilian public from mass panic." He hit the light.

An audible gasp cut through the room.

"This is what a wolf's eyes look like under the moonlight. This room is only partially darkened, just like a forest would be—you still have some visibility coming in from the sides of the shades, just like moonlight comes through the tree line. But if my eyes were red, that is not a good thing."

She walked back and forth in the front of the room. "If I have four protruding teeth—upper and lower canines—you can bet I'm a wolf or a Were from the big-cat family. If I only have two fangs, unnatural eye-teeth, I'd be a Vamp. Wave your hand in the back of the room if you can see light glinting off my teeth in a flash."

"Holy Christ!" a man shouted in the far back as half the room retreated again.

"Thank you, Lieutenant. I'll take that as an affirmative."

Sasha blew out a long breath. "Now, gentlemen. I'm about to show you something that may put you down on the ground or make you need to hit the barracks to change your fatigues." She turned to Colonel Madison. "With your permission, sir, only for training purposes."

He nodded slowly, but then stepped back, not seeming sure himself about her altered state. And then she shape-shifted.

It was a beautiful transformation, if she did say so herself . . . elegantly done with finesse. No angry lunging to strike terror in the hearts of men. She just strode across the room a few paces and transformed into her wolf, leaving her clothing to float down into a pool of fabric on the floor. Then she did give them a little theater, preening and taking a stance like a championship show dog before she threw back her head and howled. It felt so good to finally let the people she worked with see who she was and what she was—the fact that two guys passed out and one was hyperventilating while the rest were up on chairs in the back of the class was not her fault. This somehow felt even better than when she first let her small unit know what she was; this was a milestone in awareness, if not acceptance.

Loping over to her pile of clothes, Sasha picked up everything in her jaws except her boots, then went into the shadow of the front desk, shifted back to her human to dress quickly in the shadow lands, came back into the classroom through the door, and hit the lights.

"Okay, gentlemen. So now you've seen your first shape-shift. I'm a smaller version of what you'll see in combat. The males are about one and a half times my body weight—and there's a pure black three-hundred-pounder on our side. This is why it's important for you to be acclimated before you have a weapon in your hand and before a supernatural is lunging at you full-force. You have got to be able to make a split-second decision, know if it's friend or foe, and cover yourself," she said calmly. "Get those men up off the floor in the back and any soldier who needs to go clean up, no problem."

CHAPTER 20

"You did what?" Doc exclaimed into the speakerphone as the rest of the team at NORAD burst out laughing.

"OMG, Trudeau," Winters said from the background.

"How many Marines hit the floor?" Bradley asked in his typical sarcastic tone.

"In all seriousness, Sasha, did anybody need medical attention?" Clarissa asked as the only calm voice in the group.

"No," Colonel Madison said, entering the conversation. He didn't seem the least bit amused, and his gruff reply made the team on the other end of the line clear their throats. "It is not something anyone sees every day, so the fact that some of the men were a little . . . wary, cannot be held against them."

"Certainly not, Colonel," Sasha said, forcing contrition into her voice. "What they witnessed might just save their lives."

"Duly noted," Doc said.

Sasha could just imagine him giving the group the

eye along with hand signals to save the laughs for when the colonel got off the line.

"But we need your help with a theory," Sasha said, frowning. She pushed back from the colonel's desk and began to pace. It helped her think better. "I have no idea if this will work—and it's all predicated on us having any success whatsoever on the mission we intend to embark upon tonight. But as I told you, we've got two known predators hunting humans. We've made an ID on one of them, but the other is still at large . . . we have no clue as to where it could be."

She looked at Colonel Madison and ruffled the hair up off the nape of her neck, thinking out loud. "It left him alive, but for some reason didn't attach to him as a carrier. It jumped on me, though, and I had to go get it cleaned off while I was in the lab . . . It also attacked Silver Hawk when he tried to engage it while on a vision quest, and he passed it to Hunter temporarily."

"Are they clean now?" Colonel Madison asked quickly.

"You took the question right out of my mouth, sir," Doc said into the speaker.

"Affirmative," Sasha said, stopping by the window. "I don't feel anything untoward here at the base, either . . . which makes me think it probably passed over that guy—the reporter who was also a sole survivor, like the colonel."

"Russell Conway," Winters said, the sound of his keyboard clicking away in the background. "But he's not just some hotshot local-yokel reporter—he's also an anti-paranormal hothead."

"A what, Winters? Speak in plain English," Sasha

said, coming to the colonel's desk to lean closer to the speakerphone.

"This guy has a long blog in the obscure rant communities online—you know, the same folks that obsess over Big Foot sightings. Anyway, Russell Conway goes by Wolfkiller100 when he posts . . . and I was able to find some old articles in the *South Dakota Sentinel,* since he often talks about the beauty of that North Country. There was a whole front-page story about a woman and a little girl being savaged by a grizzly bear thirty years ago, leaving a young teenage boy orphaned. The article said that the boy claimed the only thing that saved him was some sort of silver-and-turquoise Native American talisman that he'd begged for and that his mother brought him at the camping lodge gift shop earlier that day. The kid also claimed it wasn't a bear, but a wolf—but authorities said a wolf couldn't have done that level of damage to a human body unless it was a pack."

"Are you serious?" Sasha sat down slowly. "How do you find this stuff out, Winters?"

"I told you, my kung fu is strong, Captain. But Russell Conway's recent TV success made it a lot easier for me to dig into his background on the Web. I wanted to personally know who this guy was that had the stones to put together a team to go out in the bayou, and after we saw what jumped out of the cooler, I definitely thought we needed to know if we had a sole survivor carrying this contagion out to the general public."

"Damn . . . I must have been slipping," Sasha said, rubbing both palms down her face. "Good looking out."

"You were infected, Captain," Clarissa said. "Is there any wonder one thing got by you? That's why you have us, your team, as backup."

"Do we need to bring this guy in?" Colonel Madison said, becoming nervous. This time he stood and was the one who began to pace.

"I don't think so," Bradley said. "More than likely, just like you were clean after your tragic incident at the Bayou House, Conway was as well. All Winters's research shows is that this man had an agenda when he came down here. He undoubtedly experienced an attack of some sort by a supernatural as a kid, and the local authorities suppressed it as a grizzly attack. Sounds like this guy has been trying to get vindicated all his life . . . sorta like the alien abduction people. He's harmless—and God bless him; he got his fifteen minutes of fame at a very high price."

"Yeah . . . and now, unfortunately," Sasha said, "in order to lure the demon to a trap, we're going to have to take that short-lived win away from the poor man."

"How so?" Colonel Madison said, turning to look at Sasha directly.

"I don't even know if it'll work," she replied with a weary sigh. "But the way we're going to bait Lady Jung Suk out of hiding is by taunting her."

"It's risky," Bradley warned, "but a good offensive move. Demons hate a challenge to their existence . . . so, a press conference saying that the U.S. military cannot authenticate the images in Russell Conway's video would make it angry."

"I'll go to Conway and personally apologize to him," Sasha said. "It's not fair to make that poor man think he's crazy when the colonel gets up on a podium and states that the Bayou House deaths are under investigation as possibly being a ferocious pack of feral dogs that have taken up residence in the bayou, post–Hurricane Katrina." She looked at the colonel. "At some point, and I suspect in the near future, the government is going to have to take a position on this secrecy thing . . . too many civilians know, too many are getting hurt, and too many of our people in uniform have been deployed and are losing their lives trying to fight this stuff without the proper training."

The colonel nodded. "I will definitely take that under advisement and pass it up the chain of command. After what I've witnessed with my own eyes, as well as how I saw those men react in the classroom, I know you're right, Captain. I just don't have the authority to do so . . . but what I don't know, I can't be responsible for."

"Thank you, sir," Sasha said and then looked at the speakerphone again.

"Bradley . . . you said your research into possession demons shows that they have a primary host, and will stay with that host body, causing it to do horrendous things until they use up the life force in it or the body is somehow destroyed."

"Yes, that is how that particular entity functions," Bradley said.

"That's why you're the man," Sasha said. She gave the colonel a quick nod. "Dude is the best dark arts spec out there. He and Clarissa with second sight make one helluva team, sir."

"Thank you, Captain," Bradley said. "That's why it probably tried you, Silver Hawk, and Hunter . . . If it could get into a strong wolf body versus some other carrier—probably a local human—then why not. I'm sure that's why it's not jumping around from human body to human body, and since wolves have souls, unlike Vampires, you're the strongest choice in the area. Hopefully the human who's currently hosting it will see the colonel's news conference tomorrow morning, which might piss the demon off."

"That's the very loosely constructed plan I had," Sasha said, letting out another frustrated breath. "Looking for this thing is like looking for a needle in a haystack. We don't even know what human it's compromised."

"I don't mind going on a fishing expedition," Colonel Madison said. "Not after what I've seen. It beats sitting around and waiting for more people to lose their lives. Don't worry, at that news conference, I'll make that thing we're hunting mad as all get-out. I'll say in no uncertain terms, we're going back to the scene of the crime with a military camera crew, and some meat as bait, in an operation to prove to the public once and for all that there's nothing out there."

Sasha nodded. "Sounds like a plan, sir. The best we've got now, anyway . . . and maybe, just maybe, we can get it to show itself again. This time we'll be ready for it."

Back-to-back missions were not something she relished, but if they wanted to strike while the iron was hot, that's what they had to do. They had to go after Lady Jung Suk first, because of the moon cycle of the Weres, as well as to have any chance of saving Amy Chen. The thing that worried her most was, if they couldn't get Lady Jung Suk separated, they'd have to make an on-the-spot decision to kill the girl to get to the disembodied Were Leopard. No one wanted to talk about that, but it was implied in the eyes of everyone involved. She was just glad that the military wouldn't be on this first mission. It was too complicated an extraction, too delicate a maneuver. One wrong move and a young girl could die, or soldiers could lose their throats in a Were Leopard's jaws.

Secreted away in the stone wizard's den beneath the palace, Sasha felt like she'd definitely tumbled into the Land of Oz. It was way freakier than the setup Sir Rodney had upstairs, where things were what they appeared to be, even if they had a little Fae topspin on them to make them more enjoyable. But sheesh, this was truly ridiculous.

His top magic advisors actually had apothecary jars labeled EYE OF NEWT with eyeballs of the tiny lizard that followed you around the room. Enchanted broomsticks perpetually kept the floors clean while cauldrons bubbled and sputtered in a walk-in fireplace.

Garth didn't have to tell anybody twice to keep their hands in their pockets and their mouths shut. He and his fellow Gnomes had been busily concocting the vision miasma during the hours she'd been gone; it hovered over a wide circle drawn on the floor and covered with cryptic sigils at the back of the room.

"We have added all of the seeing elements." Garth put a jar of chameleon eyes down on the table. "They blend in," he said with a droll little smile as Sasha studied the eyeballs that blinked and curiously studied her back. "But this," he added, holding up a small glass vial, "will ensure we get her attention."

"It is a sample from the site of the Vampire messenger demon kill," a shorter, squatter advisor said.

"A what?" Hunter cocked his head to the side.

"The plump human that the messenger demons killed."

"The kid DeWitt?" Sasha said, stunned. "The Vampires sent a messenger demon after him?"

"Of course," Garth said, seeming puzzled that she didn't know.

"They wanted to send him a message to keep his mouth shut. Messenger demons are pretty effective for that," Sir Rodney said. "They leave a cold, green slime."

"Yuck . . . like algae," Sasha said, wrinkling her nose.

Bear, Crow, and Silver Hawk just shook their heads.

"Well, we at least have evidence now that the Vampires tried to keep a witness from testifying," Silver Hawk said.

"They'll most likely claim that it had nothing to do with that," Sir Rodney said. "They'll say it was rightful retaliation for the daylight exposure of Ariel Beauchamp's mausoleum."

"Better stand back a moment," Garth warned Shogun. "Sometimes the combination sputters a bit . . . the demon gook is such a nasty element to work with. We don't want you splattered by the silver in the mirrored globe. We will call you over when it is your time to speak."

Busily working on the shimmering miasma, the Gnome opened the vial and shook a few globs into the sigil on the floor. Immediately green tendrils snaked out from the small glob, bullwhipping the area inside the circle and releasing a putrid sulfur stench. Searching for something to grasp on to, it quickly encircled the miasma, turning the shimmering metallic surface a cloudy green and causing it to wildly spark before absorbing into it.

"Damn, that's wicked," Crow Shadow murmured.

Garth cut him a scowl. "Once we begin communication and Shogun begins to speak, you will have to control yourselves. No matter what she says, you must allow her to think that he's in the room only with a witch from her coven or she will sense an ambush. Understood?"

"Understood," Hunter said, giving Crow Shadow a look.

Crow Shadow held his hands up in front of his chest. "No problem."

"Are you ready?" Garth asked, looking at Shogun.

Shogun nodded.

"And you've rehearsed what you'll say?" Sir Rodney landed a hand on his shoulder.

"I'm ready."

Shogun stepped forward and the Gnomes began a low, unintelligible chant while pointing and moving their wands as though conducting an invisible orchestra. Slowly but surely, Lady Jung Suk's face filled the center of the shimmering globe. She'd been sleeping peacefully and then suddenly her eyes snapped open, glowing green. Her cat-eye pupils elongated and a large leopard face quickly filled her once lovely mouth.

"You have not learned your lesson, little squirrels. One blinding was not enough?" She hissed and stood, sweeping off her exquisitely embroidered chaise lounge and heading down a long corridor.

Sasha studied the house as Lady Jung Suk's silk robes billowed out behind her. *Just pass something recognizable,* Sasha's mind begged. Anything, so that if the night plan didn't work, she could hunt that arrogant bitch down and kill her.

They all watched silently as Lady Jung Suk flung a heavy oak door open and entered what had to be her conjuring room. She angrily yanked a knife off a small, black lacquered table and hurried to a place on the floor where a black cat was feeding from a dead fish. She shooed the feline away with a hiss, causing it to scamper into hiding with a protesting growl. The fish was in the center of a blood-created pentagram, its eyes already caved out.

Flinging the fish to the cat, she reached out her hand, and a frightened squirrel immediately filled it. Poised in the center of the pentagram, she held the struggling animal in one hand and the point of the knife in the other, lifting them above her head as her lips moved in a silent, deadly chant.

Garth motioned to Shogun. He nodded and began the game.

"You'll only blind yourself this time," Shogun said. "I am behind a mirror—warm blood won't help you, nor will squirrel eyes!"

His aunt flung the clawing animal away. It immediately escaped her and the cat out an open window.

"So . . . you have learned. You have a stronger witch helping you this time. How interesting. But that still will not help you—you've ruined your chances to rule the United Council of Entities."

"But you will never rule any Were Federation or council," Shogun shouted. "You are a slave . . . a weak slave to the Vampires and the Unseelie queen who gave you your new body. Even that doesn't belong to you." He laughed. "You picked a weak little girl. You should have at least picked a true warrior. Your vanity, Aunt, has always been your downfall."

"I'll show you how weak this young woman's body is one night, trust me, nephew!"

"Then why not tonight, when wc can both be our true selves. One on one, you call your leopard and I will call my wolf . . . and we will see if you made the wise choice."

"I would be honored to be your master," she said in a low, cat growl.

"Teach me, old, old one . . . show me what you could not show my father or his people." Shogun laughed again. "No matter how many bodies you steal, you are an old hag. Why would I even waste my time fighting you?"

"Afraid, nephew—a coward like your father?"

Silver Hawk put his hand on Hunter's shoulder when he tensed.

"I've never been afraid of you, Aunt. The worst that I've ever done to you was pity you. But now I see why you were banished. It had less to do with the family scandal than with what you chose to be."

"And what I chose to be," she shrieked, now turning in circles clutching the small dagger, "was victorious!

I chose to be more than second—unlike you, who sit whimpering in your den over a shadow bitch you cannot have! Second to your brother in all things, and you have the nerve to challenge me?"

Shogun lunged at the miasma, but Bear Shadow and Crow Shadow silently caught him before the silver could touch him. He angrily shrugged out of their hold and pointed at the shimmering globe.

"Tonight we finish this, Aunt! In the bayou—where it all began—on the grounds of the UCE courthouse in the swamp under the full moon!"

Lady Jung Suk pressed her hands together with the dagger between them and bowed with an evil smile. "Tonight, nephew. *Zai jian.*"

CHAPTER 21

Leaving Shogun exposed in the moonlight left her unsettled. Even with Sir Rodney and his expert archers downwind in a treetop position, and she and Hunter and the other clan members just inside the shadows, there was still so much that could go so wrong.

"Aunt! Are you afraid of battle?" Shogun shouted. "Have you changed your twisted mind?"

A hurdling silver crossbow arrow whizzed past Shogun's arm, tearing the fabric of his shirt as he did a quick sideways move and allowed it to pass his chest.

"Of course you couldn't come to fight me alone," he shouted while Vampire human helpers quickly ran to take up a new position as the wind shifted.

"I saw no reason to harm this beautiful new body," Lady Jung Suk cooed as she stepped into a pool of moonlight beside Duval Hempstead. "You have been a very bad dog, and I have some friends who would like to train you."

A Vampire army exited from behind trees, their sneering laughter creating a Doppler of echoes in the night.

Duval held out his arm with a toothy smile, and Lady Jung Suk did a slow pirouette. "You like? She's beautiful, isn't she?"

"Yes . . . she is," Shogun said angrily. "And she should be returned to her mother and father."

"Forgive my nephew. He is so sentimental." She glared at Shogun with hatred brimming in her cat-green eyes. "Put him out of his misery. Kill him."

As soon as Duval left her side, Fae archers dropped the silver net on Lady Jung Suk. Hunter came out of a fold of shadow and began dragging it out of the heat of the battle toward where Silver Hawk had appeared. Sasha leaped out of a shadow, covering Shogun with a machine-gun burst of hallowed-earth hollowpoints, exploding Vampires in the air, while Sir Rodney kept the crackling white Fae electrical charge focused on the net.

Shedding their human forms, Shogun, Bear Shadow, and Crow Shadow fought off vicious Vampire attackers. They had to keep them from the screeching, twisting entity in the mesh. Shadow-jumping from tree to tree, Sasha held back her wolf. Now more effective in human form, she exited a shadow, released a short burst of gunfire, and then disappeared before an attacker could lay a hand on her.

Archers kept up the pressure from above, forcing the Vampires to remain earthbound. Each time they went into a funnel-cloud spiral to get above the fight, archers sent silver arrows into the whirling tornado, causing it to sputter to a stop with Vampire ashes and red embers.

But the battle was far from over as the Vampires

began to retreat. Amy Chen's face had distorted into that angry, fanged transition of Lady Jung Suk.

Muscles bulging, Hunter strained to hold the mesh with Silver Hawk while the Were Leopard pulled itself out of the young woman's face, hissing and roaring.

"Drop the mail!" Sir Rodney shouted. "Let her out!"

Immediately Hunter and Silver Hawk complied, but rather than run for safety, Lady Jung Suk went right for Hunter's chest.

Hunter fell backward as Silver Hawk hit the ground and then scrambled to gather the ends of the mesh to quickly begin dragging the girl away. Shogun turned just in time to see Duval send a thick branch in his direction, and he ducked, heading toward Hunter, who was locked in a ground roll with a two-hundred-pound Were Leopard on his chest.

Panic stung Sasha's nervous system. There was no way to get a shot off without killing Hunter. Silver Hawk gathered the girl in his arms and began running, a few Fae archers and Crow Shadow following orders and going with him. But Bear Shadow and Shogun circled the combatants on the ground, Shogun finally able to leap in and rip off Lady Jung Suk's ear. She let out a roar that cut through the night.

"Fall back!" Sir Rodney shouted.

The moment Shogun released the big cat, she leaped off Hunter, and went airborne to attack Shogun. Bear Shadow hit the ground, covering the fallen pack alpha with his huge wolf body. Sir Rodney caught the Were Leopard in the air in the charge, slamming her against a tree and holding her there with all the might of Garth's wand.

"Sasha, now!" Sir Rodney yelled, straining against Lady Jung Suk's strength. "Do whatever you humans do to send the bitch into the Light!"

Torn, Sasha ran headlong toward the struggling beast. She didn't know what to do, really, and only her dead mother's face came to mind.

"Please, God," Sasha said, glancing at Hunter's lifeless body and the limp girl that Silver Hawk was working on. "She's killed enough innocent people—don't allow her to take any more. Get this thing away from that poor young woman who hasn't even had a chance to start her life. Take this evil thing into the Light and make it no more. Amen!"

A supernova white light with what felt like the impact of a daisy cutter lit the swamp, felled trees, and put everyone on their faces in the dirt. Black Were soot floated to the ground, making everyone cough except Hunter. Sir Rodney had been knocked out of the tree, and he and all his archers were on the swamp floor, dazed. Duval and several henchmen were holding their charred faces, screaming and running blindly into the night.

Shogun ran to his brother as Bear Shadow slowly peeled himself off the clan leader's body. Sasha skidded to a halt, went down on her knees, and rolled Hunter over. His Adam's apple didn't move and in panic she put her ear to his shredded chest and then made a fist and pounded on it.

"No! You come back here, Max Hunter!" she shouted, between heavy thuds.

"I am not getting the girl—I'm losing her," Silver Hawk called out. "She is too afraid. She doesn't trust me!"

Tears brimming, Sasha looked from Hunter to Silver Hawk. "Come save him!" She got up and ran toward the girl, sliding down into the dirt beside her. Hugging the girl in her arms, Sasha began to rock her. "Amy, please, Amy, come back," she said quietly, panic and strain making her voice hitch. "A good man may have died for you . . . your parents need you, your mother is so upset, she is crying . . . she lit candles for you—the wolves are good. They chased away the leopard. You can come back. It's safe."

Rocking harder, Sasha kept her gaze on Silver Hawk's ministrations. Hunter hadn't let the Were go . . . he'd held its vicious jaws away from his face and had wrapped his legs around its waist tightly to keep its powerful hind legs from doing damage, but its front paws had torn at his arms, back, and chest. He'd lost so much blood . . .

Sasha nuzzled the girl's hair and wept for all the losses and all the pain that now flooded her heart. "Shogun!" she cried. "Tell her in her language. She doesn't understand me!"

She watched Shogun struggle between standing at Hunter's side while his elderly grandfather worked on him and coming to the aid of the young girl he didn't even know. Shogun dropped to his knees beside Sasha, careful not to touch the silver mail.

"I will try in Mandarin . . . ," he said, looking at Sasha. Then he spoke softly to Amy Chen. "Do you speak English—*ni hui shou ying wen ma?* I am sorry, *dui bu qi,* for what happened to you. *Qing gei wo . . .* please give me . . . a chance to take you home. *Wo mi lu le . . . wo bu zhi dao*—I am lost, I don't know what to do." Shogun hung his head. "I don't know if she can hear me and my brother is dead because of me again."

A short gasp and a muffled cry made Sasha quickly lower the girl from her embrace. Her large, startled eyes immediately filled with tears as Sasha took the mail off her face. Amy's delicate features crumbled into weeping and Sasha quickly uncovered her body, gaining help from the Fae archers who'd gathered around. But she handed her off to Shogun, then got up without a word and jogged to Silver Hawk's side.

Her hands worked with the elderly shaman's covering gashes that went down to the bone. Sir Rodney knelt beside Hunter and looked at both Sasha and Silver Hawk.

"We have to get this man to the sidhe, where our healers can assist your efforts. He's lost so much blood—"

"And has saved us the trouble," Elder Vlad said, coming out of a dark fold of night.

Canines ripped everyone's gums as the old Vampire laughed. Sasha looked along the ground for her weapon, only to see Elder Vlad standing on it.

"I call the UCE!" Sir Rodney said, glancing around at his diminished forces.

Elder Vlad shook his head as the court building began to rise in the distance. "You're early and don't have evidence gathered . . . but I guess it is wise to go for a civil alternative where the executions can be limited to the wolves, thus saving your cowardly Fae hides."

"The book must register our findings as interim . . . we still have almost ten days, maybe eleven," Sir Rodney said quickly as the wolves in his party gave him skeptical glances.

"No . . . ," Elder Vlad said with an evil grin. "You cannot ask for a continuance on a matter such as this—you present now, or you present later. If you decide that it is later, I'm sure you know that we will exercise our right to retaliate on the spot for your offenses in the glen tonight. I suggest that you, as they say, man up, and swallow your medicine."

"I call the book. This man cannot be moved," Sir Rodney said. "He's lost blood at the hands of Lady Jung Suk, who—"

"Who obviously was defending herself," Elder Vlad said coolly, "but so be it. Bring the book to record."

They waited until the huge black tome exited the front doors of the rising structure and hovered between the combatants with a black quill pen waiting in the air.

"And I want the crone as a witness—there must be someone to keep the balance, after the verdict."

"Oh, I agree, Sir Rodney. Our community has already sustained enough of a loss," Elder Vlad cooed. "We wouldn't want another violent outburst from the wolves."

They waited in silence until the massive building stopped rising out of the swamp and the old crone made her painfully slow way down the steps and to the clearing using her gnarled cane.

Sasha leaned her cheek close to Hunter's face. "He's barely breathing," she murmured, her gaze searching Silver Hawk's eyes.

The elderly shaman just nodded, placed Hunter's

amulet over his heart, and covered it with a weathered palm before closing his eyes.

"The emergency session of the United Council of Entities will come to order to hear the matter at hand—the disputed rule among the Vampire Cartel, the allied wolf Federations, and the Unseelie Fae," the crone screeched. "We have your complaint on record, Elder Vlad," she said, opening the hovering tome with a wave of her walking stick. "Therefore, the burden of proof that his claims are false rest on you, the wolf Federations."

"Fine!" Sasha shouted. "We know that Elder Vlad aided and abetted a fugitive from justice—Lady Jung Suk! She then killed two people, two humans, Tanya Mays and Jim Baton, and made it look like it was a wolf savaging. He can't come to court to ask for our removal or call for sanctions against us because his hands aren't clean."

"There are two problems with this assertion," Elder Vlad said with a smile as he held up his hand. "First, the accused is no longer able to testify on her own behalf, because once again the wolves acted prematurely, primitive creatures, and just killed her. Second, human deaths have no place in this courtroom . . . Who cares?"

The Vampires who stood behind Elder Vlad laughed as the book waited with the pen hovering over it.

"How do you plead?" the crone screeched.

"Not guilty," Shogun said, coming forward with Amy Chen. "I have a witness—the human girl my aunt tried to soul-pattern over."

Vampires erupted in angry hisses as Fae archers immediately ran forward and put the mail sheet between the girl and Elder Vlad to prevent a sudden Vampire black bolt.

"It's all right," Shogun said, holding her close to him. "You must right these wrongs by telling the truth, Amy . . . so that no one else will suffer your fate."

She looked up at Shogun with trusting eyes and held on to him tightly, and then looked at the angry monsters through the thin silver shield.

"I could see everything she was making my body do," Amy said in a small, frightened voice. She squeezed her eyes shut and retched. "She killed people . . . she . . . she ate them. She did horrible, horrible things, and she taunted me, saying that she was going to go to a brothel and give my body to men . . . but she didn't live long enough. I wanted to die—I tried to die to escape seeing any more of it," Amy said, breaking down into sobs. "I just want to go home! I didn't do anything wrong! I never hurt people—I thought Tanya was my friend!"

Shogun wrapped his arms around the distraught young woman. "Have you heard enough? Do you need her blood for the book? She's an innocent—it will never burn!"

Elder Vlad's smile faded as his eyes burned back. "Your aunt may have snatched a body and been a horror, but what has that to do with us?"

"Don't look at him," Sasha yelled. She got up, stood before Amy, and held out her amulet. "I block you from her mind. Amy, tell the court how you were abducted."

"He was there," she said with her eyes squeezed shut, pointing at Elder Vlad. "They all were . . . the monsters with the teeth. Vampires! My friends put me in a car and took me to a club, and they gave me to one of the monsters—they called him Ariel, and he brought me out in the bayou and gave me to that woman." Amy covered her face. "Please let me go. I swear I won't tell a soul. I have done things that I shouldn't live—I ate human flesh, please help me . . ."

"You didn't eat human flesh, that thing inside you did," Shogun said, "and on my life I will get you back to your parents."

"Do not make promises to the girl you cannot keep," Elder Vlad said with a sneer.

"This girl is a virgin. If I strike her blood, Vlad, and she's telling the truth, you know what will happen to your testimony, right?" the crone said with a shrug.

"There must be corroboration, because human testimony does not count . . . they are easily manipulated, paid off, tempted, and glamoured," Elder Vlad said, sweeping around the group, his black robes billowing thick, angry plumes of sulfur. "This is why they've been barred from our courts." He spun on the crone. "It was always thought that we, Vampires, would be the ones to manipulate humans to our advantage . . . but the Fae have glamour skills that match our mind-bends!"

"Then how about testimony taken by cell phone?" Sasha said, coming on the other side of the silver mail divider. She held it out to the crone. "I'm a Shadow Wolf and I can testify that there were no Fae present when I went after this kid—and if for some strange reason this doesn't play, I've got a copy back at NORAD, all right?"

The crone held up her stick before Elder Vlad could speak. "Enter this into the record. Play the human contraption."

Sasha found the video and complied, allowing everyone to see and hear Lawrence DeWitt's confession. "They snatched the girl," she said, pointing back toward Amy Chen, "for the sole purpose of giving her Lady Jung Suk's body—which is a felonious offense. It's treason, because Lady Jung Suk was wanted for other high crimes against the Fae, therefore the Vampires have mitigated any claim to justice. Plus, they killed the witness, Lawrence DeWitt. It is not a crime, per se, to kill a human in this court—but it is a crime to snuff a witness to keep him from testifying, even if he is human."

"Prove it!" Elder Vlad said through his teeth amid hisses.

Sir Rodney tossed a small glass vial to the crone, who caught it without effort. "Sniff it. That is Vampire messenger demon, something we cannot get unless they left it behind somewhere. They left it all over the human's apartment, Lawrence DeWitt's—and left him all over it as well. That young man was killed by Vampires, which is proof positive."

"Let it so be entered into the record," the crone called out as Sasha turned her wrist over to allow the pen to slash it, then write the entry in blood.

"DeWitt was killed because he opened Ariel Beauchamp's tomb to daylight!" Elder Vlad shouted, spittle flying past his fangs. "It had nothing to do with the obstruction of UCE justice!"

Any Chen shook her head as she kept her face buried against Shogun's chest. "Not true, not true, the evil one said the cold lady did it . . . that is why the one who inhabited me, Lady Jung Suk, joined a coven."

The entire bayou became silent.

"*What* did Lady Jung Suk say?" Elder Vlad hissed as he walked dangerously near the silver divider.

Wolves and archers put their bodies between Vlad and the young woman, and Shogun shoved her behind him.

"Tell him, Amy," Shogun said, glaring at the ancient Vampire. "Make us all know what happened."

"Lady Jung Suk, while inside my body, made me join a coven and participate in the rituals . . . she was angry . . . jealous that a cold lady—that's what she called her, it was not a nice name . . . she said the cold blue bitch wasn't loyal and yet she was given more respect by the Vampires than she. The queen of the Unseelie, she also called her. The evil one who took my body said the covens were beneath her when she talked to the demons in her magic room, but she needed the witches to begin to get enough power to go against the blue Faery. I don't understand—there are so many things I don't understand. She said the blue one didn't even trust the Vampires because she killed some of them—the one who brought me out to the bayou, Ariel and his mates . . . she said the cold one did that to be sure the lower Vampire wouldn't one day try to blackmail her. Lady Jung Suk said the queen did not trust the old Vampire and would never fully share power with him, because she knew he'd already betrayed her. The queen didn't make people sick, the old Vampire did in her name, but he'd blamed the queen and she hates him for that."

Amy wrapped her arms around her waist. "I pray that one day this all goes away from my mind."

Sasha shook her head and chuckled. "Now we have conspiracy, Vlad . . . you stupid, old bastard . . ."

"I could've told you that Cerridwen has trust issues and doesn't like loose ends," Sir Rodney said with a cold smile. "Beautiful though she is."

"Case dismissed," the crone said with a grunt, slamming the book shut and crooking her finger for it and the pen to follow her. "Next time you bring a charge, Vlad, come with clean hands or do not wake me up in the middle of the night!"

"Wrap him in the mail," Sasha said, glancing at Hunter as the angry Vampire contingent disappeared into a swirling black mist.

"This isn't over and the night is still young," Sir Rodney said to his men. "Bring everybody back to the sidhe, especially the girl. Put guards around her parents, and get them to go to hallowed ground until daybreak. It would be just like Vamps to seek revenge against her family for her testimony. Send advance warning to Garth—right now, we've got a badly injured man to heal."

CHAPTER 22

With Hunter in critical condition, sending the Vampires temporarily packing was such a hollow win. Who cared if the Vampires almost got them kicked out of the UCE—her man was in a silver-mesh, makeshift gurney, bleeding to death as they hurried him through the bayou. The three men on each side, holding the silver mail as steadily as possible while they ran, seemed too much like pallbearers running under a full moon.

"Lower the drawbridge," the captain of the guards shouted.

Archers flanked the men carrying Hunter, with still more ushering Shogun and the young woman to safety. The golden pathway to the sidhe revealed itself in a flash; the moment the last footfall hit it, the garrison vanished again into the night.

Garth and the other magic advisors met them on the other side of the bridge. "Get this man to our chambers. We must work quickly. It is not his body, it is his spirit. We have watched the battle from the seeing crystals."

Silver Hawk nodded and kept his hand on Hunter's chest as they rushed through the town to the castle, archers shouting "Make way," until they reached their destination.

"I've seen him busted up worse than this," Sasha said, rounding the long table as they laid Hunter on it. "But he still maintained consciousness."

"I have sealed up most of the tears to his flesh and muscle," Silver Hawk said. "But this thing that he held closely wanted in to his spirit. She knew what we were going to do to her . . . but his amulet kept her from fully entering him to escape her fate."

"Aye," Garth said. "That is what we must draw out . . . but his spirit could forever be damaged from this lesion that tried to adhere to it."

"Tell me what I can do as his brother?" Shogun said, going to the table side but having to back off because of the silver mail. "If he needs a transfusion, anything . . ."

"Hold the wholeness of his recovery in your mind. Be still," Silver Hawk said, adjusting the amulet over Hunter's heart again. "All wolves and all healers, focus on the oneness of our alpha's safe return from the dark shadows that hold him. I can fix his body, I have closed any open veins and begun to mend the flesh . . . but his spirit, that is a fight that every man and woman must fight alone."

Garth parted the bodies that had lined the side of his worktable, but Sasha climbed up on it to kneel by Hunter's face. She gently cradled his head in her hands, and then closed her eyes, resting her forehead against his.

"Hunter's spirit is the most beautiful thing about him," she murmured, finally allowing the tears to roll down the bridge of her nose without censure. "This man is kind, and wise, and gentle, and good. He is honest to a flaw, but never mean-spirited. I would give my spirit to him, if I could—rather than to see his diminished by even a fraction of the silver it contains." She kissed his forehead and took off her amulet to lay it next to the one his grandfather had placed on his chest. "Baby . . . heal . . . ," she whispered and kissed him again and then laid her cheek softly against his forehead to stare sideways at Garth. "Between you, me, and Silver Hawk, we have to fix this."

Garth reached out to her and clasped her hand within his. Silver Hawk rounded the table and took up Sasha's other hand as he reached across Hunter's body to hold Garth's gnarled grip.

"Stand at your brother's feet as closely as you can. Beware of the silver," Garth said to Shogun. Then he nodded to Crow Shadow and Bear Shadow. "Take his hands and mirror our stance. We must create sacred geometry around this man."

An advisor stood on each side of the table between the groups at Hunter's head and feet. Slowly leaning over his body until their hands were in reach to touch, they extracted stones from their brown robes.

"Rose quartz, malachite, black agate, and green tourmaline," Garth murmured. "Do your task . . . heal the heart of this man and remove the darkness, seal the legions, ignite the silver."

Silver Hawk began his low, steady healing chant as the stones lit from within. The four Gnomes standing parallel to Hunter's midsection slowly moved them up and down his body, touching one another's hands as they exchanged stones and hummed softly with their eyes shut. The low frequency of their voices sounded like bees buzzing beneath Silver Hawk's chant. Then, ever so subtly, Sasha could see the amulets on Hunter's chest begin to spark inside, until the amber glowed.

Soon the outline of his body began to pick up a thin line of light, widening as his life force aura strengthened. Sweat formed on her brow and beaded on Hunter's. Fatigue pulled at her limbs, at her body, weighting her eyes.

"Catch her before she falls," Garth said quietly, giving Sir Rodney a nod. "We are almost done. She has given much . . . she shared a part of her human soul."

She didn't remember exactly how she got to the suite, but seeing Hunter resting peacefully, breathing, albeit bandaged, made her look up from the chaise lounge and weep. He wore both amulets, and his color was good. Once he was strong enough to eat raw game, he'd be on a solid road to recovery. Even though her limbs felt like noodles, she dragged herself up and across the room to stare down at him for a while, and then brushed his lips with a tender kiss.

"I love you, Max Hunter. Don't you know that by now?"

"Please don't go," Amy whispered and grabbed both of Shogun's hands when Rupert stopped in front of her door.

"You're safe here in the sidhe . . . no Vampires or demons—"

"Just . . ." Words caught in her throat and tears seemed frozen in her stricken expression before she barreled into Shogun's arms.

"Okay, okay," he said and nodded to Rupert.

Rupert raised an eyebrow and nodded, but turned on his heel with a dignified bow. "All that you require is in your suite. As you have been our guest before, milord, please let the lady know that there are gowns for her sleeping comfort, as well as inform her of how she might order food, should she need refreshment."

"I don't want anything, just to be safe," Amy said quietly against Shogun's chest.

"Then good night, all," Rupert said and strode down the corridor with a straight spine.

"I don't think he approves because you're twenty and I'm a wolf," Shogun said, opening the door for her.

"After all that I have seen," she said, shaking her head. "Seeming as though I've lost my honor is the last thing that concerns me."

"That won't happen on my watch," he said, cradling her cheek. "I will protect you . . . will sit up all night and watch the moon until the dawn—but nothing will enter this room to harm you while I'm here."

She covered his hand with hers and openly gazed at him. "I thought I was lost. I thought I would never live to see life again . . . how will I remove this terror from my mind?"

His heart shattered as he looked into her beautiful innocent eyes. Something so horrible had tried to steal that precious gift from her and had tried to pollute her

bright mind. He let his fingers touch the silky edges of
her hair, trying to fathom a way to answer her very real
question.

"I don't know," he finally admitted. "Once you've
seen some things . . . I just don't know how to unsee
them. But you were spared for a reason."

"I was spared because you cared to find me. It would
have been easier to just trap my body and kill me to
kill her. But you and your brother almost died, so did
all those people . . . and why? I am a nobody to you—I
am—"

"A person. A being," he said quietly. "For that reason alone, you matter." He took her by the hand, brought
her to the privacy screen, and motioned toward the tub
with his chin. "You bathe, feel comfortable. I will sit
on the other side and talk to you, all right?"

She timidly peered around the small enclosure, ques-
tioning the bubble bath that was already waiting for
her. He entered the room and bent over, reaching his
hand down in the water.

"Safe," he said, but did not smile to belittle her fears.
Stooping quickly, he looked beneath the claw-footed
porcelain tub and popped back up. "Safe." He moved to
the commode and lifted the lid. "Safe." Then he walked
over to the hamper and looked in. "Safe. You put your
clothing in and it—"

"I don't want to wear her traditional silk ever again."
Amy closed her eyes.

"Give them to me and I will have Rupert burn them.
Come, let's look in the armoire and select a gown that
you can wear to sleep. In the morning, we can ask the

Faeries to bring you jeans or whatever you want. In fact, I think we should look under all the furniture together, in the armoires and drawers, and then I'll sit outside the screen so we can talk, yes?"

She nodded and gifted him with a shy but lovely smile.

It was a horrible fact, but she had to leave. Colonel Madison was waiting on an outcome report and ready to deploy a special forces unit to take a demon down. Her men were at NAS in a holding pattern. Her commanding officer was poised for a press conference that would be next to impossible to stop. Yet as she stared down at Hunter, all that dissolved. She needed to be at two places at once—here and there.

Kissing him gently as not to wake him, she slipped out of the room and headed for Silver Hawk's suite. She had to let him know where she was going and what was going on, but there was no way she'd allow Hunter to wake up alone.

The elderly shaman opened the door before she knocked. She smiled and hugged him. He was already dressed.

"Thank you," she murmured.

He patted her cheek. "My daughter-warrior, hunt well . . . and be safe . . . come back to us whole." He turned and collected a small bag of supplies. "We are forever indebted to the Fae."

She nodded and kissed his cheek. "Will you tell Sir Rodney thank you for me? You rest, let Shogun rest . . . Bear and Crow—they don't need to be out there with me. I don't know if the men I'm going with will be able to hold their fire if they shift. I can't even think about losing any of our family right now."

"And we cannot bear the thought of losing you, daughter. Please stay close to the shadows and leave the hunt if your safety is in question. I am an old man; I look forward to grandchildren, not burying my children."

"I love you, too," she said and hugged him hard. "I'll be back later tonight. Let the sun warm your face."

She rushed away from Silver Hawk before her heart broke in two. Leaving Hunter and the rest of her family there was like pulling her canine teeth sans Novocain. But as she got to the bottom of the broad stone staircase, her brother was bounding up them. He stopped and stared at her; she came close to him studying his expression.

"Can we talk before you head out?" he said.

"Yeah . . . what's wrong?"

"I need to leave and I was trying to find some staff that knew the way out—or could get word to that Rupert dude or Sir Rodney. I didn't wanna get shot trying to leave and then I didn't know how to find my way out of this magic kingdom place to get to the real world on the other side of it."

"Okay, I know how to get out, but why do you want to be out of here, Crow? I don't like the sound of this at all." She dropped the bag she was carrying and folded her arms.

He let out a hard breath. "Let's take this out in the garden, all right?"

She picked up her knapsack and flung it over her shoulder. "Follow me."

* * *

They walked until she found a small cement bench surrounded by a profusion of wildflowers. She listened closely for eavesdropping Pixies and glanced around until she was sure there was no evidence of nosy Wood Sprites.

"Okay, what's all this about?"

"I need to go into New Orleans to find somebody . . . given all this possession shit and Vampire retaliation that's been going on."

Sasha's expression mellowed. "Oh, man . . . what's her name?"

Crow Shadow looked away. "I don't exactly remember."

"Are you serious?" Sasha said and then let out an exasperated breath.

But Crow Shadow jumped up and exploded. "Don't judge me! I didn't know about humans or I would have used something, all right! Bear didn't tell me ahead of time! I thought they had seasons like she-Shadows, but they don't—and, and—I could have a kid out there. I might be just like my old man—our old man."

"Whoa, whoa," Sasha said, standing slowly to touch her brother's shoulders. "Hey, I'm sorry . . . Let's take this from the top—no judgment."

After a moment he nodded, and that was when she saw how upset he really was. Sunlight caught in his eyes and shone in the excess moisture that made them glisten.

"I swear I didn't know," he said and then flopped down on the bench. "I would have been more responsible, used precautions. I don't wanna end up like Doc one day . . . going my whole life not knowing I made a kid, missing everything about that, missing family, just because maybe the kid could come out a hybrid, ya know." He looked into her eyes with a pained expression etched in his gaze. "And how he made you . . . but couldn't claim you because of the law, because if he did, they'd take you from him and hurt him. Like, I don't even know how to talk to him, Sasha. Part of me was so mad at him when I found out, then the other part was so sorry—because he didn't know about me. Mom lied. My mother lied—there, I said it. You didn't even get to know your mom, which, to me, is fucked up, so what am I complaining about."

She didn't immediately respond with words, just pulled him into a hug and rested her head on his shoulder. "It's gonna be all right. The main thing is that you've got Doc now . . . and you should talk to him. He's a pretty cool old dude."

Her brother nodded and swallowed hard, hugging her back tightly.

"Sasha," he whispered, "I don't even know this girl's name."

"You know her scent, right?"

He nodded. She patted his back.

"Then you can track her," Sasha said calmly. "We'll find her."

"What if she's mad?" Crow Shadow sat back.

Sasha smiled. "If she's female, she's gonna be mad. If she's not pregnant, she might call you out of your name and slam the door in your face. Then you're off the hook. But if she *is* pregnant, after you man up, fall on your sword, and treat her nice . . . she'll probably be glad you went through all the trouble to come and find her. It hasn't been that long. Not like you're looking for her after five years or something."

"You think so?"

"I know so." Sasha cuffed his neck. "All you say is: I freaked out . . . left, because I realized we didn't use anything and we just met. But it messed with my mind, because you were such a nice person, a decent person, and you didn't deserve that. But then I realized that I didn't have a number, or an address, just the memory— and I didn't know how to find you . . . so I've been riding all over New Orleans looking for you for weeks."

"Damn . . . that does sound good."

"That's 'cause it's the truth," she said, shaking her head.

His muscles ached as he stretched in the window seat. He'd kept vigil all night just as he'd promised her, watching the moon, watching her sleep, glad that Sir Rodney's baths were enchanted just like his beds. Her serene beauty was simple, completely untarnished by the outside world when she'd surrendered to oblivion— that someone had tried to take that peace from her was a travesty of the worst order.

Memorizing every feature of her, he tried to begin the mental separation that he knew had to happen. She belonged in the human world; her parents would be overwhelmed to have her back. Sir Rodney could glamour away the experience from her mind. She would go back to being a vegan; he would return to his home country and go back to being a wolf.

But then she opened her eyes and smiled at him and pushed her long, mussed spill of damp blue-black hair over a creamy shoulder. She breathed in the morning and held the covers up closely, modestly, and then shyly lowered her dark velvety lashes.

"You kept watch for me all night," she said quietly.

"I promised I would."

"You have kept many promises to me, and even offered your life . . . and yet, we do not even know each other."

"Is that important?"

"To most it is."

"You deserve to live."

"Why?" She stared at him.

"Because you do." He stood, feeling uncomfortable, and walked to the table. "You should eat."

She avidly shook her head no.

"Green tea and sweet cakes," he said into a silver dome and then uncovered it.

She laughed and craned her neck to see. "How did you do that? There is so much magic, so many things that I've heard about as stories as a child . . . but you are showing me the good parts."

He stood up a little taller and brought the tray to the bed, resting it on the white, fluffy goose-down duvet. "There are good Dragons and bad, good wolves and bad," he said, pouring her tea and handing her a cup. "Good sorcerers and bad . . . good Faeries and bad . . . yin and yang, black and white, chi that runs through all, balance necessary in all."

"How did you become so wise?"

He chuckled. "I lived through good and bad. That is not wisdom, just experience." He took a sip of tea and left her bedside, not completely trusting himself.

"Then how did you become so brave?" she said, sipping her tea and peering at him over the rim of her white porcelain cup.

"I met you," he said quietly. "And I knew you deserved to live."

CHAPTER 23

"How is he doing now?" Colonel Madison asked, his worried gaze sweeping Sasha.

"Better than last night, sir. Thank you for your concern."

Woods nodded and shifted uncomfortably where he stood. "Hunter is a good man, sir. We'll miss him in the firefight tonight."

Fisher cut him a glance and then looked at Sasha. "He means a lot to all of us, Captain . . . not just as a soldier, but as a friend."

"Yeah, I know. Thanks, Lieutenant," Sasha said quietly. But she had to shake the blues, had to focus on what had to be done. Redirecting her thoughts, she brought her attention back to the colonel. "After the press conference this morning, I'll need to go check back in with our allies."

"Do what you have to do, Captain. We know our positions and where our rendezvous point is. I just hope our plan works without any more loss of human lives."

"Roger that, sir," Sasha said and then quietly slipped past the door.

* * *

"It was the closest holy site to where the Chens were that was open for evening Bible study," an exhausted Fae archer said as he motioned toward a Methodist church. "We glamoured them past the other humans and got them hunkered down in the basement until daybreak . . . got them a little food and some water. But Sir Rodney thinks that until this blows over, it may be best to bring the girl and her family back to the sidhe."

Shogun wiped his palms down his face and then looked at Amy.

"My parents will not leave their store," she said, looking up at Shogun.

"I know . . . but maybe once they see you I can convince them to go on vacation, just for a little while. Maybe if I pay for them to return to the old country to visit relatives and visit graves there?"

She nodded and took up his hand. The Fae archer thrust his shoulders back and led the way, opening the locked church door with ease. Shogun hesitated as Mr. and Mrs. Chen stood up from a pew and faced him. Stained glass let in prisms of multihued sunlight, but nothing compared to the expression on Mrs. Chen's face when she covered her mouth and then ran head-long toward her child. Shogun stepped back as Mr. Chen then ran up behind his wife, both parents crying, encircling their daughter as she openly sobbed.

"Xie xie, xie xie!" Mrs. Chen exclaimed, thanking Shogun over and over again in Mandarin. She intermittently went from frantically kissing her daughter's face to hugging Shogun and kissing his hands, clutching

them up in hers. "Bless the good police!" she said, so overcome that she had to be helped to a pew.

"My daughter . . . ," Mr. Chen said, wiping his eyes. "Did they hurt you?"

Amy's lip trembled and then she sought her father's embrace, hiding her face against his neck. But Shogun landed a hand on the older man's shoulder, knowing what he was delicately asking.

"No, sir . . . we got to her in time. Your daughter is frightened and shaken, but in the same condition as she was before she was abducted."

Mr. Chen began rocking with his child in his arms, exclaiming, *"Xie, xie,"* between sobs of relief.

The Fae archer turned and swallowed hard, and Shogun walked to the back of the church with him.

"I never really experienced humans before, you know . . . ," the archer said with a quick nod toward the Chen family. "I could never understand what Sir Rodney saw in them, why he'd put the sidhe on the line for them, but, seeing this . . ."

"I know," Shogun said quietly, reverently, his gaze on Amy Chen as his heart filled with peace. "If you just save one, the ripple in the pond to all humanity is endless. Families, friends, people that good deed touches are all connected." He chose not to say more, because it was a private knowing. Sasha had taught him that, had made him care about the human condition. And as he stood there, he became aware of a new peace that had crept up on him and entered his spirit. He still loved Sasha, but as a part of his life and family now, not as his potential mate . . . and that made everlasting peace finally possible with his half brother, Hunter.

Mr. Chen got up and came to Shogun. The Fae archer bowed deeply. "I have no way to repay this gift you have given my life," he said quietly and proudly. "You may have my store . . . I realized that the money without my child is nothing."

"Sir, no, please," Shogun said, bowing to Mr. Chen. "I am honored but cannot accept . . . uhm, it is against the law for police to accept payment for doing their jobs."

Mr. Chen seemed confused but accepted the explanation. "Are you married?"

Shogun smiled. "No, sir, I'm a lone wolf." He suspected the man would otherwise try to seek out a wife to whom he could give a gift of appreciation; it was custom to give something to someone who'd given you so much. But he had to make Mr. Chen understand that just seeing their joy had been payment enough.

The archer chuckled and folded his arms over his chest.

"All men your age are wolves," Mr. Chen said with a smile, wiping his eyes. "But I graciously give you my daughter to marry—you are the only truly honorable man I have seen since my wife and I have come to this country."

Elder Futhark held the iridescent Fae missive in his right hand and the dark, smoldering black envelope in the other as he slowly walked down the center aisle of the antechamber toward Queen Cerridwen's throne. She fixed her cool gaze on him; he could feel his steps slowing and his face becoming frostbitten as he approached the angry monarch and extended the missive.

She pointed with her icicle wand to his left hand. "I'll take the bad news first."

"Yes, Your Majesty," he said, bowing as he offered her the black envelope. "You know that I have been your faithful advisor for eons, and whatever is in this, please be lenient to the one who delivered this to you."

She snatched the missive from him without answering. "A Vampire demon messenger note from Vlad . . . how refreshing," she said coolly and opened the black letter with a snap.

Black and yellow sulfuric smoke billowed up the moment the blood wax seal was broken, and she blasted it with her wand, causing black hail to litter her ice-covered marble floor. However, her glib mood soon became serious as she read the letter through to the end.

"How did he find out about Ariel Beauchamp's tomb being opened by our forces?"

"Through the eyes of the young girl whom the late Lady Jung Suk took over. Our spies have confirmed that it is now a matter of record in the UCE tome." He peered up from his bent position and stared into her crystal-blue eyes. "Milady . . . we are now at war with the Vampires, a formidable foe."

She tossed the letter aside and reached out to snatch the iridescent parchment from Elder Futhark's other hand. "No doubt a reprimand now from Sir Rodney," she said, unfurling it with disdain.

"Milady?" Elder Futhark said, slowly standing when she sat back in her throne.

"It's not a reprimand," she said, so shocked that she laughed.

"Then . . . ?"

"It's an invitation to war. To war alongside Rodney and the wolves as an ally against Vlad."

It had taken all morning, but his nose never failed him. Scavenging his mind for whatever bits of information he could retrieve, a first name came to him—Jennifer. She'd talked about her job at the Donut Hole a little bit. Said she'd wanted to go back to school one day, and worried that at twenty-five it might be too late. She worried about money, but said she might take advantage of the president's new education plans. Odd things he remembered about her. Like scattered puzzle pieces that all had similar colors; some fit, some didn't. But the Donut Hole wasn't hard to find.

What was hard was going up to the large plate-glass window of the half-empty place and opening the door. She looked up and didn't smile. He almost turned around to walk away, but then remembered what his sister had told him.

Crow Shadow slipped into the store and stood at the counter. "Hey, Jennifer."

"So what'd you do, decide to come back and get take-out breakfast and coffee after you run out on another girl this morning?"

He listened to the wobble in her voice, studied the golden tresses and kind face he'd remembered. Hurt had hardened her pretty hazel eyes. "No, I came back to apologize and to show you this time that . . . I don't know. You didn't deserve what I did. You're a nice person. If something happened, you know . . . I'll stand by you."

She twisted the tie to the white apron that covered

her uniform and bit her lip. "I didn't do anything wrong . . . why'd you do that—just leave like that?"

Crow Shadow just closed his eyes. His wolf instincts had rarely failed him.

"Sir Rodney, Sir Rodney!" a garrison guard shouted. "Lower the drawbridge!"

Seelie guards worked quickly to bring the messenger in. The drawbridge hit the ground on the other side of the moat with a thud, and a Unicorn-riding guard took up the missive and swung his steed around to make haste to the castle. Faeries were already on the wind, bringing advance news to rouse the monarch and to get him ready. Rupert rushed around, hurrying behind Sir Rodney with his robe, helping him don it as the front guards opened the door.

The garrison commander dismounted and rushed up the steps, then went down on one knee to hand Sir Rodney the frost-covered missive. It burned his fingers with ice as he peeled it open, his top magic advisors scurrying to greet him in the castle's grand foyer.

"It is from Cerridwen," Garth said. "Be wary, milord."

"It is she who should be wary," Sir Rodney said firmly. "She is up for treason, collaboration with the Vampires against me by aiding in their scheme to embody a felon. This time, the law is on my side and I have invited her to war . . . but in a very special way."

"Her ousting from the UCE will most assuredly weaken her power," Garth said cautiously. "And you could overtake her provinces . . . but do you want to stretch your rule as far as Iceland, and to annex an entire court that will begrudge your rule?"

Sir Rodney smiled. "No. I just wanted to spank her a little, old friend."

Garth smiled. "Be careful . . . you two have always played dangerous love games."

"Well, let us see what the lady has to say," Sir Rodney quipped, shaking off the cold and unfurling Queen Cerridwen's parchment. But after a moment his smile faded and his arm slowly lowered to his side.

"Milord?" Garth said, causing the other advisors to come in closer.

"She *apologized* and does not want to war with me, but is agreeing to war beside me as an ally against the Vampires."

"Cerridwen apologized?" Garth said, eyes bulging. "*And* is agreeing to an alliance?"

"Yes," Sir Rodney said, clearly shocked. "She wants to reunite in an alliance against the Vampires, and I was only being facetious when I made the offer." He walked away a bit, running his fingers through his hair. "Then it is true . . . she was innocent and had been manipulated by the Vampires." Sir Rodney shook his head. "That old bastard will rue the day that he crossed Cerridwen. Even with immortality, he can not outlast her hatred of being made a fool."

Hunter opened his eyes and tried to sit up, but Silver Hawk gently touched his chest to make him lie back down.

"Easy, son," Silver Hawk said in a quiet voice. "There is a time to war and a time to heal. Now is the time to heal."

Hunter lay back with a wince, but his gaze searched the room.

"She did not abandon you," Silver Hawk said, reading his expression.

Hunter closed his eyes. He didn't want to suffer a lecture. He just thought she'd be there when he woke up.

"Sasha is doing what she must to protect her pack, no less than what you would do if a demon incursion were eating members of the Shadow Wolf Clan. She did not sleep all night. I could see the fatigue in her eyes. She sat vigil for you until the dawn and then came in search of me."

"Sasha will always do what duty demands," Hunter said in a raspy voice.

"No," his grandfather said, touching the dual amulets Hunter wore. "She gave you a part of her spirit . . . duty never demanded that." He stared down at Hunter, his wise eyes speaking volumes beyond his Spartan comments. "It is an immeasurable gift. Do not let your temporary disappointment or ego squander it."

Russell Conway clicked off the television remote and flung it across the room. Rage held back the tears in his eyes as he jumped up, rushed to the bathroom, and searched through his toiletries bag with shaking hands. He laughed out loud when he saw the plastic razor and then stared into the mirror for a moment before dashing out of the bathroom to the small kitchenette to locate a knife.

Holding his wrist out over the sink he pressed down on the blade. They didn't believe him; they thought he was a fraud. He'd seen what he'd seen. He had proof! A Werewolf had butchered his mother and little sister right before his eyes. He could see it as though it were yesterday. And now they were calling everything a hoax? He hadn't dedicated his life to a hoax . . . he hadn't!

"I'm not crazy," he said in a trembling voice, pressing down harder on the blade. "I'm not!"

Esmeralda touched the corridor walls lightly, taking her time as she moved timidly without her natural sight. She had to find Sir Rodney, had to let him know about her vision. Fort Shannon of Inverness, the House of Clerk—his rule would soon be under attack. Only her third-eye vision guided her past coats of armor and tapestries, and then she stopped when she heard familiar footfalls.

"Milady! My goodness! You should be recovering," Rupert said, rushing to take her elbow.

Esmeralda brought a graceful hand up to her eyes, touching the swirling colored miasma of sparkles that covered them. "Do I look horrible now?"

"Oh, no, milady . . . do not disturb the healing. It is beautiful, just like you . . . like a thousand tiny lights of the Faeries garden." Rupert soothed her with a hug. "You will forever be beautiful to all of us. You tried to help our sovereign and he will not abandon you."

She wiped at a tear that hadn't fallen and the sight of that made Rupert swallow hard.

"I've had a vision, a horrible vision that I must convey to Sir Rodney right away. I want to still be useful to him while I'm here, not just thought of as an invalid to be tucked away."

"He will keep you here in the sidhe, I'm sure . . . as, maybe, his seer. Sometimes when we lose one gift, another comes in its place. I know that Garth would try with all his might to do that for you, if it was in his powers," Rupert said delicately. "Come, let me guide you back to your room. The Pixies will help you robe while I fetch the king."

There was no explanation about why the bureaucratic side of all things government took so long. Fatigue and frustration weighed on her heavily as she double-checked rounds with Woods and Fisher to be sure that everyone on the mission had silver-dust-filled shells, understood supernatural protocols, and had a chance to get out of the bayou alive.

Late-afternoon sun took a dip behind the trees, and just seeing that made her crazy. All morning she'd been at the base, readying men, talking by VTC to the Joint Chiefs with Colonel Madison, and fact-checking demon-hunting protocols with Bradley and the NORAD team. Shogun and Crow Shadow had thankfully hit her cell with messages that they were headed back to the sidhe. That was the only way she could get a message back to Hunter, by way of a third party—and that made her stomach clench.

"Captain, we've got a problem that Lieutenant Campbell pointed out—and it's a valid concern."

Sasha briefly closed her eyes. "Give it to me with both barrels, Woods." She *had* to get back to the sidhe, and had to get to Russell Conway to give the man a ray of hope. She felt like she was stuck in molasses, walking through the day in it. Everything seemed to be conspiring to keep her from getting back to where she wanted to be most, back at Hunter's side.

"These guys are going into a firefight with night-vision goggles . . . but the goggles don't register color, just the gleam. Everything in the sight line of the goggles is a weird green tint. So they can't tell at a split-second glance if the eyes of something coming at them are red, green, or gold. That's a problem."

Sasha kicked the jeep tire hard. "Oh, just kiss my ass!"

CHAPTER 24

Functioning on hour thirty-six with no sleep, battle fatigue, worry, and delay after delay at the base, Sasha felt the Louisiana heat beginning to take its toll. Her sidearm was like an anvil, adding to the weight of everything else. It was almost dusk and there wasn't even enough time for her to grab a bite to eat; she'd been living off whatever munchies she could scavenge from vending machines. Pathetic.

She held herself up by the second-floor railing of the motel, intermittently lifting her sweat-soaked T-shirt off her back as she waited for Russell Conway to open the door. "C'mon, Mister Conway. Open up. I know you're in there. I can hear you," Sasha called out, quickly losing patience.

This was a courtesy call, one she really didn't have time for. But something moved her to do it. The poor bastard seemed like the type who might put a bullet in his skull if people didn't believe him, and she so did not need to have that on my conscience along with everything else.

"Finally," she muttered as she heard movement coming toward the door.

A bleary-eyed Russell Conway opened the door a crack. "What's this? You all coming to take me to the crazy house to keep me quiet?"

"No," Sasha said, lifting her damp hair off her neck. "I came to apologize to you for what had to be done." Sasha let out an exasperated breath. "Look, I went to a lot of trouble to find you, sir. You've moved from the hotel in town where you'd been staying to way out here in this motel. If I could just have a minute of your time, I'll be on my way."

Frowning, he peered around the door a little farther. "This is a trick, isn't it—to lure me out so you all can grab me."

Sasha stood back from the door and held her hands up in front of her chest. "Nobody wants to take you into custody, sir. In fact, I'm not even supposed to be here. But I felt bad that your story had to be discredited to keep down public panic."

"Really?" he said, opening the door wider.

Sasha's eyes went to his bloodied wrists and the gasp came out before she could stop it.

"I just gave up," he said, dropping the knife onto the motel carpet. "But I couldn't make the knife cut all the way—I need something sharper."

"Oh, God, sir," Sasha said in a rush. "Please let me in. I can help you, if you'll let me explain."

"Okay," Russell Conway said in a tone that sounded like that of a frightened child.

This was exactly what Sasha was afraid of, and she hurried in behind Russell and shut the door.

"Listen," she said. "We know you aren't crazy. There are definitely things out there that kill humans—things that aren't human."

"Oh . . . *I know*," he said and nodded, then calmly walked back toward the small kitchenette.

"But . . . sometimes we have to make deals, make compromises for the greater good."

"I understand that, too," Russell said. "I learned that as a young boy."

"I know this has been awfully difficult for you, sir . . . I'm sorry."

"Me, too," he said, picking up a backpack and extracting a nine-millimeter. He quickly put it under his chin.

"Please don't do that, Russell," Sasha said, walking toward him slowly. "It's going to be all right. Please give me the gun . . . please."

"I understand about making deals," he said with a peaceful smile. "I made a deal as a boy with something in that woods that night. It told me to take off the charm and it would keep the monsters, all of them, from coming back. Werewolves wouldn't be able to hurt me, Vampires wouldn't. I would be safe, so I took that deal. But when I wanted people to know, it kept saying, *'Feed me. That was not a part of our deal.'* So I tried to cut my wrists and they just healed up. I was about to try this when you came."

Before she could move, he pulled the trigger. Horror consumed her as the back of his head hit the cabinets in a wet thud. Sasha backed away, her mind on a crash course to call 911, but Russell's body never dropped, nor did it lose the sardonic smile on his face.

"See," he said. "Some deals are permanent."

Her back slammed against the door and then a force blew her through it. Sasha went over the rail backward, but flipped to land on all fours. A green serpent-like body bullwhipped at her over the railing, still wearing Russell Conway's disfigured head.

Sasha dove for the nearest shadow. She had to get this thing away from civilians and into the bayou. But the moment she entered the shadow lands, something sucked her into a hard spiral at breathtaking velocity. She clutched at her chest, searching for her amulet that wasn't there. A scream left her lungs. She'd given Hunter the only thing that could keep her from the wrong side of a demon door.

Tumbling, falling, she blindly reached for her side-arm and began firing. The shadows belched her out in a ground slam in the swamp, and she was up in a flash and running.

Tree limbs snatched at her, yanking at her clothes and hair as she weaved and bobbed through the treacherous maze. Leaves became razor-sharp projectiles flying at her as she dodged behind trees, and then had to flee them as they came alive. Green slime was on the move, like a high-speed serpent, twisting and turning Russell's bloodied skull in search of her.

Unable to take to the shadows, she had to opt for wolf speed, but calling her wolf was a dangerous prospect. That would leave her unarmed; there was no way her wolf could take this thing that was chasing her.

Releasing a howl to call for backup, she hoped she was in range of the sidhe as the thing chasing her thundered behind her, ripping up tree roots and swamp flooring.

Hunter got up slowly, holding his side, pushing past Silver Hawk's protests. "Something is not right."

"You are healing and allowing your worries to—"

"No, Grandfather! She is in mortal danger."

"You promised her," Silver Hawk said, holding Hunter by both arms. "You told her you wouldn't interfere with the human maneuvers, except to help. You could put her in harm's way by causing them to accidentally fire on you or her."

Hunter held on to a bedpost and leaned against it with a wince.

"You are in no condition to act on an impulse that isn't real. Rest."

"I just can't seem to, Grandfather," Hunter said, moving toward the chair to find his pants. "I cannot."

Woods had heard the howl first and relayed it to Fisher.

"Showtime, people—incoming!" Fisher yelled as Marines took their positions.

Colonel Madison watched through binoculars from a fallback position in an armored vehicle. "Hold your position," he said into a walkie-talkie. "Fire only after Captain Trudeau is on the right side of the firefight."

Sasha whizzed past Woods, grabbing him by the arm. "Go, go, go! Fall back!"

Fisher lifted a rocket-propelled grenade launcher and fired into the green slime, blowing Russell's head off the end of it.

"Fall back!" Colonel Madison shouted.

But panicked troops released hot bursts of machine-gun fire that only seemed to make the creature angrier. Sending out tentacles, it bullwhipped a jeep into the trees, sending soldiers running for cover.

Fae archers dropped down behind the demon and began a rain of silver torment that made the creature loop back and lash out at them. Before a Fae archer could be grabbed, a Marine sharpshooter hit a quick-moving tentacle with a silver-loaded bazooka shell. The archer fell; another Marine dragged him to safety as the hit tentacle burst into flames, then withered, screeching. Respect flashed between the two beings, one Fae, one human, but there wasn't time for it to mature.

Fisher pulled up the Marine, who then got the Fae archer to his feet.

"Good looking out, mate," the archer said, and then ran for the tree line.

"They've got Brits out here with us?" the young soldier asked, running for cover behind another tree.

"Something like that," Fisher said, yanking the young man out of the way of another tentacle slash.

A special forces unit was pinned down in black water as Sasha made another pass. She sprayed the tentacles behind them with a handheld Uzi burst and yelled for them to reverse their direction.

"Get out of the water!" she shouted, trying to give the men cover.

Hunter came out of a shadow holding on to a tree, then jumped out of the way when the branches tried to take his head off.

"Sasha!"

She turned to the sound of his voice. It all felt like it was happening so slowly, but time had no meaning as she dove to push Hunter out of the way of a thick root that would gore him through his back. He caught her going down into the spill of a shadow's edge. She screamed "No" as the demon left the swamp and followed behind her.

Spiraling wildly, she'd expected them to come out on the wrong side of a demon door, and clearly so had the demon. But instead they came out in the courtyard of the sidhe—apparently her lack of an amulet, combined with Hunter's having two on, had screwed up his trajectory, and now a demon was inside the garrison.

Sir Rodney was on the front line with his men as chaos broke loose. "Battle stations!"

Wolves transformed to chase the entity into the courtyard, containing the lashing tentacles with their ferocious jaws as Gnomes rushed around the perimeter with silver, sealing off its ability to gain purchase on any being. Wizard wands came out, sending hard arcs of magic discharges with lightning-bolt accuracy.

The demon burst into a cold green flame, attempting to run, and then hit the silver-dust circle and screamed a horrifying wail. Dragons from the castle turrets swooped down and kept the nemesis from an airborne escape, and it could not penetrate the group—the circle had done its job.

Garth stepped forward, his wand poised. "I command you back to Hell from whence you came—a creature lured by Vampires and conjured by covens to wreak havoc among our alliance—never to inhabit another being, never to be able to escape the dark cauldron again!"

An explosion rocked the castle, toppling Fae infantry-men and leaving a smoking black hole in the ground. Sasha transformed back slowly and touched Hunter's cheek, inspecting his wounds that had begun to bleed again.

"You shouldn't have come for me . . . but I'm glad you did."

CHAPTER 25

"You sure I can't convince you otherwise, Captain?" Colonel Madison said in a wistful tone. "That was some serious firefighting back there, Trudeau, and we could definitely use a soldier like you in uniform."

"Thank you, sir . . . but this is it for me." She smiled and glanced out the window. "As soon as my resignation papers go through, I'm gonna take a trip to China . . . my brother-in-law is thinking seriously about getting married. We need a little R and R; Hunter's ribs are still pretty banged up. Our Fae allies are in tense negotiations . . . Vampires are still an unstable regional element. Plus, I'm gonna be an aunt." She looked at him with a big smile. "You know, sir. Life."

"I hear you, Captain. I can't argue with that. But I admit that I'm glad that you won't be too far away from us. We're getting your contracts drawn up to have your firm be our sole source consultant on paranormal activity. Mark Winters is your primary contact while you're gone?"

"Yes, sir. Mark is setting up the LLC . . . and you know all of our areas of expertise. Doc Holland and

Clarissa McGill are your bio experts, in the event you run into any more green slime. Bradley has the dark arts on lock. Silver Hawk is the number-one shaman and tracker in North America, and also has wolf access, and of course Woods and Fisher are at the ready for training special units," she added with a big grin. "I won't be gone long—a month tops."

"So, this is it," he said, standing. "I wish we had met under better circumstances, Captain. Thank you for sitting in on that final meeting with the Joint Chiefs this morning. And I can't blame you, after what I saw, for needing some time off . . . I'm just glad you're not leaving us altogether."

"Couldn't do that, Colonel."

He smiled and looked out the window, where Hunter had just shown up to casually lean against a jeep. "I admire how you guys can do that." He shook his head. "He's also a damned lucky man."

Sasha tilted her head slightly, surprised that Colonel Madison of all people would have made such a comment.

The colonel smiled. "I might be in uniform, Captain, but I'm not blind."

EPILOGUE

She held up her left hand and watched the sunlight dazzle in the prisms, catching colors in a gorgeous kaleidescope display. A beautiful three-carat emerald-cut diamond was set aloft ancient turquoise and amber baguettes all wrapped in unique fusion of silver and platinum. Hunter smiled and gently brought her hand to his lips.

"There was never time to get this made and given to you properly for your birthday . . . and then all hell broke loose again." He let go of her hand and looked at her. "Do you really like it? I know it's strange—the combination of metals—but I wanted the old stones from our people, the silver merged with the human tradition of a diamond and the—"

She kissed him and stopped his awkward explanation. "It's perfect and it's beautiful."

"But do you accept it . . . in the way humans give such a token?" he said, his deep voice a rumble inside his chest and hers.

"With all my heart and soul," she murmured, kissing the naked plane of his chest.

"Good . . . then I'm glad we came here," he said quietly and closed his eyes.

"What made you choose New Hampshire?" she asked sleepily, beginning to doze on Hunter's bare chest as she breathed in his scent.

"I was tired of the Louisiana heat and all the sordid regional politics . . . just wanted to be away from the pack, away from the sidhe . . . away from other people's problems for a while." He stroked her hair with his eyes still closed, allowing it to repeatedly flow through his fingers on each pass. "This reminds me so much of the North Country, without actually being in the Uncompahgre."

It was hard to disagree as she looked out the large bay window at the glassy surface of the lake and breathed in fresh mountain air. "This is moose country," she murmured, kissing his chest. "Great trout and salmon runs up here, too, they say. Maybe later, wanna take a run . . . let our wolves out a bit?"

He smiled with his eyes closed. "Most definitely . . . that's why I wanted to come up here."

"I'm so glad you're feeling better and that you wanted to get away. I needed this, too. Thank you."

"Yeah . . . both of us did. In the fall, they tell me that the leaves turn fire red and yellow and orange—only rivaled by Japan's forests."

Sasha chuckled and then moved up his body to take his mouth. "It's early August. Mid-September is more than a month away and we've already been gone a couple of weeks."

"So . . . I rented the cabin for a bit longer than I mentioned," he said, giving her a peck on the lips and a sly half smile. "If the pack needs us, they know where to find us, and the woods here are loaded with Fae—so no chance of missing an important missive. Besides, your team still has you on an electronic leash, if anything crazy happens."

She bit his bottom lip and tugged it. "You are so not right," she said, when she released it, laughing. "And I'm *not* on a leash!"

"Hey, don't shoot the messenger. It is just a tactical observation, Captain. All I'm saying is that I wanted time for *just us* before we headed to China or wherever the next mission calls for first."

She slid her body up to blanket his. "So, just because it's quiet for now, you've just taken me hostage and are holding me captive—using great little country fairs, great wild game, fantastic blueberry pancakes at the 1785 Inn off Highway Sixteen-N, huh . . . and have handcuffed me to the region by the dazzling lakes and trails. Not fair."

"Frankly, I thought you might be handcuffed to me, but if it's the blueberry pancakes . . ." He quick-flipped her over onto her back and held her hands above her head against the goose-down mattress, and then took her mouth hard. "Not trying to be fair," he said, breaking their kiss and loving her laughter. His eyes began to glow amber as his smile widened. "Especially not this fall when you go into season. So just work with a brother, all right?"

Read on for a preview of

LEFT FOR UNDEAD

Coming from St. Martin's Press in Fall 2010

New Orleans . . . Fall

Fae archers stood at the sidhe wall and trained their arrows toward the tree line as a slow, unseasonable frost overtook the branches. A sudden hard chill sliced through the humid air all around them, keening their senses for a potential Unseelie onslaught.

The captain of the guards held up one hand, silently cautioning his archers to wait until they could tell the true direction of the enemy's approach. Skilled eyes remained focused on the minute changes in the flora as they picked up on a telltale clue. Thicker ice was forming on the branches that faced the glamour-hidden golden path to the drawbridge. But as the captain lifted an arrow from his quiver, a regal female voice rang out.

"Friend, not foe! I beseech you—I have come to seek asylum from Sir Rodney!"

The entire garrison exchanged confused but skeptical glances. Again, using hand signals, the captain sent his men into better positions while cautioning them with his eyes to look alive and not to fall for a possible Unseelie ambush.

"Then show ye-selves," the captain shouted around a stone pillar. "All of you!"

The stone path instantly glazed over with a thin covering of ice and Queen Cerridwen stood between two formidable-looking gnome bodyguards. Her hands were concealed within a white mink muff, and she was shrouded in a luxurious, full-length, hooded white mink coat that flowed out in a long train behind her. Perspiration rolled down her gnomes' faces from beneath their heavy Cossack-styled hats and furs. But the queen's composure remained eerily cool despite the Louisiana heat as she simply pushed back her hood with ease, moving slowly so that the nervous captain could observe her hands. Not a platinum strand of hair was out of place as she turned her delicate face up to the captain's and made her appeal while her intense, ice blue eyes beheld him.

"We have traveled far under dangerous conditions," she said calmly. "I need to confer with my husband on matters of national security to our Fae way of life."

"*Ex*-husband," an elderly, disembodied voice stated bluntly. Within seconds Garth became visible as he joined the standoff on the fortress outer wall.

"No matter what you may think of me, dear Garth," Queen Cerridwen cooed, "in the end, Rodney and I have a link that goes back as long as—"

"Too long," Garth snapped, cutting her off. He pulled out a wand with crooked fingers from the sleeve of his monk habit styled robe; it was a thinly veiled threat— one that, wisely, neither Cerridwen nor her gnomes responded to. "As his top advisor, there are some things that our monarch may be blind to, but that I will always see."

Queen Cerridwen allowed a tight smile to form on her pale, rosebud-shaped lips while she studied the ancient wizard. "Then see that I have come with limited guards and did not arm myself to match your rude challenge just now. My mission is much too important to be derailed at the foot of your monarch's drawbridge."

Garth arched an eyebrow and glanced at the captain of the guards, then let out a little snort of disgust. "This is not the Cerridwen I am used to. Something is clearly awry."

"There could be more of them in the trees awaiting an ambush," the worried captain murmured to Garth.

Garth nodded but spoke quietly. "But if we have their queen and a full garrison at our walls, then the odds that they will besiege the palace are tremendously reduced."

As though reading their minds, Queen Cerridwen stepped forward. Using a simple hand signal, as one would command well-trained hunting dogs, she bade her guards to stay where they stood.

"I need to speak to Rodney," she said, never blinking as she fixed her gaze on Garth. "It is a matter of utmost importance."

After a moment, the elderly gnome gave a curt nod with his bald head which was enough to signal the captain to lower the drawbridge.

"Only you," Garth said, addressing the queen.

Queen Cerridwen nodded and lifted her chin as she gracefully glided forward. "As I would only expect.

But I thank you for your limited hospitality, nonetheless."

Her ice-heeled shoes clicked against the bridge, ringing out in the deafening silence as garrison archers kept their deadly arrows trained on her. The moment she was on the other side of the bridge, anxious guards quickly drew up the only access to the castle. Then just as quickly, a phalanx of guards surrounded her.

"Your wand, Your Majesty," Garth said in a suspicious tone, then grudgingly gave her a courtesy bow before holding out his hand.

She calmly gave her muff to the closest guard beside her and then carefully reached into her flowing left sleeve with two fingers to produce a crystalline ice wand. Garth nodded and silently dispatched a runner to alert Sir Rodney as he cautiously accepted the queen's instrument of death.

"I will show you to the War Room," Garth said in a dignified tone.

Queen Cerridwen tilted her head with an amused expression. "But I was so hoping you'd show me to his private bedchamber." She released a melodramatic sigh with merriment in her eyes as the old gnome drew back, clearly shocked. "No matter, we'll wind up there sooner or later. You know Rodney almost as well as I do, and some of his notions of détente should be predictable by now even for you, dear Garth."

CHAPTER 1

Elder Vlad stood by the desecrated mausoleum, peering down at the charred male corpse. Blue blood slowly blackened beneath the visible, pulsing veins in the paper-thin skin of his bald head while his black irises completely overtook the whites of his eyes. The vampires around him were quiet and still under the blue-white wash of moonlight in the cemetery, awaiting his permission to investigate. Fury threaded through his body like dark tendrils of hatred, although the ancient vampire remained stoic.

"Who did this?" His rhetorical question was uttered between his fangs with deadly calm. He already knew the culprits; his angry query was simply a command for external confirmation. Elder Vlad glanced up, holding his top hunter lieutenant's gaze and impatiently waited for an answer.

"We believe it had to be Unseelie Fae, Your Excellency. Just like the others." Caleb dropped to one leather-clad knee, allowing his long spill of platinum hair to flow over his shoulders as he more closely examined the vampire ash. The black leather coat he wore dusted the ground, billowing out around him from supernatural fury.

"Undoubtedly death by daylight invasion," Caleb said, suddenly looking up and baring fangs as his rage kindled. "I suspect that Monroe Bonaventure went to ground, sleeping here in his mausoleum for fear that, since the mansions of so many others had been recently overrun, that his might be as well. But they found the poor bastard anyway."

"He was my sixth and last viceroy in the region." Elder Vlad paced away with silent footsteps, beginning to levitate from his unspent anger, and then he turned quickly to speak in a burst of rage to the assembled hunters. "We are of the cast Vampyre! We are the eternal night! That we fear *anything* is sacrilege! We are the definition of fear in the supernatural world! It is our kind that has always been at the top of the food chain for millennia! By all that is unholy, I vow that there will be merciless redress for this offense. Tell me, dear Mara, what clues have you uncovered, before I formally declare war? Transylvania will want to know why and I shall give them indisputable proof."

Mara traced the edges of the broken door hinges and locks around the opened crypt with her fingers. Only her long brunette hair moved in the gentle night breeze as she stopped for a second to peer at Elder Vlad, remaining momentarily, eerily still.

"This metal was fractured by sudden freezing . . . temperatures so cold that a mere tap would have shattered them," she finally said. Her smoldering dark gaze beheld Caleb's ice blue stare for a moment before returning to Elder Vlad. "Our local Seelie Fae do not work with such extreme temperatures," she murmured, her voice sounding like a seductive forensic expert's. "Nor do the wolves."

Elder Vlad narrowed his gaze and looked off into the distance. "No, they don't, do they?"

Mara shook her head. "Sir Rodney is many things, but a fool he is not," she said with a low hiss between her fangs.

"Your orders, Your Excellency?" Caleb asked, rising to stand with his head bowed before the ancient leader of the North American Vampire Cartel.

"Fix this," Elder Vlad murmured. "Make sure the Unseelie have a list of names for which we demand blood restitution. And do be sure to let Queen Cerridwen of Hecate know how very displeased I am."

Experience the dark pleasures and animal passions of

CRIMSON MOON

The acclaimed series from *New York Times* bestselling author

L.A. BANKS

BAD BLOOD
ISBN: 978-0-312-94911-2

BITE THE BULLET
ISBN: 978-0-312-94912-9

UNDEAD ON ARRIVAL
ISBN: 978-0-312-94913-6

CURSED TO DEATH
ISBN: 978-0-312-94299-1

Available from St. Martin's Paperbacks

Don't miss the Vampire Huntress Legend™ Novels
from *New York Times* Bestselling Author

L. A. BANKS

MINION
ISBN: 978-0-312-98701-5

THE FORSAKEN
ISBN: 978-0-312-94860-3

THE AWAKENING
ISBN: 978-0-312-98702-2

THE WICKED
ISBN: 978-0-312-94606-7

THE HUNTED
ISBN: 978-0-312-93772-0

THE CURSED
ISBN: 978-0-312-94772-9

THE BITTEN
ISBN: 978-0-312-99509-6

THE DARKNESS
ISBN: 978-0-312-94914-3

THE FORBIDDEN
ISBN: 978-0-312-94002-7

THE SHADOWS
ISBN: 978-0-312-94915-0

THE DAMNED
ISBN: 978-0-312-93443-9

THE THIRTEENTH
ISBN: 978-0-312-36876-0

Available from St. Martin's Paperbacks